英美成长小说导读

A Guide to British and American Bildungsromans

桂宏军　著

华中科技大学出版社
中国·武汉

图书在版编目(CIP)数据

英美成长小说导读/桂宏军著. —武汉:华中科技大学出版社,2018.9(2024.1重印)
ISBN 978-7-5680-3824-9

Ⅰ.①英… Ⅱ.①桂… Ⅲ.①小说-文学欣赏-英国②小说-文学欣赏-美国 Ⅳ.①I561.074
②I712.074

中国版本图书馆CIP数据核字(2018)第220974号

英美成长小说导读
Yingmei Chengzhang Xiaoshuo Daodu

桂宏军 著

策划编辑:刘　平
责任编辑:李文星
封面设计:刘　婷
责任校对:阮　敏
责任监印:周治超

出版发行:华中科技大学出版社(中国·武汉)　　电话:(027)81321913
　　　　　武汉市东湖新技术开发区华工科技园　　邮编:430223

录　　排:华中科技大学惠友文印中心
印　　刷:武汉邮科印务有限公司
开　　本:710mm×1000mm　1/16
印　　张:12
字　　数:218千字
版　　次:2024年1月第1版第2次印刷
定　　价:38.00元

本书若有印装质量问题,请向出版社营销中心调换
全国免费服务热线:400-6679-118　竭诚为您服务
版权所有　侵权必究

前　言

"成长"一词来源于人类学，指青少年经历了生活的一系列磨砺和考验之后，获得了独立应对社会和生活的知识、能力和信心，从而进入人生的一个新阶段，这种磨砺和考验往往具有仪式性。在西方，成长小说是一种具有悠久传统的小说类型，"成长小说"（Bildungsroman）一词来自于德语的 Bildung，Bildung 是成长的意思，而 roman 是法语词，指小说。

19世纪末20年代初，卡尔·莫根斯特恩在两篇演讲《论成长小说的本质》与《成长小说的历史》中正式提出了"成长小说"这一概念，但直到德国哲学家威廉·狄尔泰在其著名的《体验与诗》中对成长小说进行了较为详细的说明后，成长小说才成了公认的文学术语。歌德创作的《威廉·迈斯特的学习时代》被公认为是成长小说的典范。1824年，英国著名文学家托马斯·卡莱尔首次将这部作品译介到英国，随即卡莱尔发表了自传体成长小说《拼凑的裁缝》（*The Tailor Retailored*），此后成长小说作为一种文学体裁在英国发展繁荣起来。因此，英国成长小说通常被认为是德国成长小说的延伸。在我国，20世纪90年代，成长小说理论首次被引进，目前国内对成长小说的研究相对较少。

莫迪凯·马科斯在《什么是成长小说》一文中，探讨了 Bildungsroman 的定义，指出成长小说的定义主要有两类：一类把成长描绘为年轻人对外部世界的认识过程；另一类把成长解释为认知自我身份与价值，并调整自我与社会关系的过程。成长小说展示的是年轻主人公经历了某种切肤之痛的事件之后，或改变了原有的世界观，或改变了自己的性格，或两者兼有。这种改变使他摆脱了童年的天真，并最终将他引向了一个真实而复杂的成人世界。成长小说的成长内核应该是心智的成熟，而非表面意义上的年龄增长。巴赫金对成长小说有过专门研究："这里主人公的形象，不是静态的统一体，而是动态的统一体。主人公本身、他的性格，在这一小说的公式中成了变数。主人公本身的变化具有了情节意义，与此相关，小说的情节也从根本上得到了再认识、再构建。"简而言之，成长小说就是以叙述人物成长过程为主题的小说，它通过对一个人或几个人成长经历的叙述,表现个人社会化过程中的经历和感悟,反映出人物的思想和心理从幼稚走向成熟的变化过程。

巴克利指出成长小说的基本要素是一个成长和自我发现的过程,包括疏离感、与环境的格格不入、外省的一个更大社会、自身的苦难经历、对职业和工作的追求、两代人间的冲突等要素,同时巴克利认为成长小说通常是作者早期的具有自传性的作品。

成长小说是英美小说的一个重要组成部分,也是一个重要的解读视角,虽然目前国内对成长小说还没有一个公认的界定,但一般认为成长小说(如《简·爱》)大致遵循"天真—诱惑—出走流浪—迷惘困惑—考验—顿悟—失去天真—认识自我"这一叙事结构,讲述13~20岁的主人公成长历程的叙事,反映出人物的思想和心理从幼稚走向成熟的变化过程,呈现出成长主体的道德和精神发展。在这个过程中,有些主人公走向成熟,最终成功地融入社会,如狄更斯的《远大前程》、马克·吐温的《汤姆·索亚历险记》等;也有些主人公由于看到了社会本质,而选择逃避,如塞林格的《麦田里的守望者》。时代的变迁和社会的发展赋予了成长小说丰富的背景,也成为成长小说发展的土壤。

成长小说一般采用U型叙事模式,即离家出走—遭受困境—挣扎—回归,不同的故事情节有不同的表现,其原型是《圣经》里的伊甸园的故事。亚当和夏娃在伊甸园里玩耍,他们在撒旦的诱惑下偷吃了禁果,天神动怒将他们打入人间,从此过着终日劳作的生活。在人间,随着时间的过去,这种日出而作日落而息的生活不再使他们痛苦,反而使他们得到了天堂里没有的幸福,这就是从高处跌落又重回高处的U型过程。

成长小说有以下四个要素。

(一)成长中的疏离感

疏离感是成长小说的一个典型元素。这一概念最早由黑格尔和马克思提出,在整个20世纪这一概念受到了社会科学的大量关注。疏离感是个体与周围的人、自然、社会以及个体与自身之间的疏离隔阂,个体受支配控制,产生无意义感、压迫压抑感、社会孤立感等消极情感。

(二)成长中的顿悟

"顿悟"原本是一个宗教术语,指上帝在人间显灵,以昭示其现实存在。顿悟是成长小说的又一个典型元素,指在某个特定时刻由于外界的诱因突然产生的领悟,使主人公最终摆脱困惑而幡然醒悟,通常发生在心理变化的关键时刻,预示着故事的高潮。詹姆斯·乔伊斯认为顿悟是一种突发的精神现象,通过顿悟,主人公对自己的生活和某种事物的本质有了深刻的理解和认知。

(三)成长引路人

在成长小说中,主人公的经历及其切身体验是必不可少的要素,但成长路上的引路人也是一个主要的因素。成长小说中的领路人原型主要有正面领路人和反面领路人两种。正面领路人的原型可以追溯到神话或童话,从人类文明发展来看,在宗教主宰人类灵魂的时期,神被看作是至高无上的权威,统领世间万物,指引迷失的"羔羊"。到了现代社会,普通人成了"领路人",而不是充当"拯救者",他们充当指导者和教诲者的角色,对成长者产生好的或坏的影响。从社会学的角度看,处于人生初始阶段的少年,需要富于理性、阅历丰富的成年人的引导,帮助他们实现生活的拓展与生命的超越,不断跨越成长的台阶,迈向新的人生阶段。一个人的成长或多或少地受到他人的影响,这些人从正反两方面丰富、影响着主人公的生活经历和他们对社会的认识,青少年在观察这些人物扮演的社会角色中逐渐认识自我,找到自己在社会中的地位。因此,成长小说中的主人公一般都有成长引路人,例如《简·爱》中的女佣白茜和谭波尔老师。从广义上看,成长引路人分为三种:正面引路人、反面引路人、神灵。

(四)成人仪式

成人仪式是许多民族的一种古老的文化原型,是远古时代的许多部落或民族中流行着的一种为未成年人举行的仪式。举行仪式期间,这些未成年人暂时脱离团体社会,被部落中的长老或专职的巫师带到远离社会的隐秘之地,接受种种折磨和考验,并学得本部落的神话、历史、习俗和道德观念。等到仪式结束再返回原地与社会相融时,他们已经能够履行团体社会所赋予的职责和义务了。成长小说中往往有象征成长仪式的叙述和描写,通过某种具体或具有象征意义的仪式凸显出主人公在成长道路上的蜕变。

作为一种重要的小说类型,成长小说在国内目前还没有小说导读的专著。本书从成长的角度介绍了14篇原版英美成长小说(英美各7篇),选材兼顾了经典性、可读性和时代性,这些作品大多是英美文学的经典,最后两部作品创作于21世纪。这些都是作者阅读过的较为熟悉的作品,这些作品描绘了主人公的成长环境,叙述了他们的成长经历,描写了他们成长时期的心理,作品贴近生活实际,容易引起读者共鸣。作品选读前面有较为全面简洁的作家和背景介绍,作品内容介绍以及成长视角下的较为深入细致的解读。作品选读部分是作者精心挑选的作品中集中体现作品的成长主题的精彩片段,使读者在短时间内领略到原汁原味的名著。选读后面有注释和从成长角度精心设计的问题,这些问题便于读者加深理解,启发思考。通过阅读这些作品,读者在提高英语水平的同时,可以提高文学修养,陶冶情操,扩大视野,获得人生成长的启迪和指引。本书适合大学生及英美文学爱好者阅读。

  本书作者长期从事英美文学的研究和教学工作,阅读了大量的英美文学作品,目前在武汉轻工大学从事英美文学研究和教学工作。

桂宏军

2018 年 4 月

目　录

Unit 1　Robinson Crusoe ································· 1

Unit 2　Pride and Prejudice ····························· 9

Unit 3　Jane Eyre ··· 21

Unit 4　Great Expectations ······························ 45

Unit 5　A Portrait of an Artist as a Young Man ······· 61

Unit 6　Sons and Lovers ································· 73

Unit 7　Of Human Bondage ····························· 83

Unit 8　Gone with the Wind ···························· 95

Unit 9　Adventures of Huckleberry Finn ··············· 103

Unit 10　The Great Gatsby ······························ 111

Unit 11　The Catcher in the Rye ······················· 125

Unit 12　Beloved ·· 137

Unit 13　The Kite Runner ································ 145

Unit 14　A Thousand Splendid Suns ··················· 165

参考文献 ··· 182

Robinson Crusoe

作者及背景简介

丹尼尔·笛福(Daniel Defoe)(1660—1731)被誉为"英国与欧洲小说之父"。在18世纪英国四大著名小说家中,笛福名列第一(其余三人分别是乔纳森·斯威夫特、塞缪尔·理查逊和亨利·菲尔丁)。这一时期的思想文化背景是倡导理性、平等、科学的启蒙主义,强调文学作品的教育作用。笛福生于伦敦一个油烛商家庭,年轻的时  候,是一个成功的商人。他广泛游历,早年经营内衣、烟酒、羊毛织品、制砖业,曾到欧洲大陆各国经商。在从事商业的同时,他还从事政治活动,代表当时日益上升的资产阶级出版了大量的政治性小册子,并因此被捕。笛福直到晚年才开始创作小说。写《鲁滨孙漂流记》时,他已经59岁了。此后,他又创作了《辛格顿船长》《杰克上校》《摩尔·弗兰德斯》等小说,这些小说对英国及欧洲小说的发展都起了巨大的影响及作用。

选读作品简介

鲁滨孙出身于一个体面的商人家庭,从小渴望航海,想去海外见识一番。鲁滨孙偷偷瞒着父亲出海,到了伦敦,在那儿购买了一些假珠子、玩具带到非洲做生意。第四次航海时,船在途中遇到风暴触礁,船上同伴全部遇难,唯有鲁滨孙幸存,只身漂流到一个荒无人烟的孤岛上。鲁滨孙用沉船的桅杆做了木筏,一次又一次地把船上的食物、衣服、枪支弹药等运到岸上,并在小山边搭起帐篷定居下来。接着他用削尖的木桩在帐篷周围围上栅栏,在帐篷后挖洞居住。他用简单的工具制作桌、椅等家具,猎野味为食,饮小溪里的淡水,渡过了最初遇到的困难。

鲁滨孙开始在岛上种植大麦和稻子，自制木臼、木杵、筛子，加工面粉，烘出了粗糙的面包。他捕捉并驯养野山羊，让其繁殖。他还制作陶器等，保证了自己的生活需要。还在荒岛的另一端建了一个"乡间别墅"和一个养殖场。虽然这样，鲁滨孙一直没有放弃寻找离开孤岛的办法。他砍倒一棵大树，花了五六个月的时间做成了一只独木舟，但船实在太重，无法拖下海去。鲁滨孙在岛上独自生活了15年后，一天他发现岛边海岸上有一个脚印，不久他又发现了人骨和灰烬。原来外岛的一群野人曾在这里举行过人肉宴。鲁滨孙惊愕万分。此后他便一直保持警惕，更加留心周围的事物。直到第24年，岛上又来了一群野人，带着准备杀死并吃掉的俘虏。鲁滨孙发现后，救出了其中的一个。因为那一天是星期五，所以鲁滨孙把被救的俘虏取名为"星期五"。此后，"星期五"成了鲁滨孙忠实的仆人和朋友。接着，鲁滨孙带着"星期五"救出了一个西班牙人和"星期五"的父亲。不久有条英国船在岛附近停泊，船上水手叛乱，把船长等三人抛弃在岛上，鲁滨孙与"星期五"帮助船长制服了那帮叛乱水手，夺回了船只。他把那帮水手留在岛上，自己带着"星期五"和船长等离开荒岛回到英国。此时鲁滨孙已离家35年（在岛上居住了28年）。他在英国结了婚，生了三个孩子。妻子死后，鲁滨孙又一次出海经商，途经他住过的荒岛，这时留在岛上的水手和西班牙人都已安家繁衍生息。鲁滨孙又送去一些新的移民，将岛上的土地分给他们，并留给他们各种生活必需品，满意地离开了小岛。

成长主题解读

启蒙主义强调文学作品的教育作用，相信人有自我完善提高的能力，小说用生动的细节描写塑造了一个充满劳动热情、坚毅勇敢的人。鲁滨孙在荒无人烟的孤岛上生活了28年，其间也曾悲观绝望，他凭借自立自强的精神，最终战胜了自我和艰苦的环境，在荒岛上创造了文明。小说从以下几方面体现了成长小说要素。

一、疏离感

小说中的疏离首先体现在人与自然的关系上。鲁滨孙和岛上的动物之间的关系，更像是控制、征服、操纵甚至是无情的杀戮。鲁滨孙在岛屿上的统治和剥削是人类对大自然的侵略和征服的体现，面对岛上美丽的风景，鲁滨孙不懂得欣赏岛上各种动物、鸟类、昆虫和河流的美和存在价值，对他来说，岛屿仅仅被视为主宰自然的发生地。在鲁滨孙到来之前，岛屿充满了生机和活力，在自然界中具有其自身的价值，不依附于任何人存在。然而，鲁滨孙把小岛的一切都看作有待利用和开发的对象,对他而言,自然仅仅是一个仆人。鲁滨孙杀死山羊时,山羊幼崽就在旁边,但是鲁滨孙坚持杀死了山羊母亲。(见选读)鲁滨孙没有意识到自然的价值,所以毫无怜悯地杀死动物。鲁滨孙在岛上的行为体现了人类中心论的思想,人类优于一切,是宇宙的中心,是仅次于上帝的存在。作为岛屿的国王,"整个岛屿都是我的臣民;我对于岛上的一切都有支配权,岛上的任何东西我都可以做标记、放生、扔掉……"自然遭受了鲁滨孙不公平的对待,对他来说,整个岛屿仅仅是其意志的支配场所,自然的存在只是为了人类实现个人目标,人类对一切具有绝对控制权。

其次,疏离体现在殖民统治上。鲁滨孙在海岛上的生活不仅破坏了自然界,而且还对原住民推行殖民统治。他通过对资源的掠夺和思想意识改造来推行殖民统治。鲁滨孙第一次出海到非洲,就用大约价值40英镑的小玩物和零碎货物换回了五磅零九盎司的金沙,这些金沙在伦敦换了300英镑。此次海外贸易带来的甜头使鲁滨孙更加野心勃勃,他还把英国的工业品在巴西卖了高价,赚取了4倍的利润,买下了一个种植园。当他听说在几内亚的海岸同黑人做生意时,只需一些像假珠子、刀子、玻璃、玩具之类的物品,就可以换得象牙、金沙,甚至还有黑奴时,就冒险去了几内亚。鲁滨孙甚至还以60西班牙金币的价格贩卖了一名奴隶。鲁滨孙除了进行贩卖黑奴等殖民贸易外,还占有殖民地的土地,当发现自己落难的荒岛没有人类的足迹时就无比喜悦地声称"这一切将属于我",并用篱笆等修筑围墙来防备土著人。而实际上土著人在鲁滨孙之前就经常光顾这一小岛,在西方殖民者将其并不视为人的情况下,他们的土地也被无情地剥夺。殖民者在占有了土地、使土著人沦为奴隶之后,按照西方的文化模式开始对殖民地人民进行思想改造和意识控制。

最后,小说中的疏离也体现在男女关系上。小说从头至尾体现了鲁滨孙的男性精神,对他的婚姻只用一句话匆匆带过。作品中还提到三位与鲁滨孙有关的女性人物,一位寡妇和两个姐姐,而其中的一个姐姐也是寡妇,另一个姐姐生活得也不好。那个时代女性似乎没有享受幸福生活的权利,女性的脆弱和低下的社会地位在作者看来是天经地义的,这种女性的边缘化充分体现了男性霸权话语。另外,小说中的鲁滨孙善于处理日常生活中的各种事务,像通常需要女人来完成的加工面包、制作奶油和酪干及晾晒葡萄干等,鲁滨孙都处理得井井有条,"他的生活并不需要女人"。在鲁滨孙看来,女性的作用只不过是繁衍后代,文明是男性创造的,自然和女性都是男性征服的对象。

二、成长引路人

宗教信仰在鲁滨孙的成长过程中起着重要作用。在鲁滨孙的成长过程中,宗教扮演着精神支柱和引领的作用,对宗教的理解和皈依使主人公从鲁莽的不信教者,成长为一名遇事不惊、审时度势、充满理性的文明社会成员。(见选读)宗教使鲁滨孙能积极乐观地面对困难,他认为自己遭受了种种磨难,每次都能逢凶化吉,这是上帝想通过这些磨炼促使他更好地成长。鲁滨孙想到上帝既然创造了一切,也就引导和支配这一切,天地间的一切事情和自己的一切遭遇也是在他的安排之中,自己落到这个地步是上帝的旨意。鲁滨孙从宗教那里得到了心灵的慰藉,他相信,只要向上帝祈祷,皈依上帝,必能得到上帝的搭救。鲁滨孙救下了星期五,不知疲倦地对其灌输基督教的思想,对星期五的教育也有助于他的自我教育与深思。他的宗教思想的成熟以及对宗教的皈依是和他的逐步成熟并行与相互促进的。随着其宗教思想的成熟,他最终成为理性和成熟的个体。

三、成长仪式

小说对疾病的描写具有成长仪式意义。疾病在表象上是生理出了问题,但在更深的层次上,暗喻着主人公在精神上的残缺。正是这场持续了十余天的大病,不仅把主人公推向了精神炼狱,而且促使他开始了一场灵魂与道德的"驱魔"活动,疾病是导向主人公最终获得自由的重要途径。在小说接近尾声处,船长主持了带有狂欢意味的送礼仪式,并表示可以带领鲁滨孙返回英国。船长带领主人公回归群体,这与古老部落长老执行成人仪式相似,同时也与小说开头对那位船长的描写形成呼应。在仪式中,主人公将船长送的衣服穿在身上,他觉得全世界再也没有什么事情比这个更不舒服、更别扭的了。衣服是文明社会的象征,穿上衣服就等于恢复了社会身份。在成人仪式过程中,鲁滨孙在精神上成长了,但还没有在其他方面成为一个真正的社会人,当小说中船长说"我们等这些仪式过去以后"时,预示着成人仪式的结束。

选读部分出自第四章描写了鲁滨孙在岛上安家的情景以及他从对上帝的信仰中得到了精神力量。

My thoughts were now wholly employed about securing myself against either savages, if any should appear, or wild beasts, if any were in the island; and I had many thoughts of the method how to do this, and what kind of dwelling to make—whether I should make me a cave in the earth, or a tent upon the earth; and, in short, I resolved upon both; the manner and description of which, it may not be improper to give an account of.

I soon found the place I was in was not fit for my settlement, because it was upon a low, moorish ground, near the sea, and I believed it would not be wholesome, and more particularly because there was no fresh water near it; so I resolved to find a more healthy and more convenient spot of ground.

I consulted several things in my situation, which I found would be proper for me: 1st, health and fresh water, I just now mentioned; 2ndly, shelter from the heat of the sun; 3rdly, security from ravenous creatures, whether man or beast; 4thly, a view to the sea, that if God sent any ship in sight, I might not lose any advantage for my deliverance,[1] of which I was not willing to banish all my expectation yet.

In search of a place proper for this, I found a little plain on the side of a rising hill, whose front towards this little plain was steep as a house-side, so that nothing could come down upon me from the top. On the one side of the rock there was a hollow place, worn a little way in, like the entrance or door of a cave but there was not really any cave or way into the rock at all.

On the flat of the green, just before this hollow place, I resolved to pitch my tent. This plain was not above a hundred yards broad, and about twice as long, and lay like a green before my door; and, at the end of it, descended irregularly every way down into the low ground by the seaside. It was on the N. N. W. side of the hill; so that it was sheltered from the heat every day, till it came to a W. and by S. sun, or thereabouts, which, in those countries, is near the setting.

Before I set up my tent I drew a half-circle before the hollow place, which took in about ten yards in its semi-diameter from the rock, and twenty yards in its diameter from its beginning and ending.

In this half-circle I pitched two rows of strong stakes, driving them into the ground till they stood very firm like piles, the biggest end being out of the ground above five feet and a half, and sharpened on the top. The two rows did not stand above six inches from one another.

……

In the interval of time while this was doing, I went out once at least every day with my gun, as well to divert myself as to see if I could kill anything fit for food; and, as near as I could, to acquaint myself with what the island produced. The first time I went out, I presently discovered that there were goats in the island, which was a great satisfaction to me; but then it was attended with this misfortune to me—viz.[2] that they were so shy, so subtle, and so swift of foot, that it was the most difficult thing in the world to come at them; but I was not discouraged at this, not doubting but I might now and then shoot one, as it soon happened; for after I had found their haunts a little, I laid wait in this manner for them: I observed if they saw me in the valleys, though they were upon the rocks, they would run away, as in a terrible fright; but if they were feeding in the valleys, and I was upon the rocks, they took no notice of me; from whence I concluded that, by the position of their optics, their sight was so directed downward that they did not readily see objects that were above them; so afterwards I took this method—I always climbed the rocks first, to get above them, and then had frequently a fair mark.

The first shot I made among these creatures, I killed a she-goat, which had a little kid by her, which she gave suck to, which grieved me heartily; for when the old one fell, the kid stood stock still by her, till I came and took her up; and not only so, but when I carried the old one with me, upon my shoulders, the kid followed me quite to my enclosure; upon which I laid down the dam,[3] and took the kid in my arms, and carried it over my pale,[4] in hopes to have bred it up tame; but it would not eat; so I was forced to kill it and eat it myself. These two supplied me with flesh a great while, for I ate sparingly, and saved my provisions, my bread especially, as much as possibly I could.

Having now fixed my habitation, I found it absolutely necessary to provide a place to make a fire in, and fuel to burn: and what I did for that, and also how I enlarged my cave, and what conveniences I made, I shall give a full account of in its place; but I must now give some little account of myself, and of my thoughts about living, which, it may well be supposed, were not a few.

I had a dismal prospect of my condition; for as I was not cast away upon that island without being driven, as is said, by a violent storm, quite out of the course of our intended voyage, and a great way, viz. some hundreds of leagues, out of the ordinary course of the trade of mankind, I had great reason to consider it as a determination of Heaven, that in this desolate place, and in this desolate manner, I should end my life. The tears would run plentifully down my face when made these reflections; and sometimes I would expostulate[5] with myself why Providence [6]should thus completely ruin His creatures, and render them so absolutely miserable; so without help, abandoned, so entirely depressed, that it could hardly be rational to be thankful for such a life.

But something always returned swift upon me to check these thoughts, and to reprove me; and particularly one day, walking with my gun in my hand by the seaside, I was very pensive upon the subject of my present condition, when reason, as it were, expostulated with me the other way, thus: "Well, you are in a desolate condition, it is true; but, pray remember, where are the rest of you? Did not you come, eleven of you in the boat? Where are the ten? Why were they not saved, and you lost? Why were you singled out? Is it better to be here or there?" And then I pointed to the sea. All evils are to be considered with the good that is in them, and with what worse attends them.

I now began to consider seriously my condition, and the circumstances I was reduced to; and I drew up the state of my affairs in writing, not so much to leave them to any that were to come after me—for I was likely to have but few heirs—as to deliver my thoughts from daily poring[7] over them, and afflicting[8] my mind; and as my reason began now to master my despondency, I began to comfort myself as well as I could, and to set the good against the evil, that I might have something to distinguish my case from worse; and I stated very impartially, like debtor and creditor, the comforts I enjoyed against the miseries I suffered.

Upon the whole, here was an undoubted testimony that there was scarce any condition in the world so miserable but there was something negative or something positive to be thankful for in it; and let this stand as a direction from the experience of the most miserable of all conditions in this world: that we may always find in it something to comfort ourselves from, and to set, in the description of good and evil, on the credit side[9] of the account.

Notes:

1. deliverance:解救

2. viz.:也就是,即

3. dam:母羊

4. pale:栅栏,即鲁滨孙的家

5. expostulate:规劝

6. Providence:上帝

7. pore:细想,凝思

8. afflict:使痛苦

9. credit side:贷款方,这里指看到积极的一面

Questions:

1. What is the alienation in the novel?

2. What is his epiphany here?

3. How did Robinson's attitude towards his circumstance change?

2

Pride and Prejudice

作家及背景简介

简·奥斯汀(Jane Austen,1775—1817)是英国浪漫主义时期最重要的现实主义小说家之一,父亲是当地教区牧师。奥斯汀没有上过正规学校,但受到较好的家庭教育,主要教材就是父亲的文学藏书。奥斯汀一家爱读流行小说,多半是庸俗的消遣品。她少女时期的习作就是对这类流行小说的滑稽模仿,这样就形成了她作品中嘲讽的基调。她20岁左右开始写作,共发表了6部长篇小说。1811年出版的《理智与情感》是她的处女作,随后又接连发表了《傲慢与偏见》(1813)、《曼斯菲尔德花园》(1814)和《爱玛》(1815)。《诺桑觉寺》和《劝导》(1818)是在她去世后第二年发表的,并署上了作者真名。

奥斯汀终身未婚,家道小康。由于居住在乡村小镇,接触到的是中小地主、牧师等人物以及他们恬静、舒适的生活环境,因此她的作品里没有重大的社会矛盾。她以女性特有的细致入微的观察力,真实地描绘了她周围世界的小天地,尤其是绅士淑女间的婚姻和爱情风波。她的作品格调轻松诙谐,富有喜剧性冲突,深受读者欢迎。

从18世纪末到19世纪初,庸俗无聊的"感伤小说"和"哥特式小说"充斥英国文坛,而奥斯汀的小说破旧立新,一反常规地展现了当时尚未受到资本主义工业革命冲击的英国乡村中产阶级的日常生活和田园风光。她的作品往往通过喜剧性的场面嘲讽人们的愚蠢、自私、势利和盲目自信等可鄙可笑的弱点。奥斯汀的小说出现在19世纪初叶,一扫风行一时的假浪漫主义潮流,继承和发展了英国18世纪优秀的现实主义传统,为19世纪现实主义小说的高潮做了准备。虽然其作品反映的广度和深度有限,但她的作品如"两寸牙雕",从一个小窗口中窥视到整个社会形态和人情世故,对改变当时小说创作中的庸俗风气起了好的作用,在英国小说的发展史上有承上启下的意义,被誉为地位可与莎士比亚平起平坐的作家。

选读作品简介

乡绅班纳特有五个待嫁闺中的千金,班纳特太太整天操心着为女儿们物色称心如意的丈夫。新来的邻居宾利是个有钱的单身汉,他立即成了班纳特太太追猎的目标。在一次舞会上,宾利对班纳特家的大女儿简一见钟情,班纳特太太为此欣喜若狂。

参加舞会的还有宾利的好友达西,达西仪表堂堂,非常富有,许多姑娘纷纷向他投去秋波。但达西不愿意和在场的任何女孩跳舞,因此达西给自尊心很强的伊丽莎白留下了傲慢的印象。不久,达西对她活泼可爱的举止产生了好感,在另一次舞会上主动请她同舞,伊丽莎白同意和达西跳一支舞,达西由此而逐渐对伊丽莎白改变了看法。

宾利的妹妹卡罗琳一心想嫁给达西,而达西对她十分冷漠。她发现达西对伊丽莎白有好感后,决意从中阻挠。达西虽然欣赏伊丽莎白,但却无法忍受她的母亲以及妹妹们粗俗无礼的举止,达西担心简看上宾利并非出自真情,便劝说宾利放弃娶简。在妹妹和好友达西的劝说下,宾利不辞而别。

班纳特先生没有儿子,根据当时法律,班纳特家的财产是只能由男性继承,而班纳特家的女儿们仅仅只能得到五千英镑作为嫁妆,因此他的家产将由远亲柯林斯继承。柯林斯古板平庸,善于谄媚奉承,依靠权势当上了牧师。他向伊丽莎白求婚,遭拒绝后,马上与她的密友夏洛特结婚。

附近小镇的民团联队里有个英俊潇洒的青年军官威克汉姆。一天,威克汉姆对伊丽莎白说,他父亲是达西家的总管,达西的父亲曾在遗嘱中建议达西给他一笔财产,从而体面地成为一名神职人员,而这笔财产却被达西吞没了。(其实是威克汉姆自己把那笔遗产挥霍殆尽,还企图勾引达西的妹妹乔治安娜私奔)伊丽莎白听后,对达西更加反感。

柯林斯夫妇请伊丽莎白去他们家作客,伊丽莎白在那里遇到达西的姨妈凯瑟琳夫人,并且被邀去她的罗辛斯山庄做客。在那里,伊丽莎白又见到了来过复活节的达西。达西无法抑制自己对伊丽莎白的爱慕之情,向她求婚,但态度还是比较傲慢,加之伊丽莎白之前对他有严重偏见,他的求婚被断然拒绝了。这一打击使达西第一次认识到骄傲自负所带来的恶果,他痛苦地离开了伊丽莎白,临走前留下一封长信做解释:他承认宾利不辞而别是他促使的,原因是他不满班纳特太太和班纳特小姐们的轻浮和粗鄙（不包括简和伊丽莎白），并且认为简并没有真正钟情于宾利；威克汉姆说的却全是谎言，事实是威克汉姆自己把那笔遗产挥霍殆尽，还企图勾引达西的妹妹乔治安娜私奔。伊丽莎白读信后十分后悔，既对错怪达西感到内疚，又为母亲和妹妹的行为感到羞愧。

第二年夏天，伊丽莎白随舅父母来到达西的庄园彭伯里，在管家那里了解到达西在当地很受人们尊敬，而且对他妹妹乔治安娜非常爱护。伊丽莎白在树林中偶遇刚回到家的达西，本以为达西不在家的伊丽莎白见到达西尴尬万分，而达西态度大为改变，对他们彬彬有礼，渐渐地伊丽莎白对他的偏见消除了。正当其时，伊丽莎白接到家信，说小妹莉迪亚与负债累累的威克汉姆私奔了。这种家丑使伊丽莎白非常难堪，以为达西会更瞧不起自己。出乎意料的是，达西得知上述消息以后，便想办法替她解决了难题——不仅替威克汉姆还清赌债，还给了他一笔巨款，让他与莉迪亚完婚。自此以后，伊丽莎白往日对达西的种种偏见通通化为真诚的爱。

宾利和简经过一番周折，言归于好，一对情人沉浸在欢乐之中。而一心想把自己的女儿嫁给达西的凯瑟琳夫人匆匆赶来，蛮横地要伊丽莎白保证不与达西结婚，伊丽莎白对这一无理要求断然拒绝。达西因此知道伊丽莎白已经改变了对他的看法，诚恳地再次向她求婚。至此，一对曾因傲慢和偏见而延搁婚事的有情人终成眷属。

成长主题解读

《傲慢与偏见》中主要人物的性格不是简单化和概念化的，而是随着故事情节层层推进的。男女主人公原有的思想和道德意识受到了挑战，他们开始意识到了各自在性格和心理上的弱点与不足，进而积极地调整自己的思想和行为，最终使自己在心理和道德上成熟起来。

一、达西的成长

小说的开始，达西在舞会上表现得非常傲慢，当许多姑娘被他的富有和俊朗的外貌吸引时，他骄傲地认为这里所有的女孩都不配做他的舞伴。之后，达西仅凭自己的片面之见，断然推测生活在普通家庭中的人都爱慕钱财和虚荣，又单凭简的母亲及姐妹的举止和言行就断定简并不钟情于好朋友宾利，认为简的婚姻都只是为了钱财，于是达西从中作梗，劝说好朋友宾利放弃娶简，导致宾利最终不辞而别，丢下简去了伦敦。伊丽莎白对求婚的拒绝使得达西不得不重新反思自身。达西意识到自己的不可一世、自高自大、目中无人、傲慢无礼都是自己喜欢的人所反感和厌恶的。达西决定改变自己,首先最重要的是要改变自己傲慢无礼的态度。他决定先离开伊丽莎白,在临走之前,他向伊丽莎白解释了自己阻止简和宾利婚礼的原因,同时也澄清了威克汉姆对自己的诋毁和污蔑,使得伊丽莎白对达西的态度稍有改变。第二年夏天,伊丽莎白跟随舅父母来到达西的庄园,此时达西充满爱心,受人尊敬,关心和爱护家人。见到伊丽莎白时,达西变得彬彬有礼,和蔼可亲。同时,在处理伊丽莎白妹妹私奔事件上,达西不仅没有因为伊丽莎白的家丑而嘲笑她,而且竭尽全力帮助她解决难题。达西的改变使伊丽莎白对达西的误解和偏见得以解除,从而也为两人关系的进一步发展打下了基础。在达西的态度改变的同时,其精神思想也有了进一步的提升。

二、伊丽莎白的成长

小说的开始可以看出伊丽莎白性格上的闪光点。首先是敏锐的观察力,她敏锐地觉察到宾利姐妹的傲慢自负虚伪;她看出了好朋友夏洛特为了追逐世俗利益而在道德上做出的"聪明的让步";她指出了达西"一旦与人结怨,永难忘却"的缺点;她从柯林斯的信中推测出他"既奴颜婢膝又妄自尊大"的性格特点。这些都说明了伊丽莎白有明达的理性头脑和敏锐的观察力。她不顾路途艰险孤身一人步行三英里(1 英里≈1609.34 米)去内瑟菲尔德庄园看望生病的姐姐以致弄得浑身泥泞,这突出了她的真诚与直率;面对达西无端的怠慢与侮辱她毫不在意,反而能把这事"兴致勃勃"地讲给自己的同伴听,表现了她的幽默与活泼;即使此后与达西相见,她也既不像其他小姐那样自作多情也没有伺机报复,体现了她的成熟与大度;她为母亲的粗俗和妹妹们的轻浮感到难堪更说明了她有良好的道德修养。这些都使她比那些矫揉造作的所谓"淑女"更胜一筹。在故事的开头,她就以活泼聪慧而又自尊自重的性格赢得了读者的认可和喜爱。另一方面,她的聪慧和机敏又成为她傲慢性格的基础。她从不放弃挪揄打趣的任何机会而且总是傲慢地拒绝他人的提醒。伊丽莎白傲慢的性格又为她的偏见埋下了伏笔。她的偏见可分为两种:第一种是对达西的反感和对韦汉姆的偏爱与同情。伊丽莎白对达西的反感无疑会在以后影响伊丽莎白对他品行的客观认识与评价,甚至会影响到对自己感情的正确认知。第二种偏见则来源于她的年龄。不满 21 岁的伊丽莎白生活阅历还不是很丰富,和其他年轻姑娘一样很容易被韦汉姆优雅的举止和迷人的风度所吸引。和达西的冷嘲热讽相反,韦汉姆的殷勤备至更容易使伊丽莎白的虚荣心得到满足,于是她从一开始就对韦汉姆流露出好感。伊丽莎白对达西的偏见导致了对韦汉姆的偏爱。在把韦汉姆的话转告姐姐后,她尖刻地嘲讽姐姐为达西所做的辩解,否认自己可能受骗,并且宣称"从他的神色就可以看出这些都是实情"。伊丽莎白没有意识到她的偏见已经深深影响了她的判断力。对达西的偏见使她曲解了达西对她的一切行为和表示,她将达西对她的不断注视看作挑剔,认为达西邀请她跳舞是想借机讥笑她的轻佻,还指责达西对韦汉姆存有偏见。这种偏见也让她一开始便倾向于相信韦汉姆对达西的指责,认定达西是一个冷酷无情的家伙。伊丽莎白听不进达西所做的任何解释,固执地认为达西阻挠简和宾利的婚事的动机是出于自负和势利,指责是达西一手造成了韦汉姆今日的不幸。这一切都严重阻碍了她对自我、达西、韦汉姆的正确认知。

　　达西的信成为她自我认知的转折点,此后她的心理逐渐趋于成熟。当她真正平静客观冷静地阅读那封信时,她终于意识到并开始克服性格中的弱点。她羞愧地发现自己过去判断事情的片面性和以貌取人的弱点,意识到自己必须学会通过事物的现象去认识本质。伊丽莎白意识到了自己的愚蠢与无知,客观地评价了达西,看出了韦汉姆的虚伪,对自我和他人的认识有了质的飞跃,她的道德随之升华。由于摆脱了傲慢与偏见,伊丽莎白更加清楚地认识到自己的优点。于是当凯瑟琳夫人要求她保证不同达西订婚时,她不卑不亢地拒绝了,这说明她意识到自己的才智和修养足以弥补自己低俗的家庭带来的不利,她与富人是完全平等的。她的心理终于成熟起来,消除了对达西的偏见,伊丽莎白清楚地感受到自己和达西之间的感情。伊丽莎白心理成长在于她终于克服了自己性格的傲慢与偏见,达到了正确的自我认知,忠实地面对自己的感情,完成了心理发展成熟过程,最终赢得了幸福。

下面选读是小说第 1 章,描述了故事的背景以及班纳特夫妇的性格特征。

IT is a truth universally acknowledged, that a single man in possession of a good fortune must be in want of a wife.

However little known the feelings or views of such a man may be on his first entering a neighbourhood, this truth is so well fixed in the minds of the surrounding families, that he is considered as the rightful property of some one or other of their daughters.

"My dear Mr. Bennet," said his lady to him one day, "have you heard that Netherfield Park is let at last?"[1]

Mr. Bennet replied that he had not.

"But it is," returned she, "for Mrs. Long has just been here, and she told me all about it."

Mr. Bennet made no answer.

"Do not you want to know who has taken it?" cried his wife impatiently.

"You want to tell me, and I have no objection to hearing it."

This was invitation enough.

"Why, my dear, you must know, Mrs. Long says that Netherfield is taken by a young man of large fortune from the north of England; that he came down on Monday in a chaise and four to see the place, and was so much delighted with it that he agreed with Mr. Morris immediately; that he is to take possession before Michaelmas,[2] and some of his servants are to be in the house by the end of next week."

"What is his name?"

"Bingley."

"Is he married or single?"

"Oh! single, my dear, to be sure! A single man of large fortune; four or five thousand a year. What a fine thing for our girls!"

"How so? how can it affect them?"

"My dear Mr. Bennet," replied his wife, "how can you be so tiresome! You must know that I am thinking of his marrying one of them."

"Is that his design in settling here?"

"Design! nonsense, how can you talk so! But it is very likely that he may fall in love with one of them, and therefore you must visit him as soon as he comes."

"I see no occasion for that. You and the girls may go, or you may send them by themselves, which perhaps will be still better; for, as you are as handsome as any of them, Mr. Bingley might like you the best of the party."[3]

"My dear, you flatter me. I certainly have had my share of beauty, but I do not pretend to be any thing extraordinary now. When a woman has five grown up daughters, she ought to give over thinking of her own beauty."

"In such cases, a woman has not often much beauty to think of."

"But, my dear, you must indeed go and see Mr. Bingley when he comes into the neighbourhood."

"It is more than I engage for, I assure you."

"But consider your daughters. Only think what an establishment it would be for one of them. Sir William and Lady Lucas are determined to go, merely on that account, for in general, you know they visit no new comers. Indeed you must go, for it will be impossible for us to visit him, if you do not."

"You are over-scrupulous, surely. I dare say Mr. Bingley will be very glad to see you; and I will send a few lines by you to assure him of my hearty consent to his marrying which ever he chooses of the girls; though I must throw in a good word for my little Lizzy."

"I desire you will do no such thing. Lizzy is not a bit better than the others; and I am sure she is not half so handsome as Jane, nor half so good humoured as Lydia. But you are always giving her the preference."

"They have none of them much to recommend them," replied he; "they are all silly and ignorant like other girls; but Lizzy has something more of quickness than her sisters."

"Mr. Bennet, how can you abuse your own children in such way? You take delight in vexing me. You have no compassion on my poor nerves."

"You mistake me, my dear. I have a high respect for your nerves. They are my old friends. I have heard you mention them with consideration these twenty years at least."

"Ah! you do not know what I suffer."

"But I hope you will get over it, and live to see many young men of four thousand a year come into the neighbourhood."

"It will be no use to us if twenty such should come, since you will not visit them."

"Depend upon it, my dear, that when there are twenty I will visit them all."

Mr. Bennet was so odd a mixture of quick parts, sarcastic humour, reserve, and caprice, that the experience of three and twenty years had been insufficient to make his wife understand his character. Her mind was less difficult to develop. She was a woman of mean understanding, little information, and uncertain temper. When she was discontented, she fancied herself nervous. The business of her life was to get her daughters married; its solace was visiting and news.

Notes:

1. Netherfield Park is let at last:尼日斐花园终于租出去了

2. he is to take possession before Michaelmas:他要在米迦勒节以前搬进来。米迦勒节在大约每年的9月29日,在中世纪,米迦勒节被强制性地当作一个圣日来庆祝,在英格兰、威尔士和爱尔兰,米迦勒节同时也是每年的四个账目结算日之一。

3. 注意此处以及下面班纳特先生对妻子的嘲讽语气。

Questions:

1. What are the ironies in this chapter?

2. How did the author present the Bennets' characters?

以下的选读为第 60 章,伊丽莎白接受达西的求婚后二人谈论他们感情发展的过程。

ELIZABETH's spirits soon rising to playfulness again, she wanted Mr. Darcy to account for his having ever fallen in love with her. "How could you begin?" said she. "I can comprehend your going on charmingly, when you had once made a beginning; but what could set you off in the first place?"

"I cannot fix on the hour, or the spot, or the look, or the words, which laid the foundation. It is too long ago. I was in the middle before I knew that I had begun."

"My beauty you had early withstood, and as for my manners—my behaviour to you was at least always bordering on the uncivil, and I never spoke to you without rather wishing to give you pain than not. Now be sincere; did you admire me for my impertinence[1]?"

"For the liveliness of your mind, I did."

"You may as well call it impertinence at once. It was very little less. The fact is, that you were sick of civility, of deference, of officious[2] attention. You were disgusted with the women who were always speaking, and looking, and thinking for your approbation[3] alone. I roused, and interested you, because I was so unlike them. Had you not been really amiable, you would have hated me for it; but in spite of the pains you took to disguise yourself, your feelings were always noble and just; and in your heart, you thoroughly despised the persons who so assiduously courted you. There—I have saved you the trouble of accounting for it; and really, all things considered, I begin to think it perfectly reasonable. To be sure, you knew no actual good of me—but nobody thinks of that when they fall in love."

"Was there no good in your affectionate behaviour to Jane while she was ill at Netherfield?"

"Dearest Jane! Who could have done less for her? But make a virtue of it by all means. My good qualities are under your protection, and you are to exaggerate them as much as possible; and, in return, it belongs to me to find occasions for teasing and quarrelling with you as often as may be; and I shall begin directly by asking you what made you so unwilling to come to the point at last. What made you so shy of me, when you first called, and afterwards dined here? Why, especially, when you called, did you look as if you did not care about me?"

"Because you were grave and silent, and gave me no encouragement."

"But I was embarrassed."

"And so was I."

"You might have talked to me more when you came to dinner."

"A man who had felt less, might."

"How unlucky that you should have a reasonable answer to give, and that I should be so reasonable as to admit it! But I wonder how long you would have gone on, if you had been left to yourself. I wonder when you would have spoken, if I had not asked you! My resolution of thanking you for your kindness to Lydia had certainly great effect. Too much, I am afraid; for what becomes of the moral, if our comfort springs from a breach of promise? For I ought not to have mentioned the subject. This will never do."

"You need not distress yourself. The moral will be perfectly fair. Lady Catherine's unjustifiable endeavours[4] to separate us were the means of removing all my doubts. I am not indebted for my present happiness to your eager desire of expressing your gratitude. I was not in a humour to wait for any opening of yours. My aunt's intelligence had given me hope, and I was determined at once to know every thing."

"Lady Catherine has been of infinite use, which ought to make her happy, for she loves to be of use. But tell me, what did you come down to Netherfield for? Was it merely to ride to Longbourn and be embarrassed? Or had you intended any more serious consequence?"

"My real purpose was to see you, and to judge, if I could, whether I might ever hope to make you love me. My avowed[5] one, or what I avowed to myself, was to see whether your sister were still partial to Bingley, and if she were, to make the confession to him which I have since made."

Notes:

1. impertinence: 鲁莽，无理
2. officious: 多管闲事的
3. approbation: 批准，这里指一些女孩希望得到达西的好感

4. Catherine's unjustifiable endeavours:指凯瑟琳夫人为了让自己的女儿嫁给达西而蛮横地要伊丽莎白保证不与达西结婚

5. avowed:公开宣称的,这里指达西以去看好友宾利为借口去看伊丽莎白

Questions:

1. How did their feeling for each other develop according to their recalling?

2. How was Elizabeth alienated from her surrounding?

3 Jane Eyre

作家及背景简介

夏洛蒂·勃朗特(Charlotte Brontë, 1816—1855)是英国批判现实主义小说家,批判现实主义作家描写劳资矛盾,揭露资本家对工人的残酷剥削和政治欺骗,正面描写工人的生活和斗争。善于描写"小人物"的命运,表现小资产阶级的痛苦挣扎和个人奋斗,具有温和的人道主义和浓厚的改良主义倾向。英国批判现实主义一般是从资产阶级人道主义

立场出发对社会进行批判和揭露的。作家们谴责资产阶级的不人道,要求剥削者和被剥削者之间互相宽容。他们并不要求消灭剥削制度,只要求剥削阶级恢复被金钱势力所腐蚀了的"人的天性",宽容地对待劳动者,让他们身心得到发展。批判现实主义作家歌颂劳动人民的某些品质,同情他们的遭遇,但是他们反对任何过激行为,反对暴力革命。

夏洛蒂·勃朗特生于英国北部约克郡的豪渥斯的一个乡村牧师家庭。母亲早逝,8岁的夏洛蒂被送进一所专收神职人员孤女的慈善性机构——柯文桥女子寄宿学校。在那里,她的两个姐姐玛丽亚和伊丽莎白因染上肺病而先后死去。夏洛蒂和妹妹艾米莉回到家乡,15岁时,她进入了伍勒小姐办的学校读书,几年后又在这个学校当教师。后来她当过家庭教师,最终投身于文学创作的道路。夏洛蒂·勃朗特有两个姐姐、两个妹妹和一个弟弟。两个妹妹艾米莉·勃朗特和安妮·勃朗特也是著名作家,因而在英国文学史上常有"勃朗特三姐妹"之称。

夏洛蒂·勃朗特善于利用当时现实生活中所提供的题材与人物,正确表现了那个时代的大事件,作品富有时代气息,叙述描写具有强

烈的感情色彩和感染力,这种激情是作者内心情感的自然流露,有很强的抒情色彩,她崇尚内心燃烧着精神火焰的人,夏洛蒂擅长描写景物,擅长用景物烘托气氛,衬托人物心理。

夏洛蒂·勃朗特小说的主人公都是女性。夏洛蒂认为,女性不是消极地适应环境和社会,不是无原则地妥协和牺牲;女性要勇于维护自己的尊严和权利,要学会依靠自己,独立面对人生和社会的各种挑战。女性要在情感、心理、精神上告别软弱、依赖和无助,克服各种限制人成长的羁绊。在勃朗特的小说中,最突出的主题就是女性要求独立自主的强烈愿望,将女性的呼声作为小说主题,这在她之前的英国文学史上是不曾有过的,夏洛蒂·勃朗特是表现这一主题的第一人。

选读作品简介

《简·爱》是一部具有自传色彩的作品,是夏洛蒂·勃朗特"诗意生平的写照"。作品讲述了一位从小变成孤儿的英国女子在各种磨难中不断追求自由与尊严,坚持自我,最终获得幸福的故事。小说引人入胜地展现了女主人公曲折起伏的爱情经历,塑造了一个摆脱一切旧习俗和偏见,敢于反抗,敢于争取自由和平等地位的妇女形象。

幼小的简·爱是个孤女,出身于一个穷牧师家庭。不久父母相继去世,简·爱寄居在舅妈家里,度过了10年备受歧视和虐待的生活。一次和舅妈争吵后,简·爱被舅妈送去了洛伍德孤儿院,在那里,简·爱经历了孤儿院的孩子所受的精神和肉体上的摧残,她最好的朋友海伦在一次大的伤寒中去世了,这次斑疹伤寒也使孤儿院有了大的改善。简·爱在孤儿院接受了六年的教育,并在这所学校任教两年。由于唯一关心简·爱的谭波尔小姐的离开,简·爱厌倦了孤儿院里的生活,简·爱登广告谋求家庭教师的工作,应聘到桑菲尔德庄园做了家庭教师,与庄园主人罗切斯特相爱。当婚礼在教堂悄然进行时,突然有人指证罗切斯特先生15年前已经结婚,他的妻子原来就是那个被关在三楼密室里的疯女人,简·爱不能接受一个有妇之夫,在一个风雨之夜,简·爱离开了罗切斯特。在寻找独立的生活出路的途中,简·爱在荒原上风餐露宿,历经磨难,最后被牧师圣·约翰收留,在当地一所小学校任教。不久,简·爱得知叔父去世并给她留下一笔遗产,同时还发现圣·约翰是她的表兄,简·爱决定将财产平分。圣·约翰是个狂热的教徒,打算去印度传教。他请求简·爱嫁给他并和他同去印度,理由只是简·爱适合做一位传教士的妻子,简·爱拒绝了他。简·爱在梦中听到了罗切斯特的呼唤,回到了桑菲尔德庄园,那座宅子已被烧成废墟,疯女人放火后坠楼身亡,罗切斯特也致残。简·爱最终和罗切斯特结婚,得到了自己理想的幸福生活。

成长主题解读

一、疏离感和顿悟

《简·爱》是关于女主人公成长历程的故事。小说的开头描写了一个被疏远在欢乐家庭生活圈子之外的孩子,她独自一人躲在帷幔后面看书。即使这样,这个寄人篱下的孩子也被人从她的躲避处拖了出来,受到无故的责骂和殴打。起初简·爱逆来顺受,"我听惯了约翰·里德的责骂,从未想回嘴;我盘算的只是:怎样来忍受那一定会跟着谩骂而来的殴打。"但随着年龄的增长,简·爱内心逐渐萌发了反抗意识,对里德少爷的专横有一天终于忍无可忍了。在简·爱用拳头回击了表兄之后,简·爱被舅妈关进了死去的舅舅住过的传说闹鬼的红房子,她和其他的孩子一样恐惧、害怕、痛苦、沮丧。但是她的反抗意识战胜了恐惧,冲破了痛苦,这是简·爱第一次精神顿悟,她开始意识到自我的存在,萌发了反抗意识。

在洛伍德孤儿院,简·爱和其他孩子们受到了身心的虐待,好友海伦的死亡促使了她对生命的首次沉思和顿悟。简·爱在欣赏着初夏的美好时,脑子里第一次想到"现在病危躺在床上,那是多么悲哀啊!世界真可爱,被迫离开世界,不得不到那谁也不知道的地方去,将是凄惨的",她的脑子"做出第一次认真的努力,要理解灌输给她的有关天堂和地狱事"。简·爱的意识里只能感觉到现世,还没有对死亡的清晰概念。当护士告诉她海伦即将死去时,简·爱经历了一次心灵的顿悟,也是其成长的标志。海伦告诉简·爱,她要回到"永久的家"和"最后的家",并以自己的宗教信仰来安慰简·爱:每个人都会死,像自己这样总是犯错的人在世上也不会有很大成就,死反而减轻了痛苦;人死后都会去到天国,那里有仁慈的上帝。海伦的死和她的信仰促使简·爱开始思考生死和信仰的问题,海伦的死是简·爱成长道路上的一次思想顿悟和启蒙。

为了追求经济独立以实现自我,简·爱离开了孤儿院来到了桑菲尔德庄园当了一名家庭女教师。来到庄园后第一次与男主人罗切斯特的对话中,可以看出简·爱的反叛且勇于表现自我的性格。当罗切斯特问她觉得他长得怎么样时,简·爱答道:"不太好看,先生,我说得太坦率了,请你原谅。"简·爱出身卑微、地位低下、相貌平平,但她在主人面前却始终不卑不亢,保持做人的尊严和独立人格。罗切斯特把她当作朋友、独立的人,他能对她坦诚相待,简·

爱非常感激他平等对待自己,她很珍视自己的独立人格和做人的尊严。罗切斯特也爱上了这位善良、自强不息的女孩。当罗切斯特拐弯抹角地向简·爱求婚时,简·爱天真地误以为罗切斯特要将她解雇,以为罗切斯特要和门当户对非常漂亮的布兰奇小姐结婚。简·爱以为自己将离开心爱的桑菲尔德庄园和她暗恋着的主人,简·爱直率地表达了自己的留恋和伤心,"离开桑菲尔德我很伤心,我爱桑菲尔德庄园——我爱它是因为我在这里过着充实而愉快的生活——至少有一段时间。我没有遭人践踏,也没有弄得古板僵化,没有混迹于志趣低下的人之中,也没有被排斥在同光明、健康、高尚的心灵交往的一切机会之外。我已面对面同我所敬重的人、同我所喜欢的人,同一个独特、活跃、博大的心灵交谈过。"同时她也勇敢维护了自己人格尊严:"你觉得因为我贫穷、低微、不美、矮小,我就没有灵魂,没有感情吗?你错了!我和你一样有灵魂和感情……我不是在传统和习俗的意义上和你对话,而是我的精神在和你的精神对话,就像我们死后平等地站在上帝面前一样,因为我们本来就是平等的!"(见选读二),这段爱情宣言,大胆、直率,丝毫没有自卑感,冲破了世俗及传统偏见,打破了以往女人被动角色,表现了她与众不同的新女性特征。她开始从男权社会中女性被赋予的温柔、被动性格中脱离出来,她凭着自己坚强的人生信念,勇于向传统世俗挑战:"我不是鸟,没有网能够捕捉我,我是一个有独立意志的自由人。"在当时物欲横流、道德沦丧的资本主义社会,人们往往根据财产、社会地位来判断人的价值,而简·爱有勇气面对世俗,维护自己的人格尊严,靠的是坚定独立的信念。当罗切斯特和简·爱在教堂举行婚礼时,罗切斯特却被揭露早已结婚,简·爱从幸福巅峰坠入了痛苦深渊。虽然罗切斯特表达了对简·爱真挚爱情并要求她留下与他共同生活,但自尊、自强不息的简·爱没有成为感情的奴隶,尽管她深爱着罗切斯特,尽管在当时的英国婚姻被认为是妇女唯一的出路,在经过痛苦的抉择后,她毫不犹豫将爱情深埋在心里,她不愿当第三者,不愿做情人,毅然离开桑菲尔德庄园去寻找自由、平等之路。此刻的简·爱经历了情感与理智、美丽的想象与残酷的现实的剧烈冲突,简·爱抵抗住了诱惑,离开了罗切斯特,经过这一痛苦的选择,简·爱得到了磨炼和成长。

离开桑菲尔德庄园后,简·爱在荒原上风餐露宿,历经磨难,最后被牧师圣·约翰收留,经过一段时间接触,圣·约翰开始向她求婚,圣·约翰以上帝使者自居,认为传教是他的天职,他假借上帝旨意强迫简·爱嫁给他,要求简·爱和他一起去印度传教。简·爱断然拒绝了他,她认清了他冷酷自私伪善的面目,也看破了这种婚姻的殉道本质,简·爱知道圣·约翰并不是真心爱她,只是认为她非常适合做传教士的妻子。在当时英国社会,无依无靠的简·爱和牧师结婚是一个非常体面的归宿,但是简·爱已意识到他们之间精神上极不和谐,她所追求是平等的、心灵相通的、真心相爱的婚姻,这表明了简·爱不随波逐流,敢于坚持自己人生信念的人格。

简·爱出走一段时间后,她内心感到罗切斯特在真诚召唤她,她再无法控制住自己的情感,在真挚的爱情的感召下,简·爱回到了桑菲尔德庄园,回到了阔别已久的罗切斯特身边,此时简·爱已经从她叔叔那继承了一些财产,有了些财富,罗切斯特却由于大火一贫如洗且双目失明,罗切斯特的妻子也在大火中丧生,简·爱却不顾他肢体的残缺及贫穷,义无反顾地与他结婚。简·爱认为婚姻应建立在平等基础上,而不应取决于人的社会地位、财富和外貌,只有男女彼此真心相爱,才能在婚姻中得到真正的幸福。

二、成长引路人

在成长小说中,主人公的经历及其切身体验是必不可少的要素,但成长路上的引路人也是一个主要的条件。简·爱在认识自我的成长过程中有着三类引路人。

一是神灵。每当她有所思考时,简·爱的思绪都会自然地转向上帝,渴求神灵的指引和帮助。"除了这个尘世,除了人类,还有一个看不见的世界,还有一个神灵的王国。这个世界就在我们周围,它无所不在;那些神灵守护着我们,因为它们有保护我们的任务。"

二是女性引路人。在盖茨海德,简·爱倍感孤独,女佣白茜是她幼小心灵的唯一感情慰藉,也是她心目中第一个母亲形象。当简·爱在红房子里时,白茜抚慰她、保护她。在洛伍德孤儿院,从海伦·彭斯身上,简·爱看到了近乎清教徒式的安静、善良、隐忍,尽管简·爱并不认同和赞成海伦的这种"不抵抗"态度,但她还是在无形中受到了海伦的影响。谭波尔小姐是这所阴暗的慈善学校里唯一闪亮的灯光,她的善良、温柔、和蔼给简·爱带来了无限的温暖。于是简·爱努力学习,尽量做到最好,以博得谭波尔小姐的喜爱,同时赢得别人的友谊和尊敬。当谭波尔小姐离开时,简·爱回顾她们多年来的友谊,认为"她是我的母亲、保护人,后来又是我的伴侣"。当简·爱逃离桑菲尔德庄园后,她经历了人生中最为困苦的时刻,贫穷、饥饿、流浪使她走投无路,在一所名叫沼泽居的乡村住宅前,被黛安娜和玛丽挽救。在这姐妹俩身上,简·爱又找到了母亲的影子。

三是男性引路人。在简·爱的成长过程中,有两个主要男性人物威胁到她对平等和尊严的追求:布洛克赫斯特校长和圣·约翰。这两位男性是其反面意义上的引路人。布洛克赫斯特校长以虚伪的虔诚控制他人,他不让学生吃饱穿暖,不给她们足够的休息时间,还强制她们剪掉自然卷曲的头发,给她们穿质地最粗、式样最丑的服装,企图扼杀她们身上少女最后一点爱美的天性。他对女性流露出一种本能的敌意,显示了一种极端的男权压迫。逃离了罗切斯特以后,圣·约翰又以传教的名义来压迫简·爱,其残忍程度不亚于当年的布洛克赫斯特校长,他不允许简·爱追求世俗的乐趣,不承认简·爱有自主选择生活道路的权利,他把自己的目标以崇高的名义强加于简·爱。简·爱奋起反抗,"要是我嫁了你,你会害死我的。你现在就害死我"。《简·爱》中的主人公体验了成长中的孤独感,受到正面形象和反面形象引路人的影响,经历了顿悟,获得了身心的成长。

下面选读出自第 7 章，描写了慈善学校的虚伪和女孩受到的身心虐待。

"Madam, allow me an instant. You are aware that my plan in bringing up these girls is, not to accustom them to habits of luxury and indulgence, but to render them hardy, patient, self-denying. Should any little accidental disappointment of the appetite occur, such as the spoiling of a meal, the under or the over dressing of a dish[1], the incident ought not to be neutralised by replacing with something more delicate the comfort lost[2], thus pampering the body and obviating the aim of this institution; it ought to be improved to the spiritual edification of the pupils, by encouraging them to evince fortitude under temporary privation. A brief address on those occasions would not be mistimed, wherein a judicious instructor would take the opportunity of referring to the sufferings of the primitive Christians;[3] to the torments of martyrs; to the exhortations of our blessed Lord Himself[4], calling upon His disciples to take up their cross and follow Him; to His warnings that man shall not live by bread alone, but by every word that proceedeth out of the mouth of God; to His divine consolations, 'If ye suffer hunger or thirst for my sake, happy are ye.' " "Oh, madam, when you put bread and cheese, instead of burnt porridge, into these children's mouths, you may indeed feed their vile bodies, but you little think how you starve their immortal souls!"

Mr. Brocklehurst again paused—perhaps overcome by his feelings. Miss Temple had looked down when he first began to speak to her; but she now gazed straight before her, and her face, naturally pale as marble, appeared to be assuming also the coldness and fixity of that material;[5] especially her mouth, closed as if it would have required a sculptor's chisel to open it, and her brow settled gradually into petrified severity.

Meantime, Mr. Brocklehurst, standing on the hearth with his hands behind his back, majestically surveyed the whole school. Suddenly his eye gave a blink, as if it had met something that either dazzled or shocked its pupil;[6] turning, he said in more rapid accents than he had hitherto used—

"Miss Temple, Miss Temple, what—what is that girl with curled hair? Red hair, ma'am, curled—curled all over?" And extending his cane he pointed to the awful object[7], his hand shaking as he did so.

"It is Julia Severn," replied Miss Temple, very quietly.

"Julia Severn, ma'am! And why has she, or any other, curled hair?

Why, in defiance of every precept and principle of this house, does she conform to the world so openly—here in an evangelical, charitable establishment—as to wear her hair one mass of curls?"

"Julia's hair curls naturally," returned Miss Temple, still more quietly.

"Naturally! Yes, but we are not to conform to nature; I wish these girls to be the children of Grace[8]; and why that abundance? I have again and again intimated that I desire the hair to be arranged closely, modestly, plainly. Miss Temple, that girl's hair must be cut off entirely; I will send a barber tomorrow; and I see others who have far too much of the excrescence—that tall girl, tell her to turn round. Tell all the first form to rise up and direct their faces to the wall."

Miss Temple passed her handkerchief over her lips, as if to smooth away the involuntary smile that curled them; she gave the order, however, and when the first class could take in what was required of them, they obeyed. Leaning a little back on my bench, I could see the looks and grimaces with which they commented on this manoeuvre: it was a pity Mr. Brocklehurst could not see them too; he would perhaps have felt that, whatever he might do with the outside of the cup and platter, the inside was further beyond his interference than he imagined[9].

He scrutinised the reverse of these living medals[10] some five minutes, then pronounced sentence. These words fell like the knell of doom—

"All those top-knots must be cut off."

Miss Temple seemed to remonstrate.

"Madam," he pursued, "I have a Master to serve whose kingdom is not of this world[11]; my mission is to mortify in these girls the lusts of the flesh; to teach them to clothe themselves with shame-facedness and sobriety, not with braided hair and costly apparel; and each of the young persons before us has a string of hair twisted in plaits which vanity itself might have woven; these, I repeat, must be cut off; think of the time wasted, of—"

Mr. Brocklehurst was here interrupted: three other visitors, ladies, now entered the room. They ought to have come a little sooner to have heard his lecture on dress, for they were splendidly attired in velvet, silk, and furs. The two younger of the trio (fine girls of sixteen and seventeen) had grey beaver hats, then in fashion, shaded with ostrich plumes, and from under the brim of this graceful head-dress fell a profusion of light tresses, elaborately curled; the elder lady was enveloped in a costly velvet shawl, trimmed with ermine, and she wore a false front of French curls.

These ladies were deferentially received by Miss Temple, as Mrs. and the Misses Brocklehurst, and conducted to seats of honour at the top of the room. It seems they had come in the carriage with their reverend relative, and had been conducting a rummaging scrutiny of the room upstairs, while he transacted business with the housekeeper, questioned the laundress, and lectured the superintendent. They now proceeded to address divers remarks and reproofs to Miss Smith, who was charged with the care of the linen and the inspection of the dormitories: but I had no time to listen to what they said; other matters called off and enchanted my attention.

Hitherto, while gathering up the discourse of Mr. Brocklehurst and Miss Temple, I had not, at the same time, neglected precautions to secure my personal safety; which I thought would be effected, if I could only elude observation. To this end, I had sat well back on the form, and while seeming to be busy with my sum, had held my slate in such a manner as to conceal my face: I might have escaped notice, had not my treacherous slate somehow happened to slip from my hand, and falling with an obtrusive crash, directly drawn every eye upon me; I knew it was all over now, and, as I stooped to pick up the two fragments of slate, I rallied my forces for the worst. It came.

"A careless girl!" said Mr. Brocklehurst, and immediately after—"It is the new pupil, I perceive." And before I could draw breath, "I must not forget I have a word to say respecting her." Then aloud: how loud it seemed to me! "Let the child who broke her slate come forward!"

Of my own accord I could not have stirred; I was paralysed: but the two great girls who sit on each side of me, set me on my legs and pushed me towards the dread judge[12], and then Miss Temple gently assisted me to his very feet, and I caught her whispered counsel—

"Don't be afraid, Jane, I saw it was an accident; you shall not be punished."

The kind whisper went to my heart like a dagger.

"Another minute, and she will despise me for a hypocrite," thought I; and an impulse of fury against Reed, Brocklehurst, and Co.[13] bounded in my pulses at the conviction. I was no Helen Burns.

"Fetch that stool," said Mr. Brocklehurst, pointing to a very high one from which a monitor had just risen: it was brought.

"Place the child upon it."

And I was placed there, by whom I don't know: I was in no condition to note particulars; I was only aware that they had hoisted me up to the height of Mr. Brocklehurst's nose, that he was within a yard of me, and that a spread of shot orange and purple silk pelisses and a cloud of silvery plumage extended and waved below me.

Mr. Brocklehurst hemmed.

"Ladies," said he, turning to his family, "Miss Temple, teachers, and children, you all see this girl?"

Of course they did; for I felt their eyes directed like burning-glasses against my scorched skin.

"You see she is yet young; you observe she possesses the ordinary form of childhood; God has graciously given her the shape that He has given to all of us; no signal deformity points her out as a marked character. Who would think that the Evil One[14] had already found a servant and agent in her? Yet such, I grieve to say, is the case."

A pause—in which I began to steady the palsy of my nerves, and to feel that the Rubicon was passed[15]; and that the trial, no longer to be shirked, must be firmly sustained.

"My dear children," pursued the black marble clergyman, with pathos, "this is a sad, a melancholy occasion; for it becomes my duty to warn you, that this girl, who might be one of God's own lambs, is a little castaway: not a member of the true flock, but evidently an interloper and an alien. You must be on your guard against her; you must shun her example; if necessary, avoid her company, exclude her from your sports, and shut her out from your converse. Teachers, you must watch her: keep your eyes on her movements, weigh well her words, scrutinise her actions, punish her body to save her soul; if, indeed, such salvation be possible, for (my tongue falters while I tell it) this girl, this child, the native of a Christian land, worse than many a little heathen who says its prayers to Brahma[16] and kneels before Juggernaut[17]—this girl is—a liar!"

Now came a pause of ten minutes, during which I, by this time in perfect possession of my wits, observed all the female Brocklehursts produce their pocket-handkerchiefs and apply them to their optics, while the elderly lady swayed herself to and fro, and the two younger ones whispered, "How shocking!" Mr. Brocklehurst resumed.

"This I learned from her benefactress; from the pious and charitable lady who adopted her in her orphan state, reared her as her own daughter, and whose kindness, whose generosity the unhappy girl repaid by an ingratitude so bad, so dreadful, that at last her excellent patroness was obliged to separate her from her own young ones, fearful lest her vicious example should contaminate their purity: she has sent her here to be healed, even as the Jews of old sent their diseased to the troubled pool of Bethesda[18]; and, teachers, superintendent, I beg of you not to allow the waters to stagnate round her."

With this sublime conclusion, Mr. Brocklehurst adjusted the top button of his surtout, muttered something to his family, who rose, bowed to Miss Temple, and then all the great people sailed in state[19] from the room. Turning at the door, my judge said—

"Let her stand half-an-hour longer on that stool, and let no one speak to her during the remainder of the day."

There was I, then, mounted aloft; I, who had said I could not bear the shame of standing on my natural feet in the middle of the room, was now exposed to general view on a pedestal of infamy. What my sensations were no language can describe; but just as they all rose, stifling my breath and constricting my throat, a girl came up and passed me; in passing, she lifted her eyes. What a strange light inspired them! What an extraordinary sensation that ray sent through me! How the new feeling bore me up! It was as if a martyr, a hero, had passed a slave or victim, and imparted strength in the transit. I mastered the rising hysteria, lifted up my head, and took a firm stand on the stool.

Notes:

1. the under or over dressing of a dish:菜没做熟或做糊了

2. Miss Temple should not have given the pupils a lunch of bread and cheese("something more delicate") after they had taken burnt porridge("the

comfort lost")即使粥煮糊了,谭波尔小姐也不应该给学生更好吃的面包和奶酪作为赔偿。此话表现了校长以宗教之名对学生的虐待。

3. the sufferings of the primitive Christians:指早期基督教在未被接受时基督教徒受到的折磨

4. Lord Himself:指耶稣本人

5. material:指前面的 the marble(大理石)

6. pupil:瞳孔

7. the awful object:指这里的红色卷发的学生

8. children of grace:孩子在上帝的庇护下长大

9. 他可以在一定程度上控制这些女孩的外在行为,但她们的内心不是他能操控的。

10. living medals:这是比喻女孩们的站姿

11. I have a Master to serve whose kingdom is not of this world. 我所服待的上帝的王国不在这个世界,意指这些孩子不应该有尘世的享受。

12. the dread judge:指布洛克赫斯特校长

13. Co. 指简·爱认为与她为敌的 Reed 和 Broklehurst 等那一帮人。

14. the Evil One:恶魔撒旦

15. The decisive step had been taken.(源自于恺撒带领军队越过 Rubicon 河)

16. Brahma:印度神,这里指异教神

17. Juggernaut:印度神话中的克利须那神

18. 在圣经中,耶路撒冷的生病的穷人聚集在毕士大池,当地人认为天使会在某个季节到来搅动池水,最先进入池水的人会恢复健康。

19. sail in state:这里比喻校长的女儿们走路的姿势。in state,庄重地,此处描写讽刺了校长一家人的虚伪。

Questions:

1. How was Jane Eyre alienated from the environment here?

2. What did she realize from the experience?

下面选读出自第 23 章,描写了罗切斯特先生向简·爱求婚的情景。

A SPLENDID Midsummer shone over England: skies so pure, suns so radiant as were then seen in long succession, seldom favour even singly, our wave-girt[1] land. It was as if a band of Italian days had come from the South, like a flock of glorious passenger birds,[2] and lighted to rest[3] them on the cliffs of Albion. The hay was all got in; the fields round Thornfield were green and shorn; the roads white and baked; the trees were in their dark prime; hedge and wood, full-leaved and deeply tinted, contrasted well with the sunny hue of the cleared meadows between.

On Midsummer-eve, Adele, weary with gathering wild strawberries in Hay Lane half the day, had gone to bed with the sun. I watched her drop asleep, and when I left her, I sought the garden.

It was now the sweetest hour of the twenty-four:-'Day its fervid fires had wasted,' and dew fell cool on panting plain and scorched summit. Where the sun had gone down in simple state-pure of the pomp of clouds-spread a solemn purple, burning with the light of red jewel and furnace flame at one point, on one hill-peak, and extending high and wide, soft and still softer, over half heaven. The east had its own charm of fine deep blue, and its own modest gem, a rising and solitary star: soon it would boast the moon; but she was yet beneath the horizon.

I walked a while on the pavement; but a subtle, well-known scent-that of a cigar-stole from some window; I saw the library casement open a hand-breadth; I knew I might be watched thence; so I went apart into the orchard. No nook in the grounds more sheltered and more Eden-like; it was full of trees, it bloomed with flowers: a very high wall shut it out from the court, on one side; on the other, a beech avenue screened it from the lawn. At the bottom was a sunk fence; its sole separation from lonely fields: a winding walk, bordered with laurels and terminating in a giant horse-chestnut, circled at the base by a seat, led down to the fence. Here one could wander unseen. While such honey-dew fell, such silence reigned, such gloaming gathered, I felt as if I could haunt such shade for ever; but in threading the flower and fruit parterres at the upper part of the enclosure, enticed there by the light the now rising moon cast on this more open quarter, my step is stayed-not by sound, not by sight, but once more by a warning fragrance.

Sweet-brier and southernwood,[4] jasmine, pink, and rose have long been yielding their evening sacrifice of incense: this new scent is neither of shrub nor flower; it is-I know it well-it is Mr. Rochester's cigar. I look round and I listen. I see trees laden with ripening fruit. I hear a nightingale warbling in a wood half a mile off; no moving form is visible, no coming step audible; but that perfume increases: I must flee. I make for the wicket leading to the shrubbery, and I see Mr. Rochester entering. I step aside into the ivy recess; he will not stay long: he will soon return whence he came, and if I sit still he will never see me.

But no—eventide is as pleasant to him as to me, and this antique garden as attractive; and he strolls on, now lifting the gooseberry-tree branches to look at the fruit, large as plums, with which they are laden; now taking a ripe cherry from the wall; now stooping towards a knot of flowers, either to inhale their fragrance or to admire the dew-beads on their petals. A great moth goes humming by me; it alights on a plant at Mr. Rochester's foot: he sees it, and bends to examine it.

'Now, he has his back towards me,' thought I, ' and he is occupied too; perhaps, if I walk softly, I can slip away unnoticed.'

I trode on an edging of turf that the crackle of the pebbly gravel might not betray me: he was standing among the beds at a yard or two distant from where I had to pass; the moth apparently engaged him. 'I shall get by very well,' I meditated. As I crossed his shadow, thrown long over the garden by the moon, not yet risen high, he said quietly, without turning-

'Jane, come and look at this fellow.'

I had made no noise: he had not eyes behind-could his shadow feel?

I started at first, and then I approached him.

'Look at his wings,' said he, 'he reminds me rather of a West Indian insect; one does not often see so large and gay a night-rover in England; there! he is flown.'

The moth roamed away. I was sheepishly retreating also; but Mr. Rochester followed me, and when we reached the wicket, he said-

'Turn back: on so lovely a night it is a shame to sit in the house; and surely no one can wish to go to bed while sunset is thus at meeting with moonrise.'

It is one of my faults, that though my tongue is sometimes prompt enough at an answer, there are times when it sadly fails me in framing an excuse; and always the lapse occurs at some crisis, when a facile word or plausible pretext is specially wanted to get me out of painful embarrassment. I did not like to walk at this hour alone with Mr. Rochester in the shadowy orchard; but I could not find a reason to allege for leaving him. I followed with lagging step, and thoughts busily bent on discovering a means of extrication; but he himself looked so composed and so grave also, I became ashamed of feeling any confusion: the evil-if evil existent or prospective there was-seemed to lie with me only; his mind was unconscious and quiet.

'Jane,' he recommenced, as we entered the laurel walk, and slowly strayed down in the direction of the sunk fence and the horse-chestnut,' Thornfield is a pleasant place in summer, is it not?'

'Yes, sir.'

'You must have become in some degree attached to the house,-you, who have an eye for natural beauties, and a good deal of the organ of Adhesiveness?'[5]

'I am attached to it, indeed.'

'And though I don't comprehend how it is, I perceive you have acquired a degree of regard for that foolish little child Adele, too; and even for simple dame Fairfax?'[6]

'Yes, sir; in different ways, I have an affection for both.'

'And would be sorry to part with them?'

'Yes.'

'Pity!' he said, and sighed and paused. 'It is always the way of events in this life,' he continued presently: 'no sooner have you got settled in a pleasant resting-place, than a voice calls out to you to rise and move on, for the hour of repose is expired.'

'Must I move on, sir?' I asked. 'Must I leave Thornfield?'

'I believe you must, Jane. I am sorry, Janet, but I believe indeed you must.'

This was a blow; but I did not let it prostrate me.

'Well, sir, I shall be ready when the order to march comes.'

'It is come now-I must give it to-night.'

'Then you are going to be married, sir?'

'Ex-act-ly-pre-cise-ly: with your usual acuteness, you have hit the nail straight on the head.'[7]

'Soon, sir?'

'Very soon, my-that is, Miss Eyre: and you'll remember, Jane, the first time I, or Rumour, plainly intimated to you that it was my intention to put my old bachelor's neck into the sacred noose, to enter into the holy estate of matrimony-to take Miss Ingram to my bosom, in short (she's an extensive armful: but that's not to the point-one can't have too much of such a very excellent thing as my beautiful Blanche): well, as I was saying-listen to me, Jane!

You're not turning your head to look after more moths, are you? That was only a lady-clock,[8] child, 'flying away home.' I wish to remind you that it was you who first said to me, with that discretion I respect in you-with that foresight, prudence, and humility which befit your responsible and dependent position-that in case I married Miss Ingram, both you and little Adele had better trot forthwith. I pass over[9] the sort of slur conveyed in this suggestion on the character of my beloved; indeed, when you are far away, Janet, I'll try to forget it: I shall notice only its wisdom; which is such that I have made it my law of action. Adele must go to school; and you, Miss Eyre, must get a new situation.'

'Yes, sir, I will advertise immediately: and meantime, I suppose-' I was going to say, 'I suppose I may stay here, till I find another shelter to betake myself to': but I stopped, feeling it would not do to risk a long sentence, for my voice was not quite under command.

'In about a month I hope to be a bridegroom,' continued Mr. Rochester; 'and in the interim, I shall myself look out for employment and an asylum for you.'

'Thank you, sir; I am sorry to give-'

'Oh, no need to apologise! I consider that when a dependant[10] does her duty as well as you have done yours, she has a sort of claim upon her employer for any little assistance he can conveniently render her; indeed I have already, through my future mother-in-law, heard of a place that I think will suit: it is to undertake the education of the five daughters of Mrs.

Dionysius O'Gall of Bitternutt Lodge, Connaught, Ireland. You'll like Ireland, I think; they're such warmhearted people there, they say.'

'It is a long way off, sir.'

'No matter-a girl of your sense will not object to the voyage or the distance.'

'Not the voyage, but the distance; and then the sea is a barrier-'

'From what, Jane?'

'From England and from Thornfield; and-'

'Well?'

'From you, sir.'

I said this almost involuntarily, and, with as little sanction of free will, my tears gushed out. I did not cry so as to be heard, however; I avoided sobbing. The thought of Mrs. O'Gall and Bitternutt Lodge struck cold to my heart; and colder the thought of all the brine and foam, destined, as it seemed, to rush between me and the master at whose side I now walked, and coldest the remembrance of the wider ocean-wealth, caste, custom intervened between me and what I naturally and inevitably loved.

'It is a long way,' I again said.

'It is, to be sure; and when you get to Bitternutt Lodge, Connaught, Ireland, I shall never see you again, Jane; that's morally certain. I never go over to Ireland, not having myself much of a fancy for the country. We have been good friends, Jane; have we not?'

'Yes, sir.'

'And when friends are on the eve of separation, they like to spend the little time that remains to them close to each other. Come! we'll talk over the voyage and the parting quietly half an hour or so, while the stars enter into their shining life up in heaven yonder: here is the chestnut tree: here is the bench at its old roots.

Come, we will sit there in peace to-night, though we should never more be destined to sit there together.' He seated me and himself.

'It is a long way to Ireland, Janet, and I am sorry to send my little friend on such weary travels; but if I can't do better, how is it to be helped? Are you anything akin to me, do you think, Jane?'

I could risk no sort of answer by this time; my heart was still.

'Because,' he said, 'I sometimes have a queer feeling with regard to you-especially when you are near me, as now: it is as if I had a string somewhere under my left ribs, tightly and inextricably knotted to a similar string situated in the corresponding quarter of your little frame. And if that boisterous Channel and two hundred miles or so of land come broad between us, I am afraid that cord of communion will be snapped; and then I've a nervous notion I should take to bleeding inwardly. As for you,-you'd forget me.'

'That I never should, sir: you know-' Impossible to proceed.

'Jane, do you hear that nightingale singing in the wood? Listen!'

In listening, I sobbed convulsively; for I could repress what I endured no longer; I was obliged to yield, and I was shaken from head to foot with acute distress. When I did speak, it was only to express an impetuous wish that I had never been born, or never come to Thornfield.

'Because you are sorry to leave it?'

The vehemence of emotion, stirred by grief and love within me, was claiming mastery, and struggling for full sway, and asserting a right to predominate, to overcome, to live, rise, and reign at last: yes,-and to speak.

'I grieve to leave Thornfield: I love Thornfield:-I love it, because I have lived in it a full and delightful life,-momentarily at least. I have not been trampled on. I have not been petrified. I have not been buried with inferior minds, and excluded from every glimpse of communion with what is bright and energetic and high. I have talked, face to face, with what I reverence, with what I delight in,-with an original, a vigorous, an expanded mind. I have known you, Mr. Rochester; and it strikes me with terror and anguish to feel I absolutely must be torn from you for ever. I see the necessity of departure; and it is like looking on the necessity of death.'

'Where do you see the necessity?' he asked suddenly.

'Where? You, sir, have placed it before me.'

'In what shape?'

'In the shape of Miss Ingram; a noble and beautiful woman,-your bride.'

'My bride! What bride? I have no bride!'

'But you will have.'

'Yes;-I will!'-I will!' He set his teeth.

'Then I must go;-you have said it yourself.'

'No; you must stay! I swear it-and the oath shall be kept.'

'I tell you I must go!' I retorted, roused to something like passion. 'Do you think I can stay to become nothing to you? Do you think I am an automaton? -a machine without feelings? And can bear to have my morsel of bread snatched from my lips, and my drop of living water dashed from my cup? Do you think, because I am poor, obscure, plain, and little, I am soulless and heartless? You think wrong! -I have as much soul as you,-and full as much heart! And if God had gifted me with some beauty and much wealth, I should have made it as hard for you to leave me, as it is now for me to leave you. I am not talking to you now through the medium of custom, conventionalities, nor even of mortal flesh;-it is my spirit that addresses your spirit; just as if both had passed through the grave, and we stood at God's feet, equal,-as we are!'

'As we are!' repeated Mr. Rochester-'so,' he added, enclosing me in his arms, gathering me to his breast, pressing his lips on my lips: 'so, Jane!'

'Yes, so, sir,' I rejoined: 'and yet not so; for you are a married man-or as good as a married man, and wed to one inferior to you-to one with whom you have no sympathy-whom I do not believe you truly love; for I have seen and heard you sneer at her. I would scorn such a union: therefore I am better than you-let me go!'

'Where, Jane? To Ireland?'

'Yes-to Ireland. I have spoken my mind, and can go anywhere now.'

'Jane, be still; don't struggle so, like a wild frantic bird that is rending its own plumage in its desperation.'

'I am no bird; and no net ensnares me; I am a free human being with an independent will, which I now exert to leave you.'

Another effort set me at liberty, and I stood erect before him.

'And your will shall decide your destiny,' he said: 'I offer you my hand, my heart, and a share of all my possessions.'

'You play a farce, which I merely laugh at.'

'I ask you to pass through life at my side-to be my second self, and best earthly companion.'

'For that fate you have already made your choice, and must abide by it.'

'Jane, be still a few moments: you are over-excited: I will be still too.'

A waft of wind came sweeping down the laurel-walk and trembled through the boughs of the chestnut: it wandered away-away-to an indefinite distance-it died. The nightingale's song was then the only voice of the hour: in listening to it, I again wept.

Mr. Rochester sat quiet, looking at me gently and seriously. Some time passed before he spoke; he at last said-

'Come to my side, Jane, and let us explain and understand one another.'

'I will never again come to your side: I am torn away now, and cannot return.'

'But, Jane, I summon you as my wife: it is you only I intend to marry.'

I was silent: I thought he mocked me.

'Come, Jane-come hither.'

'Your bride stands between us.'

He rose, and with a stride reached me.

'My bride is here,' he said, again drawing me to him, 'because my equal is here, and my likeness. Jane, will you marry me?'

Still I did not answer, and still I writhed myself from his grasp: for I was still incredulous.

'Do you doubt me, Jane?'

'Entirely.'

'You have no faith in me?'

'Not a whit.'

'Am I a liar in your eyes?' he asked passionately. 'Little sceptic, you shall be convinced. What love have I for Miss Ingram? None; and that you know. What love has she for me? None: as I have taken pains to prove: I caused a rumour to reach her that my fortune was not a third of what was supposed, and after that I presented myself to see the result; it was coldness both from her and her mother. I would not-I could not-marry Miss Ingram. You-you strange, you almost unearthly thing! -I love as my own flesh. You-poor and obscure, and small and plain as you are-I entreat to accept me as a husband.'

'What, me!' I ejaculated, beginning in his earnestness-and especially in his incivility-to credit his sincerity: 'me who have not a friend in the world but you-if you are my friend: not a shilling but what you have given me?'

'You, Jane, I must have you for my own-entirely my own. Will you be mine? Say yes, quickly. '

'Mr. Rochester, let me look at your face: turn to the moonlight. '

'Why?'

'Because I want to read your countenance-turn!'

'There! you will find it scarcely more legible than a crumpled, scratched page. Read on: only make haste, for I suffer. '

His face was very much agitated and very much flushed, and there were strong workings in the features, and strange gleams in the eyes.

'Oh, Jane, you torture me!' he exclaimed. 'With that searching and yet faithful and generous look, you torture me!'

'How can I do that? If you are true, and your offer real, my only feelings to you must be gratitude and devotion-they cannot torture. '

'Gratitude!' he ejaculated; and added wildly-'Jane, accept me quickly. Say, Edward-give me my name-Edward-I will marry you. '

'Are you in earnest? Do you truly love me? Do you sincerely wish me to be your wife?'

'I do; and if an oath is necessary to satisfy you, I swear it. '

'Then, sir, I will marry you. '

'Edward-my little wife!'

'Dear Edward!'

'Come to me-come to me entirely now,' said he; and added, in his deepest tone, speaking in my ear as his cheek was laid on mine, 'Make my happiness-I will make yours. '

'God pardon me!' he subjoined ere long; 'and man meddle not with me: I have her, and will hold her. '

'There is no one to meddle, sir. I have no kindred to interfere. '

'No-that is the best of it, ' he said. And if I had loved him less I should have thought his accent and look of exultation savage; but, sitting by him, roused from the nightmare of parting-called to the paradise of union-I thought only of the bliss given me to drink in so abundant a flow. Again and again he said, 'Are you happy, Jane?'

And again and again I answered, 'Yes,' After which he murmured, 'It will atone-it will atone. Have I not found her friendless, and cold, and comfortless? Will I not guard, and cherish, and solace her? Is there not love in my heart, and constancy in my resolves? It will expiate at God's tribunal. I know my Maker[11] sanctions what I do.

For the world's judgment-I wash my hands thereof.[12] For man's opinion-I defy it.'

But what had befallen the night? The moon was not yet set, and we were all in shadow: I could scarcely see my master's face, near as I was. And what ailed the chestnut tree? it writhed and groaned; while wind roared in the laurel walk, and came sweeping over us.

'We must go in,' said Mr. Rochester: 'the weather changes. I could have sat with thee till morning, Jane.'

'And so,' thought I, 'could I with you.' I should have said so, perhaps, but a livid, vivid spark leapt out of a cloud at which I was looking, and there was a crack, a crash, and a close rattling peal; and I thought only of hiding my dazzled eyes against Mr. Rochester's shoulder.

The rain rushed down. He hurried me up the walk, through the grounds, and into the house; but we were quite wet before we could pass the threshold. He was taking off my shawl in the hall, and shaking the water out of my loosened hair, when Mrs. Fairfax emerged from her room. I did not observe her at first, nor did Mr. Rochester. The lamp was lit. The dock was on the stroke of twelve.

'Hasten to take off your wet things,' said he: 'and before you go, good-night-good-night, my darling!'

He kissed me repeatedly. When I looked up, on leaving his arms, there stood the widow, pale, grave, and amazed. I only smiled at her, and ran upstairs. 'Explanation will do for another time,' thought I. Still, when I reached my chamber, I felt a pang at the idea she should even temporarily misconstrue what she had seen. But joy soon effaced every other feeling; and loud as the wind blew, near and deep as the thunder crashed, fierce and frequent as the lightning gleamed, cataract-like as the rain fell during a storm of two hours' duration, I experienced no fear and little awe. Mr. Rochester came thrice to my door in the course of it, to ask if I was safe and tranquil:

and that was comfort, that was strength for anything.

　　Before I left my bed in the morning, little Adele came running in to tell me that the great horse-chestnut at the bottom of the orchard had been struck by lightning in the night, and half of it split away.

Notes:
1. wave-girt:波浪环绕的
2. passenger bird:候鸟
3. light to rest:歇脚
4. southernwood:青蒿
5. adhesiveness:依恋之情
6. Fairfax:费尔法克斯(男子名、姓氏)桑菲尔德庄园的管家
7. hit the nail straight on the head:说中了
8. lady-clock:瓢虫
9. pass over:不在意
10. dependant:家眷,侍从
11. Maker:造物主
12. wash one's hands there of:不理睬

Questions:
1. What's the implication of the environment description?
2. How do the characters' conversations reveal their mind?

4

Great Expectations

作者及背景简介

查尔斯·狄更斯(Charles John Huffam Dickens,1812—1870)是英国批判现实主义文学的代表作家之一,狄更斯注重描写生活在英国社会底层受到剥削和压迫的"小人物"的生活遭遇,深刻地反映了维多利亚时期英国复杂的社会现实,他的作品对英国文学发展起到了深远的影响。

狄更斯出身贫寒,父亲是英国海军部门的一名小职员,薪水微薄,经常入不敷出,狄更斯10岁时,父亲因负债被关进债务拘留所,狄更斯经常去那里看望父亲,狱中的阴森恐怖使他永生难忘,狄更斯被关进一家黑鞋油作坊当童工,整天洗刷玻璃瓶,在瓶身上贴鞋油商标,狄更斯在贫困和痛苦中度过了童年,生活的磨难使他对英国贫苦儿童和劳动人民的痛苦和屈辱有了深刻的了解,狄更斯小说中的主人公的种种不幸他大都经历过。后来狄更斯的一位亲属去世,他父亲得到了一笔遗产,从而还清了贷款并获释出狱。狄更斯因此进入一所私立学校就读。15岁时,狄更斯又因家庭经济拮据不得不辍学,到伦敦的一个律师事务所当了办事员,这份工作不仅使他学会了速记,而且还使他有机会走遍城市的大街小巷,同形形色色的人接触,充分体验社会各阶层的生活。与此同时,狄更斯依靠自学来充实自己,在伦敦的图书馆内博览群书,几年后狄更斯担任了一家报社的采访记者,经常在英国议会中列席采访,目睹了英国议会政治的肮脏内幕。

狄更斯18岁时,同一位银行家的女儿玛丽亚·皮特奈尔相爱,但对方家长因嫌狄更斯当"采访记者"的卑微身份而坚决反对,狄更斯以为双方互相钟情,鼓足勇气向玛丽亚表白,却遭遇到了冷淡的拒绝。这次经历在狄更斯的心灵上刻下了深刻的烙印,以至于他轻蔑现实中的女子而幻想理想中的女性,这在他的一些小说中有所反映。狄更斯于1836年同《晨报》经纪人的女儿凯瑟琳·霍德斯相遇,两人一见钟情,于当年结婚,婚后最初几年还算幸福,但后来凯瑟琳逐渐爱慕虚荣,贪图享乐,热衷于投身上流社会,两人之间的隔阂渐深,最终因感情破裂离婚。狄更斯与凯瑟琳的妹妹却处得非常好,在他与凯瑟琳结婚以后,16岁的玛丽(凯瑟琳有两个妹妹,玛丽排行老三)经常来家中作客,这让他有了足够的与玛丽相处的机会,玛丽在狄更斯的心目中是理想女性的化身,小说《老古玩店》中的耐尔就是以玛丽为原型塑造的。

狄更斯生活和创作的时间正是19世纪中叶维多利亚女王时代前期,这一时期也是英国工业革命时期,英国经济快速发展,成为"世界工厂",另一方面贫富差距日益加大,经济剥削和政治压迫等社会问题加剧。狄更斯以写实的笔法揭露社会上层和资产阶级的虚伪、贪婪、凶残,满怀激愤和深切的同情揭示了下层社会,特别是妇女、儿童和老人的悲惨处境,描写开始觉醒的劳苦大众的抗争。与此同时,他还以理想主义和浪漫主义的豪情讴歌人性中的真善美,憧憬更合理的社会和更美好的人生。狄更斯体现了英国人的核心精神,一种发自内心的快乐和满足,但狄更斯身上还有英国人的另一种精神,一种自觉的反思和批判精神。他为弱势群体发声,追求社会正义,探寻能使人类和谐相处的核心价值。

狄更斯描写了数量众多的中下层社会的小人物,这在文学作品中是空前的。狄更斯以高度的艺术概括、生动的细节描写、妙趣横生的幽默和细致入微的分析,塑造了许多令人难忘的形象,真实地反映了英国19世纪初叶的社会面貌,具有巨大的感染力和认识价值,并形成了独特的风格。狄更斯不采用说教或概念化的方式表现他的倾向性,而往往以生动的艺术形象激发读者的愤慨、憎恨、同情和热爱。狄更斯笔下的人物大多有鲜明的个性,狄更斯善于运用艺术夸张的手法突出人物形象的某些特征,用他们习惯的动作、姿势和用语等揭示他们的内心生活和思想面貌,狄更斯还善于从生活中汲取生动的群众语言,以人物特有的语言表现人物的特点和性格。

选读作品简介

《远大前程》大致可分成三个部分。第一部分记述了皮普在乡间质朴的童年生活。皮普父母双亡,寄居在姐姐家,姐姐脾气暴躁,一直唠叨他;而姐夫善良淳朴,给了他无私的关爱和帮助。童年时期的皮普天真善良,并没有什么远大理想,只希望自己长大后能和姐夫一样有一份让自己生活稳定的工作。一次偶然的机会皮普遇见了一名逃犯,并偷了家里的东西帮助他。不久皮普遇到了郝薇香小姐和她的女儿艾斯黛拉小姐,皮普的思想开始出现大幅波动,他憧憬那些漂亮高傲的女人,迷恋上了艾斯黛拉,沙提斯庄园富丽堂皇的装饰使皮普对自己贫寒的家庭出身和粗俗的言谈举止自惭形秽,皮普向往上流社会的绅士生活,开始觉得他姐姐家生活低俗,甚至认为他姐姐家的社会处境就是他的耻辱。就在这时,一位不知名的恩人希望把皮普抚养成为一个有教养的绅士。因此皮普成了一位有"远大前程"的人。当律师贾格斯告诉皮普将继承一笔财产时,皮普兴奋不已,他开始变得高傲,瞧不起抚养他的姐姐和姐夫,也不愿意让他姐夫到车站送他到伦敦,因为姐夫会影响他的形象,皮普已经彻底失去了童年的纯真和朴实。

故事的第二部分主要描写了皮普在伦敦接受教育的经历。由于受到上层社会势利习气的感染,皮普过着奢靡堕落的生活,道德品质也变得低下。虽然已经成为一个上等人,皮普却越来越不自信,越来越不快乐,对自己的所作所为开始后悔。"对于姐夫的无理和傲慢,我长期心神不定,对于毕蒂,我感到良心上有愧。"但即使皮普挥金如土,债台高筑,他仍然在暗地里支持赫伯特开店经商,皮普还没有完全失去善良的本性。皮普一直以为是郝薇香小姐匿名资助他接受教育,真正的"恩人"马格韦契的出现使皮普回到了现实。马格韦契使他认识到自己的恩人不是郝薇香小姐,而是他曾经救助过的逃犯马格韦契,而郝薇香小姐根本无意把艾斯黛拉许配给他,原来郝薇香小姐年轻时被抛弃,一直未婚,艾斯黛拉是她的养女,是她报复男人的工具。

小说最后一部分记叙了皮普保护潜逃回国的流放犯马格韦契的经过。虽然马格韦契最终难逃被捕的命运,但经过一系列的变故,皮普最终恢复了善良的本性,认识到了友情和亲情的可贵。在帮助马格韦契偷渡出境的过程中,皮普在心理上成熟了很多。天真、善良、怯懦的皮普变成了一个有勇有谋自信的大男人。皮普的价值观也有了巨大变化,皮普虽然失去"远大前程",但获得了善良淳朴的回归。当马格韦契被捕后,皮普仍然和他联系,照料这位垂死的病人。皮普向马格韦契保证:只要监狱允许我和你在一起,我绝不会离开你。至此,皮普已经完成了从天真无邪、充满幻想的少年到思想成熟、经得起考验的成年人的转变。

狄更斯在《远大前程》中揭露了19世纪中叶英国上流社会的势利虚伪,歌颂了纯朴善良的广大劳苦大众,同时小说也表明了狄更斯的社会改良主义的观点:如果每个人都献出自己的爱和仁慈,让整个世界充满爱,他也会得到同样甚至更多的爱。

成长主题解读

　　主人公皮普自幼失去双亲，在姐姐家长大，姐姐脾气暴躁，皮普常常遭到她的漫骂和踢打，但姐夫乔·葛吉瑞是个老实人，给予了他无私的爱和帮助，皮普的童年生活还算无忧无虑。生活在和自己一样的乡下人中间，皮普丝毫没有觉得自己的手有多么粗糙、靴子有多么笨重。不久这种纯真快乐却在无意中被打破了，一位富有的老小姐郝薇香找到了他，这位老小姐年轻时在婚礼前遭情人遗弃，多年来她一直生活在当年她结婚的那一天，时间在她那儿永远是静止的。在和富有的郝薇香相处的过程中，皮普逐渐受到上层社会的影响，开始讨厌自己粗糙的双手和笨重的靴子，开始羞于自己对世事的无知和浅薄。他感到迷茫，幼小的心灵里充满了对上层社会生活的憧憬和渴望，皮普对郝薇香的养女——漂亮的艾斯黛拉充满青睐和爱慕。虽然皮普只在那儿待了几个小时，却给他纯真的心灵带来了巨大的冲击和震撼。像亚当和夏娃一样，皮普受到了外界的巨大诱惑。

　　意想不到的幸运之神光顾了皮普，一位不能透露姓名的朋友给了皮普一大笔财产，皮普离开了成长的故乡，只身来到令人向往的大都市伦敦，过上了令人羡慕的绅士生活，步入了上等人的社会。随着自己"远大前程"的突然实现，皮普的纯洁真爱逐渐消失了，他羞于见故乡的亲人和朋友，甚至连一直都非常关爱他的姐夫都被抛到脑后。当皮普最后得知现在的一切财产都来自自己童年时曾救过的囚犯时，他感到迷茫和震惊，觉得自己的美好期望马上就要彻底破灭了。罪犯马格韦契的突然回来粉碎了他的黄金梦，同时使他的道德感得以复苏。在与马格韦契最初交往的过程中，皮普内心充满了惶恐和不安，马格韦契父亲般的关怀使皮普意识到了自己的背叛，恢复了善良的天性。经过一番痛苦的心理斗争，皮普决心帮助他逃离英国。但计划失败了，马格韦契被送上了电椅。失去了财产的皮普在亲人的感召下回到了家乡，找到了真正的自我。

　　皮普的成长历程在很大程度上体现了成长小说的原型特征：天真无邪的主人公受到外面世界的诱惑，走出家门来到陌生的地方，开始了自己的人生之旅，在寻求自我的道路上，遇到了考验和磨难，甚至为此付出极大的代价，也因此获得了成长。

　　在这部体现青少年成长的现实主义小说中，狄更斯塑造了两个出色的"父亲"形象：铁匠乔·葛吉瑞和罪犯马格韦契，这两个人在皮普的成长道路上充当了正面领路人的角色，他们给予了皮普无私的"父爱"，指引着皮普的成长。

姐夫乔·葛吉瑞目不识丁，举止粗俗，但却是唯一可以让皮普信赖、给他慰藉的人。乔·葛吉瑞拥有一颗博大无私的心，他把皮普当成一个无话不说的朋友和一个弱小的对象，尽自己最大的力量来保护他。在乔·葛吉瑞身上体现了成长小说正面引路人的特征：他们能够以平等身份与比自己年纪小的人相处；他们乐于助人，富有同情心；他们的身份都比较特殊，正是这种特殊性使他们与主流社会保持一定距离，而乐于和年轻人交往，他们与被帮助的年轻人一样，也属于社会边缘人物。当皮普受到资助去伦敦，过上了上等人的生活，不愿意和乔·葛吉瑞相见时，乔没有责怪和记恨；而当他去伦敦看皮普时，竟然手足无措，不知如何面对这个曾是自己老朋友的"上等人"，一直称皮普为"先生"，这一称呼表明了他们之间的距离。而此时的皮普则认为他们之间已经没有了沟通的桥梁，乔的到来只会给他增添尴尬和不快，他们之间不可能像以前那样亲密无间了。但姐夫乔·葛吉瑞仍诚恳地对待亲爱的"绅士"皮普，此时的皮普却没有体会到他深沉的"父爱"。（见选读）直到姐姐下葬的那一天，皮普才回家见到了乔。而当过上了绅士生活的皮普债台高筑时，乔默默地伸出了友爱之手，数日照料病中的老朋友，用自己微薄的积蓄替皮普偿还了债务。乔·葛吉瑞用自己朴实的言行影响着皮普的成长，用仁爱的力量感化皮普的无知和困惑。这种仁爱使皮普意识到了自己的势利，过上普通人的生活是多么的可贵，皮普终于从自己"远大前程"的美梦中醒来。

　　在皮普的成长道路上，另一个有很大影响的引路人是马格韦契。马格韦契虽然是个罪犯，却拥有一颗慈爱和感恩的心，用无私的爱来帮助皮普。马格韦契把自己多年在海外的积蓄都留给了皮普，他这样做是为了报答皮普小时候的帮助，童年的皮普曾经出于善良的天性给了一顿让他活命的饭和一把救命的锉刀让他得以逃生。马格韦契虽然身在异国他乡孤独牧羊，却一心想着怎样把皮普培养成上等人，想在皮普身上实现自己的"伟大前程"。马格韦契和皮普一样，都出身于贫穷的家庭，都不知道自己的父母是谁，都没有人关爱；他们都处于社会的边缘地位，游离于主流社会之外，正是这种特殊的身份，使马格韦契愿意为皮普奉献赤诚的爱。在和马格韦契短暂的相处过程中，皮普开始用成熟的目光重新审视他，发现这个当初看起来吃东西像狗，打起人来像野兽的逃犯似乎充满了仁爱精神。受到这种仁爱精神的感化，皮普决心帮助他获得自由。尽管营救失败了，皮普获得了良心上的醒悟，完成了自身的成长。

　　在成长小说中，对主人公的成长起引导作用的并不总是正面人物，反面人物也同样可以对主人公的成长产生影响，但这种影响多是消极的。成长小说中，反面引路人的原型可以追溯到撒旦，由于魔鬼撒旦的诱惑，亚当和夏娃偷食了禁果,上帝把他们逐出了伊甸园,让他们承受人类生存之苦。小说《远大前程》中的反面引路人是堪称富有而心灵扭曲的老小姐郝薇香,这一撒旦式的人物对皮普的引诱就像撒旦对亚当和夏娃的引诱一样,使天真的皮普坠入了世俗中,陷入了对自己远大前程的幻想中。为了报复新婚之夜抛弃她的男人,郝薇香收养了艾斯黛拉,决心把她培养成一个骄傲、自私、冷酷却又魅力无比的上层社会女子,用她作为报复男人的工具。郝薇香选中了孤儿皮普,用自己的优越地位来诱惑他,让她精心打造的艾斯黛拉去征服他、引诱他。善良、天真的皮普没有经得起美色的诱惑,爱上了艾斯黛拉,为了与她匹配,皮普一心想成为上等人。如果没有这位老小姐的引诱,皮普也许会一直过着无忧无虑的普通人的生活。正是这位心理变态的老小姐郝薇香的诱惑使皮普迷失了自己,陷入了迷茫的深渊,失去了天真纯朴的本性。经历了人生的诱惑和切肤之痛的磨砺和考验,在父辈们的关爱和感召下,皮普走出了迷茫,完成了人生道路上的成长。

  选读选自第 27 章,描写了皮普的姐夫乔来伦敦看成为"上等人"的皮普的情景。

'MY DEAR MR PIP,

'I write this by request of Mr Gargery,[1] for to let you know that he is going to London in company with Mr Wopsle[2] and would be glad if agreeable to be allowed to see you. He would call at Barnard's Hotel Tuesday morning at nine o'clock, when if not agreeable please leave word. Your poor sister is much the same as when you left. We talk of you in the kitchen every night, and wonder what you are saying and doing. If now considered in the light of a liberty, excuse it for the love of poor old days. No more, dear Mr Pip, from

'Your ever obliged, and affectionate servant,

'BIDDY. '[3]

'P. S. He wishes me most particular to write what larks. He says you will understand. I hope and do not doubt it will be agreeable to see him even though a gentleman, for you had ever a good heart, and he is a worthy worthy man. I have read him all excepting only the last little sentence, and he wishes me most particular to write again what larks. '

I received this letter by post on Monday morning, and therefore its appointment was for next day. Let me confess exactly, with what feelings I looked forward to Joe's coming.

Not with pleasure, though I was bound to him by so many ties; no; with considerable disturbance, some mortification, and a keen sense of incongruity. If I could have kept him away by paying money, I certainly would have paid money. My greatest reassurance was, that he was coming to Barnard's Inn, not to Hammersmith, and consequently would not fall in Bentley Drummle's way.[4] I had little objection to his being seen by Herbert[5] or his father, for both of whom I had a respect; but I had the sharpest sensitiveness as to his being seen by Drummle, whom I held in contempt. So, throughout life, our worst weaknesses and meannesses are usually committed for the sake of the people whom we most despise.

I had begun to be always decorating the chambers in some quite unnecessary and inappropriate way or other, and very expensive those wrestles with Barnard proved to be. By this time, the rooms were vastly different from what I had found them, and I enjoyed the honour of occupying a few prominent pages in the books of a neighbouring upholsterer. I had got on so fast of late, that I had even started a boy in boots-top boots-in bondage and slavery to whom I might have been said to pass my days. For, after I had made the monster (out of the refuse of my washerwoman's family) and had clothed him with a blue coat, canary waistcoat, white cravat, creamy breeches, and the boots already mentioned, I had to find him a little to do and a great deal to eat; and with both of those horrible requirements he haunted my existence.

This avenging phantom was ordered to be on duty at eight on Tuesday morning in the hall (it was two feet square, as charged for floorcloth), and Herbert suggested certain things for breakfast that he thought Joe would like. While I felt sincerely obliged to him for being so interested and considerate, I had an odd half-provoked sense of suspicion upon me, that if Joe had been coming to see him, he wouldn't have been quite so brisk about it.

However, I came into town on the Monday night to be ready for Joe, and I got up early in the morning, and caused the sitting-room and breakfast-table to assume their most splendid appearance. Unfortunately the morning was drizzly, and an angel could not have concealed the fact the Barnard was shedding sooty tears outside the window, like some weak giant of a Sweep.

As the time approached I should have liked to run away, but the Avenger pursuant to orders was in the hall, and presently I heard Joe on the staircase. I knew it was Joe, by his clumsy manner of coming up-stairs-his state boots being always too big for him-and by the time it took him to read the names on the other floors in the course of his ascent. When at last he stopped outside our door, I could hear his finger tracing over the painted letters of my name, and I afterwards distinctly heard him breathing in at the keyhole. Finally he gave a faint single rap, and Pepper-such was the compromising name of the avenging boy-announced 'Mr Gargery!' I thought he never would have done wiping his feet, and that I must have gone out to lift him off the mat, but at last he came in.

'Joe, how are you, Joe?'

'Pip, how AIR you, Pip?'

With his good honest face all glowing and shining, and his hat put down on the floor between us, he caught both my hands and worked them straight up and down, as if I had been the last patented pump.

'I am glad to see you, Joe. Give me your hat. '

But Joe, taking it up carefully with both hands, like a bird's-nest with eggs in it, wouldn't hear of parting with that piece of property, and persisted in standing talking over it in a most uncomfortable way.

'Which you have that growed, '[6] said Joe, 'and that swelled, and that gentle-folked;' Joe considered a little before he discovered this word; 'as to be sure you are a honour to your king and country. '

'And you, Joe, look wonderfully well. '

'Thank God, ' said Joe, 'I'm ekerval to most[7]. And your sister, she's no worse than she were. And Biddy, she's ever right and ready. And all friends is no backerder, if not no for arder. [8] 'Ceptin 'Wopsle;[9] he's had a drop. '[10]

All this time (still with both hands taking great care of the bird's-nest), Joe was rolling his eyes round and round the room, and round and round the flowered pattern of my dressing-gown.

'Had a drop, Joe?'

'Why yes, ' said Joe, lowering his voice, 'he's left the Church, and went into the playacting.[11] Which the playacting have likeways brought him to London along with me. And his wish were, ' said Joe, getting the bird's-nest under his left arm for the moment and groping in it for an egg with his right; 'if no offence, as I would 'and you that. '

I took what Joe gave me, and found it to be the crumpled playbill of a small metropolitan theatre, announcing the first appearance, in that very week, 'of the celebrated Provincial Amateur of Roscian renown, whose unique performance in the highest tragic walk of our National Bard has lately occasioned so great a sensation in local dramatic circles. '

'Were you at his performance, Joe?' I inquired.

'I were, ' said Joe, with emphasis and solemnity.

'Was there a great sensation?'

'Why, ' said Joe, 'yes, there certainly were a peck of orange peel. Partickler,[12] when he see the ghost. Though I put it to yourself, sir, whether it were calculated to keep a man up to his work with a good heart, to be continually cutting in betwixt him and the Ghost with Amen! " A man may have had a misfortune and been in the Church,' said Joe, lowering his voice to an argumentative and feeling tone, 'but that is no reason why you should put him out at such a time. Which I meantersay,[13] if the ghost of a man's own father cannot be allowed to claim his attention, what can, Sir? Still more, when his mourning 'at is unfortunately made so small as that the weight of the black feathers brings it off, try to keep it on how you may.'

A ghost-seeing effect in Joe's own countenance informed me that Herbert had entered the room. So, I presented Joe to Herbert, who held out his hand; but Joe backed from it, and held on by the bird's-nest.

'Your servant, Sir,' said Joe, 'which I hope as you and Pip'—here his eye fell on the Avenger,[14] who was putting some toast on table, and so plainly denoted an intention to make that young gentleman one of the family, that I frowned it down and confused him more—'I meantersay, you two gentlemen which I hope as you get your elths[15] in this close spot? For the present may be a very good inn, according to London opinions,' said Joe, confidentially, 'and I believe its character do stand i; but I wouldn't keep a pig in it myself not in the case that I wished him to fatten wholesome and to eat with a mellower flavour on him.'

Having borne this flattering testimony to the merits of our dwelling place, and having incidentally shown this tendency to call me 'sir,' Joe, being invited to sit down to table, looked all round the room for a suitable spot on which to deposit his hat—as if it were only on some very few rare substances in nature that it could find a resting place—and ultimately stood it on an extreme corner of the chimney-piece, from which it ever afterwards fell off at intervals.

'Do you take tea, or coffee, Mr Gargery?' asked Herbert, who always presided of a morning.

'Thankee, Sir,' said Joe, stiff from head to foot, 'I'll take whichever is most agreeable to yourself.'

'What do you say to coffee?'

'Thankee, Sir,' returned Joe, evidently dispirited by the proposal, 'since you are so kind as make choice of coffee, I will not run contrary to your own opinions. But don't you never find it a little 'eating?'

'Say tea then,' said Herbert, pouring it out.

Here Joe's hat tumbled off the mantel-piece, and he started out of his chair and picked it up, and fitted it to the same exact spot. As if it were an absolute point of good breeding that it should tumble off again soon.

'When did you come to town, Mr Gargery?'

'Were it yesterday afternoon?' said Joe, after coughing behind his hand, as if he had had time to catch the whooping-cough since he came. 'No it were not. Yes it were. Yes. It were yesterday afternoon' (with an appearance of mingled wisdom, relief, and strict impartiality).

'Have you seen anything of London, yet?'

'Why, yes, Sir,' said Joe, 'me and Wopsle went off straight to look at the Blacking Ware'us.[16] But we didn't find that it come up to its likeness in the red bills at the shop doors; which I meant to say,' added Joe, in an explanatory manner, 'as it is there drawn too architectural.'

I really believe Joe would have prolonged this word (mightily expressive to my mind of some architecture that I know) into a perfect Chorus, but for his attention being providentially attracted by his hat, which was toppling. Indeed, it demanded from him a constant attention, and a quickness of eye and hand, very like that exacted by wicket-keeping. He made extraordinary play with it, and showed the greatest skill; now, rushing at it and catching it neatly as it dropped; now, merely stopping it midway, beating it up, and humouring it in various parts of the room and against a good deal of the pattern of the paper on the wall, before he felt it safe to close with it; finally, splashing it into the slop-basin, where I took the liberty of laying hands upon it.

As to his shirt-collar, and his coat-collar, they were perplexing to reflect upon-insoluble mysteries both. Why should a man scrape himself to that extent, before he could consider himself full dressed? Why should he suppose it necessary to be purified by suffering for his holiday clothes? Then he fell into such unaccountable fits of meditation, with his fork midway between his plate and his mouth; had his eyes attracted in such strange directions; was afflicted with such remarkable coughs; sat so far from the table, and dropped so much more than he ate, and pretended that he hadn't dropped it; that I was heartily glad when Herbert left us for the city.

I had neither the good sense nor the good feeling to know that this was all my fault, and that if I had been easier with Joe, Joe would have been easier with me. I felt impatient of him and out of temper with him; in which condition he heaped coals of fire on my head.

'Us two being now alone, Sir,'-began Joe.

'Joe,' I interrupted, pettishly, 'how can you call me, Sir?'

Joe looked at me for a single instant with something faintly like reproach. Utterly preposterous as his cravat was, and as his collars were, I was conscious of a sort of dignity in the look.

'Us two being now alone,' resumed Joe, 'and me having the intentions and abilities to stay not many minutes more, I will now conclude-leastways begin-to mention what have led to my having had the present honour. For was it not,' said Joe, with his old air of lucid exposition, 'that my only wish were to be useful to you, I should not have had the honour of breaking vittles[17] in the company and abode of gentlemen.

I was so unwilling to see the look again, that I made no remonstrance against this tone.

'Well, Sir,' pursued Joe, 'this is how it were. I were at the Bargement' other night, Pip;' whenever he subsided into affection, he called me Pip, and whenever he relapsed into politeness he called me Sir; 'when there come up in his shay-cart, Pumblechook. Which that same identical,' said Joe, going down a new track, 'do comb my'air the wrong way sometimes, awful, by giving out up and down town as it were him which ever had your infant companion and were looked upon as a playfellow by yourself.'

'Nonsense. It was you, Joe.'

'Which I fully believed it were, Pip,' said Joe, slightly tossing his head, 'though it signify little now, Sir. Well, Pip; this same identical, which his manners is given to blusterous, come to me at the Bargemen (wot[18] a pipe and a pint of beer do give refreshment to the working-man, Sir, and do not over stimulate), and his word were, "Joseph, Miss Havisham she wish to speak to you."'

'Miss Havisham, Joe?'

'"She wish," were Pumblechook's word, "to speak to you."' Joe sat and rolled his eyes at the ceiling.

'Yes, Joe? Go on, please.'

'Next day, Sir,' said Joe, looking at me as if I were a long way off, 'having cleaned myself, I go and I see Miss A.'

'Miss A., Joe? Miss Havisham?'

'Which I say, Sir,' replied Joe, with an air of legal formality, as if he were making his will, 'Miss A., or otherways Havisham. Her expression air them as hollering: "Mr Gargery. You are in correspondence with Mr Pip?" Having had a letter from you, I were able to say "I am." (When I married your sister, Sir, I said "I will," and when I answered your friend, Pip, I said "I am.") "Would you tell him, then," said she, "that which Estella has come home and would be glad to see him."

I felt my face fire up as I looked at Joe. I hope one remote cause of its firing, may have been my consciousness that if I had known his errand, I should have given him more encouragement.

'Biddy,' pursued Joe, 'when I got home and asked her fur to write the message to you, a little hung back. Biddy says, "I know he will be very glad to have it by word of mouth, it is holiday time, you want to see him, go!" I have now concluded, Sir,' said Joe, rising from his chair, 'and, Pip, I wish you ever well and ever prospering to a greater and a greater height.'

'But you are not going now, Joe?'

'Yes I am,' said Joe.

'But you are coming back to dinner, Joe?'

'No I am not,' said Joe.

Our eyes met, and all the 'Sir' melted out of that manly heart as he gave me his hand.

'Pip, dear old chap, life is made of ever so many partings welded together, as I may say, and one man's a blacksmith, and one's a whitesmith, and one's a goldsmith, and one's a coppersmith. Divisions among such must come, and must be met as they come. If there's been any fault at all to-day, it's mine. You and me is not two figures to be together in London; nor yet anywhere else but what is private, and be known, and understood among friends. It ain't that I am proud, but that I want to be right, as you shall never see me no more in these clothes. I'm wrong in these clothes. I'm wrong out of the forge, the kitchen, or off the 'meshes. You won't find half so much fault in me if you think of me in my forge dress, with my hammer in my hand, or even my pipe. You won't find half so much fault in me if, supposing as you should ever wish to see me, you come and put your head in at the forge window and see Joe the blacksmith, there, at the old anvil, in the old burnt apron, sticking to the old work. I'm awful dull, but I hope I've beat out something nigh the rights of this at last. And so GOD bless you, dear old Pip, old chap, GOD bless you!'

I had not been mistaken in my fancy that there was a simple dignity in him. The fashion of his dress could no more come in its way when he spoke these words, than it could come in its way in Heaven. He touched me gently on the forehead, and went out. As soon as I could recover myself sufficiently, I hurried out after him and looked for him in the neighbouring streets; but he was gone.

Notes：

1. Gargery：Joe Gargery，皮普的姐夫

2. Mr Wopsle：皮普老家的教堂职员，后来在伦敦当演员

3. Biddy：皮普小时候的朋友，纯朴善良，与皮普所追求的艾斯黛拉形成对比

4. Bentley Drummle：本特莱·德鲁莫尔和皮普一起上过绅士培训课，是贵族阶层中的小人物，自负、冷酷、心理畸形，令人厌恶，受到皮普鄙视，后来和艾斯黛拉结婚

5. Herbert Pocket：皮普进入上流社会后的好朋友，是郝薇香小姐的侄儿

6. Which you have that growed，意为你现在长大了。皮普的姐夫乔没受过教育，说的不标准的英语。

7. I'm ekerval to most：我倒是还不错

8. And all friends is no backerder, if not no for arder：不好不坏

9. ceptin Wopsle：除 Wopsle 以外

10. He's had a drop：运气不佳

11. playacting：演戏

12. partickler：尤其是（particularly）

13. meantersay:我的意思是(mean to say)
14. Avenger:指前面说的 avenging phantom,即皮普的仆人
15. elth:elf(侏儒)
16. Blacking Ware'us 鞋油厂
17. breaking vittles:进餐
18. wot:意思是

Questions

1. How was Pip's attitude toward Joe?
2. How did what Joe behavior and words reveal his character?

5

A Portrait of an Artist as a Young Man

作者及背景简介

詹姆斯·乔伊斯(James Joyce,1882—1941),爱尔兰小说家,20世纪伟大的作家之一,后现代文学的奠基者之一,其作品及"意识流"创作思想对世界文坛影响巨大。

乔伊斯主要作品为《都柏林人》《一个青年艺术家的肖像》《尤利西斯》《芬尼根的守灵夜》。短篇小说集《都柏林人》(1914)描写了底层市民的日常生活,表现了社会环境对人的理想和希望的幻灭。自传体小

说《一个青年艺术家的肖像》(1916)以大量内心独白描写了成长时期的心理及其周围世界。代表作长篇小说《尤利西斯》(1922)表现现代社会中人的孤独与悲观。后期作品长篇小说《芬尼根的守灵夜》(1939)借用梦境表达对人类的存在和命运的终极思考,语言极为晦涩难懂。其作品结构复杂,用语奇特,作品中有很多独创的具有特殊含义的词汇,语言极富独创性和颠覆性。

詹姆斯·乔伊斯出生在爱尔兰的都柏林。乔伊斯一生颠沛流离,辗转于欧洲各地,1920年起定居巴黎,依靠教授英语和写作糊口,晚年饱受眼疾之痛,几近失明。乔伊斯的父亲对民族主义有坚定的信念,母亲则是虔诚的天主教徒。乔伊斯出生时,爱尔兰这个风光绮丽的岛国是英国的殖民地,战乱不断,民不聊生。乔伊斯在天主教教会学校上学,成绩出众,并初步表现出非凡的文学才能,一度想当神父。19世纪以来,在都柏林形成了以叶芝、格雷戈里夫人及辛格为中心的爱尔兰文艺复兴运动,乔伊斯直接或间接地受到影响。通过友人,乔伊斯也受到爱尔兰民族独立运动的影响。受19世纪末出现在欧洲文学中的自由思想的影响,他对宗教信仰产生了怀疑。1898年,乔伊斯进入都柏林大学专攻哲学和语言。1900年,英国文学杂志《半月评

论》发表他的关于易卜生作品《当我们死而复醒时》的评论《易卜生的新戏剧》,获得年过七旬的易卜生的称许,乔伊斯深受鼓舞,从而坚定了走文学道路的决心。1901年,乔伊斯发表《喧嚣的时代》,批评爱尔兰文艺剧院的狭隘的民族主义。

乔伊斯的文学生涯始于他1904年开始创作的短篇小说集《都柏林人》。在写给出版商理查兹的一封信中,他明确地表述了这本书的创作原则:"我的宗旨是要为我国的道德和精神史写下自己的一章。"这实际上也成了他一生文学追求的目标。在乔伊斯眼中,处于大英帝国和天主教会双重压迫和钳制下的爱尔兰是一个不可救药的国家,而都柏林则是它"瘫痪的中心",在这个城市里每时每地都上演着麻木、苦闷、沦落的一幕幕生活剧。

乔伊斯1908年起在都柏林开始创作长篇小说《一个青年艺术家的肖像》,1914年完稿于意大利的里雅斯特,历时10年。《一个青年艺术家的肖像》有强烈的自传色彩,乔伊斯通过斯蒂芬·迪达勒斯的故事,提出了艺术家与社会、与生活的关系问题,并且揭示了这样一个事实:斯蒂芬·迪达勒斯本人就是他力图逃避的都柏林世界所造就的。

1922年创作的长篇小说《尤利西斯》借用古希腊史诗《奥德赛》的框架,把布卢姆一天18个小时在都柏林的游荡比作希腊史诗英雄尤利西斯10年的海上漂泊,但小说中的主人公布卢姆不是尤利西斯那样的英雄,而是现代社会的"反英雄"。小说通过布卢姆和斯蒂芬一天的琐碎猥琐的生活,嘲讽了现代生活的堕落和徒劳以及现代人的漂泊和孤独感。小说中的现代人不再是传统的英雄或坏人,他们粗俗琐碎,人格分裂,理想幻灭,内心猥琐,家庭破裂,在一个腐朽的世界里徒劳地寻求和谐的人际关系和精神支柱。

1939年出版的长篇小说《芬尼根的守灵夜》借用意大利18世纪思想家维柯关于世界在四种不同社会形态中循环的观点,以此为框架展开庞杂的内容。书中暗喻《圣经》、莎士比亚、古代宗教、近代历史、都柏林地方志等,大量借用外国词语甚至自造词汇,通过夸张的联想,喻示爱尔兰乃至全人类的历史和全宇宙的运动。

选读作品简介

作为一部成长小说,《一个青年艺术家的肖像》展现了主人公斯蒂芬从童年到青少年期的成长历程,描写了一个爱尔兰天主教家庭的孩子成长的故事,它既是一部自传体小说,也是一部虚构的作品。这部小说主要描写都柏林青年斯蒂芬·迪达勒斯如何试图摆脱妨碍他发展的各种影响——家庭束缚、宗教传统和狭隘的民族主义情绪——去追求艺术与美的真谛。主人公斯蒂芬的姓氏是迪达勒斯,与古希腊神话传说的能工巧匠迪达勒斯同名。相传迪达勒斯是一名工匠,曾为克里特国王造了一座迷宫,建好后被国王囚禁在自己造的迷宫中,迪达勒斯用自己造的蜡翼飞离了迷宫。斯蒂芬所处的时代正值爱尔兰社会处于瘫痪状态,它反映在爱尔兰社会政治、经济、意识形态等各个领域。政治上,爱尔兰的民族自治运动陷入低谷;经济上,爱尔兰人生活异常困苦;意识形态上,天主教势力使爱尔兰社会死气沉沉,人民无所事事。迷宫便成为爱尔兰社会的象征,它是主人公斯蒂芬成长的囚笼,严重阻碍了他的自由成长。小说主要由两条叙事线索构成:一条是男主人公斯蒂芬的成长过程,另一条则是斯蒂芬的心理活动。小说的第一章描写的是斯蒂芬的出生和成长,第二章描写了他青少年时的经历和渐渐萌发的对女性的追求,使他走向妓院去寻求欢乐。第三章主要描写了斯蒂芬去妓院满足了性饥渴,但内心的矛盾却变得更加尖锐。一天,他听了阿纳尔长老关于死亡、审判、地狱和天堂的布道,胆战心惊,斯蒂芬经过激烈的思想斗争,到礼拜堂向牧师忏悔了自己的罪过,最终获得了心灵的平静。第四章是全书的高潮,充满着斯蒂芬走宗教之路还是艺术之路的思想斗争,乔伊斯运用了大量的意识流手法发掘人类的内心生活,斯蒂芬呼唤人类精神的家园,这是与命运搏斗的声音,人类只有返璞归真,才能找到自己失去的本性获得自由。这促使斯蒂芬走上反传统的自由艺术之路,斯蒂芬眼前的那个小姑娘变得像一只神秘的海鸟,成为生命的象征,斯蒂芬的内心被激发起比宗教更虔诚的艺术创作的欲望,要从"生命中创造出生命"。小说的最后一章描述了17岁到20岁的斯蒂芬,斯蒂芬思索着人生的价值和目标,决心追求精神上的真善美。乔伊斯在这部分里,主要以对话讨论和日记的形式展示斯蒂芬的艺术观,即中世纪神学家和经院哲学家托马斯·阿奎那所说的:完整、和谐和光彩。斯蒂芬一直在追求这一美的最高特征,最终走向流亡他乡的艺术之路。这一章也折射出乔伊斯的后现代思维特征:多元性和不断地否定。乔伊斯在想象(fantasy)和现实(realism)的矛盾中,不断地否定现实世界,让一位艺术家的高贵品质自然显露。在这里,可以看到两面对立的景象:一面是艺术家的想象世界,自己的路、自己创造出的生命;另一面是现实的世俗世界。斯蒂芬这样表明自己与家庭、宗教和国家彻底决裂的决心:"你听我说,克兰利,我不愿意去为我已经不再相信的东西卖力……我将试图在某种生活方式中,某种艺术形式中尽可能自由地表现我自己,那就是沉默、流亡和机智。"斯蒂芬大学毕业后就离开爱尔兰侨居国外,寻找自己未来的事业。

成长主题解读

作为一部描述年轻人内心历程的成长小说,《一个青年艺术家的肖像》深刻地描绘了青年艺术家斯蒂芬从婴儿朦胧时期到青年成熟时期的心理成长过程。在20世纪追溯年轻人内心历程的成长小说之中,《一个青年艺术家的肖像》可以说是最有深度的一部。这部小说讲述了主人公斯蒂芬·迪达勒斯从一名牧师转变为一名杰出的艺术家的故事,深刻地展示了主人公斯蒂芬是如何在庸俗、闭塞、压抑的都柏林社会环境中,受到了来自家庭、学校、教会和社会等各方面的压力,并在与之反抗的斗争中逐渐成长,最终在艺术创作中找到自己的归宿的过程。作者以生动细腻的笔触,描述了斯蒂芬从童年到青年的成长过程,以及他在道德瘫痪世界中精神发育和心理发展的过程。小说自始至终以斯蒂芬心理矛盾和精神感受为基本内容,揭示了他隐秘的内心世界及与各种社会势力之间的激烈冲突,这不仅是作者本人成长中精神发育和心理发展的真实写照,也是现代西方社会中艺术家们的共同遭遇。小说在描写主人公内心世界和精神冲突时,采用了自由联想、内心独白等意识流技巧及精神顿悟和语体变化等方法,小说的题材也因此从现实真实转变和升华到心灵真实。斯蒂芬的漫长而痛苦的心灵旅程可以分为5个阶段:无知(ignorance)—堕落(degradation)—忏悔(repentance)—复活(resurrection)—流亡(exile)。小说体现了以下成长小说要素。

一、疏离感

疏离感是成长小说的一个典型元素,疏离感是个体与周围的人、社会、自然以及个体与自身之间的疏离隔阂,个体被支配控制,产生无意义感、压迫压抑感、社会孤立感等消极情感。

《一个青年艺术家的肖像》第一、第二章初步展示了斯蒂芬与学校、家庭和爱尔兰的宗教环境的疏离。第一章记述了斯蒂芬的幼年和童年时期。儿时的经验看似琐碎,却反复出现在斯蒂芬的回忆之中,也对斯蒂芬后来的生活产生了很大的影响。他因为不肯满足三年级学生韦尔斯换鼻烟盒的要求,被恶意地撞倒,掉进臭水沟里,并因此感染风寒病倒了。韦尔斯怕老师追究原因而受到惩罚,问斯蒂芬会不会告发他,斯蒂芬想到爸爸对他说的"永远不要告发同学"的告诫,就表示不会告发。学校让他感到孤独,在经历了孤独的学校寄宿生活后,斯蒂芬回到家中参加了人生第一次圣诞节家庭聚会。但是,本该温馨的聚会却充满了关于政治和宗教的争吵。爱尔兰受到天主教会和英国殖民政府的双重压迫,爱尔兰民族主义与爱尔兰天主教之间的矛盾一触即发,虚伪的天主教压迫着每一位爱尔兰人。斯蒂芬的母亲是一位虔诚的天主教徒,一心希望儿子能够像她一样笃信天主教并且能够担任神职。斯蒂芬隐约感觉到无助和绝望,感觉到了来自家庭、学校、教会各方面的压力,而斯蒂芬也正是在反抗这些方面的压力的过程中逐渐成长起来了。

二、顿悟

顿悟是成长小说的又一个典型元素,指在每个特定时刻由于外界的诱因突然产生的领悟,使主人公最终摆脱困惑而幡然醒悟,通常发生在心理变化的关键时刻。《一个青年艺术家的肖像》中的顿悟出现在主人公的内心挣扎斗争的时刻。在第二章,随着性意识的觉醒,斯蒂芬开始憧憬与异性的接触。在和一位他心仪的女孩同车回家的途中,他的心随着她的脚步向她走近又走远,像浪尖上的软木塞一样跳跃不止。他想伸手去拥抱她,亲吻她,但理智的无形约束使他不敢这么做。事后他感到很后悔,把车票撕成碎片来发泄,这为他后来放任感情埋下了伏笔。由于一再错失与女孩接触的机会,他的情感像被堵住了的洪水一样在他心中翻腾激荡,寻找着出口,他开始在妓女出没的后街上游荡,寻找爱情的替代品,投入到了妓女的怀抱里。在这一章中,斯蒂芬的性意识以顿悟的形式苏醒,情感和艺术的力量在他内心中也以顿悟的形式苏醒。

在第三章中,顿悟出现在斯蒂芬与天主教价值观的抗争中,斯蒂芬进入精神错乱期,他经常出入妓院,性饥渴得到了满足,他明知自己罪孽深重,却始终拒绝忏悔。直到他听到阿纳尔长老的布道。阿纳尔教导孩子们要把尘世间的诱惑通通逐出脑海,思考神圣的宗教教义。斯蒂芬开始恨自己,极度地厌恶自己。最终斯蒂芬到礼拜堂向牧师忏悔了自己的罪过,在宗教的怀抱里得到了"美好与安宁"。顿悟之后的斯蒂芬投入了宗教的怀抱。

第四章是小说的高潮,顿悟出现在斯蒂芬在献身宗教还是投身艺术的内心斗争中。选择牧师作为终身职业,意味着"一种严肃的、有秩序的和毫无热情的生活,一种没有物质烦恼的生活"。母亲希望他能接受圣职,而斯蒂芬向往的却是一种富于激情和创造的丰富多彩的生活。文中重复出现的"头盖骨"暗示如果斯蒂芬开始他的宗教圣职,也就意味着他精神的死亡。斯蒂芬站在了个体发展的十字路口,他对美和人体的敏感注定了他不适合成为牧师。在海边,面对天上的流云和海中翻滚的浪涛,斯蒂芬感到一种大自然的启示。他感到自己的心飞上了云霄,他要翱翔四野,浪迹天涯。他要用心灵的自由来创造生活,而不是把心灵禁锢在死板的牧师生活里,他凝神观望伫立在水中央的像海鸟一样的美丽清纯少女,感到她是新生活的象征,他顿悟到生活和艺术对他的感召,他要追求美与激情的生活,"去生活,去创造,去堕落,去战胜,去从生命中创造生命。"(见选读)斯蒂芬决定挣脱一切来自于家庭、民族、宗教的束缚,到艺术中寻求理想,他决心和他同名的希腊神话人物迪达勒斯一样向着艺术的理想飞翔,即使粉身碎骨也在所不惜。斯蒂芬的思想在这一章产生飞跃,对人生有了崭新的认识,最激烈的内心斗争以主人公再一次的顿悟而结束。

—Stephanos Dedalos! Bous Stephanoumenos! Bous Stephaneforos!

Their banter was not new to him and now it flattered his mild proud sovereignty. Now, as never before, his strange name seemed to him a prophecy. So timeless seemed the grey warm air, so fluid and impersonal his own mood, that all ages were as one to him. A moment before the ghost of the ancient kingdom of the Danes[1] had looked forth through the vesture of the hazewrapped[2] city. Now, at the name of the fabulous artificer, he seemed to hear the noise of dim waves and to see a winged form flying above the waves and slowly climbing the air. What did it mean? Was it a quaint device opening a page of some medieval book of prophecies and symbols, a hawk-like man flying sunward[3] above the sea, a prophecy of the end he had been born to serve and had been following through the mists of childhood and boyhood, a symbol of the artist forging a new in his workshop out of the sluggish matter of the earth a new soaring impalpable imperishable being?

His heart trembled; his breath came faster and a wild spirit passed over his limbs as though he was soaring sunward. His heart trembled in an ecstasy of fear and his soul was in flight. His soul was soaring in an air beyond the world and the body he knew was purified in a breath and delivered of incertitude and made radiant and commingled with the element of the spirit. An ecstasy of flight made radiant his eyes and wild his breath and tremulous and wild and radiant his windswept limbs.

—One! Two! ... Look out!

—Oh, Cripes, I'm drowned!

—One! Two! Three and away!

—The next! The next!

—One! ... UK!

—Stephaneforos!

His throat ached with a desire to cry aloud, the cry of a hawk or eagle on high, to cry piercingly of his deliverance to the winds. This was the call of life to his soul not the dull gross voice of the world of duties and despair, not the inhuman voice that had called him to the pale service of the altar. An instant of wild flight had delivered him and the cry of triumph which his lips withheld cleft his brain.

—Stephaneforos!

What were they now but cerements shaken from the body of death—the fear he had walked in night and day, the incertitude that had ringed him round, the shame that had abased him within and without—cerements, the linens of the grave?

His soul had arisen from the grave of boyhood, spurning her graveclothes. Yes! Yes! Yes! He would create proudly out of the freedom and power of his soul, as the great artificer whose name he bore, a living thing, new and soaring and beautiful, impalpable[4], imperishable.

He started up nervously from the stone-block for he could no longer quench the flame in his blood. He felt his cheeks aflame and his throat throbbing with song. There was a lust of wandering in his feet that burned to set out for the ends of the earth. On! On! His heart seemed to cry. Evening would deepen above the sea, night fall upon the plains, dawn glimmer before the wanderer and show him strange fields and hills and faces. Where?

He looked northward towards Howth. The sea had fallen below the line of sea wrack on the shallow side of the breakwater[5] and already the tide was running out fast along the foreshore. Already one long oval bank of sand lay warm and dry amid the wavelets. Here and there warm isles of sand gleamed above the shallow tide and about the isles and around the long bank and amid the shallow currents of the beach were lightclad[6] figures, wading and delving.

In a few moments he was barefoot, his stockings folded in his pockets and his canvas shoes dangling by their knotted laces over his shoulders and, picking a pointed salt-eaten stick out of the jetsam among the rocks, he clambered down the slope of the breakwater.

There was a long rivulet in the strand and, as he waded slowly up its course, he wondered at the endless drift of seaweed. Emerald and black and russet and olive, it moved beneath the current, swaying and turning. The water of the rivulet was dark with endless drift and mirrored the high-drifting clouds. The clouds were drifting above him silently and silently the seatangle was drifting below him and the grey warm air was still and a new wild life was singing in his veins.

Where was his boyhood now? Where was the soul that had hung back from her destiny, to brood alone upon the shame of her wounds and in her house of squalor and subterfuge to queen it in faded cerements and in wreaths that withered at the touch? Or where was he?

He was alone. He was unheeded, happy and near to the wild heart of life. He was alone and young and wilful and wild-hearted, alone amid a waste of wild air and brackish waters and the sea-harvest of shells and tangle and veiled grey sunlight and gayclad lightclad figures of children and girls and voices childish and girlish in the air.

A girl stood before him in midstream, alone and still, gazing out to sea. She seemed like one whom magic had changed into the likeness of a strange and beautiful seabird. Her long slender bare legs were delicate as a crane's and pure save where an emerald trail of seaweed had fashioned itself as a sign upon the flesh. Her thighs, fuller and soft-hued as ivory, were bared almost to the hips, where the white fringes of her drawers were like feathering of soft white down. Her slate-blue skirts were kilted boldly about her waist and dovetailed behind her. Her bosom was as a bird's, soft and slight, slight and soft as the breast of some dark-plumaged dove. But her long fair hair was girlish: and girlish, and touched with the wonder of mortal beauty, her face.

She was alone and still, gazing out to sea; and when she felt his presence and the worship of his eyes her eyes turned to him in quiet sufferance of his gaze, without shame or wantonness. Long, long she suffered his gaze and then quietly withdrew her eyes from his and bent them towards the stream, gently stirring the water with her foot hither and thither. The first faint noise of gently moving water broke the silence, low and faint and whispering, faint as the bells of sleep; hither and thither, hither and thither; and a faint flame trembled on her cheek.

—Heavenly God! cried Stephen's soul, in an outburst of profane joy.

He turned away from her suddenly and set off across the strand. His cheeks were aflame; his body was aglow; his limbs were trembling. On and on and on and on he strode, far out over the sands, singing wildly to the sea, crying to greet the advent of the life that had cried to him. Her image had passed into his soul forever and no word had broken the holy silence of his ecstasy. Her eyes had called him and his soul had leaped at the call. To live, to err, to fall, to triumph, to recreate life out of life! A wild angel had appeared to him, the angel of mortal youth and beauty, an envoy from the fair courts of life, to throw open before him in an instant of ecstasy the gates of all the ways of error and glory. On and on and on and on!

He halted suddenly and heard his heart in the silence. How far had he walked? What hour was it?

There was no human figure near him nor any sound borne to him over the air. But the tide was near the turn and already the day was on the wane. He turned landward and ran towards the shore and, running up the sloping beach, reckless of the sharp shingle, found a sandy nook amid a ring of tufted sand knolls and lay down there that the peace and silence of the evening might still the riot of his blood.

He felt above him the vast indifferent dome and the calm processes of the heavenly bodies; and the earth beneath him, the earth that had borne him, had taken him to her breast.

He closed his eyes in the languor of sleep. His eyelids trembled as if they felt the vast cyclic movement of the earth and her watchers, trembled as if they felt the strange light of some new world. His soul was swooning into some new world, fantastic, dim, uncertain as under sea, traversed by cloudy shapes and beings. A world, a glimmer or a flower? Glimmering and trembling, trembling and unfolding, a breaking light, an opening flower, it spread in endless succession to itself, breaking in full crimson and unfolding and fading to palest rose, leaf by leaf and wave of light by wave of light, flooding all the heavens with its soft flushes, every flush deeper than the other.

Evening had fallen when he woke and the sand and arid grasses of his bed glowed no longer. He rose slowly and, recalling the rapture of his sleep, sighed at its joy.

He climbed to the crest of the sandhill and gazed about him. Evening had fallen. A rim of the young moon cleft the pale waste of skyline, the rim of a silver hoop embedded in grey sand; and the tide was flowing in fast to the land with a low whisper of her waves, islanding[7] a few last figures in distant pools.

Notes:

1. Danes: 丹麦人,英国的原始部落来自于丹麦海盗
2. hazewrapped: 烟雾笼罩的

3. sunward: 向着太阳
4. impalpable: 无形的
5. breakwater: 防波堤
6. lightclad: clad 为穿衣的、覆盖的, lightclad 在这里指暮色中的
7. island: 孤立, 使成岛状

Questions:

1. What images in the excerpt convey Steven's aspiration?
2. What is the epiphany here?

6 Sons and Lovers

作者及背景简介

戴维·赫伯特·劳伦斯（David Herbert Lawrence,1885—1930）是英国现代主义代表作家之一,出生于诺丁汉郡的一个煤乡,父亲是煤矿工人,母亲当过小学教师,劳伦斯父母文化水平差异较大,父亲性情暴躁,经常在醉酒后打骂妻儿,由于婚姻生活的不幸,劳伦斯母亲把所有的爱转移到了儿子身上。劳伦斯和他的母亲关系非常亲密,他的很多作品中可以看到他母亲的影子,他最著名的作品之一《儿子与情人》(1913)曾引发西方评论界关于"恋母情结"的争议。16岁中学毕业后,劳伦斯当过两年的工厂职员和小学教员,后靠奖学金念完诺丁汉大学。读书期间劳伦斯便开始创作小说,他的第一部小说《白孔雀》因表现儿女之情而受到批评,直到1911年才出版,此后劳伦斯开始专门从事文学创作。

1912年,劳伦斯和他在诺丁汉大学教授现代语言学的妻子弗丽达·冯·里希托芬私奔至德国。第一次世界大战爆发后,两人返回英国,并于1914年7月13日结婚。由于在一战中德国和英国是交战国,劳伦斯夫妇始终生活在官方的监视之下。他们的生活非常贫困,他们被指控在康沃尔海岸向德国潜艇传送谍报信息。战争之后,劳伦斯开始了他的所谓"原始朝圣"计划,劳伦斯认为僵化的欧洲基督教已经逐渐失去了活力,并试图用原始的、部族的信仰来改造它,这就是他开始"原始朝圣"的原因之一。他偕同妻子离开英国,开始四处旅行,仅短暂回国两次。他们旅行的足迹遍布法国、意大利、斯里兰卡、澳大利亚、美国和新墨西哥。劳伦斯曾梦想在新墨西哥建立一个乌托邦式的社区,他在新墨西哥居住了几年后,因肺炎复发而不得不回到欧洲,1930年因肺炎在法国南部去世。

劳伦斯的创作受到了弗洛伊德心理学的较大影响，他的小说力图表现潜意识和无意识，表现精神与肉体以及光明与黑暗之间的对立与冲突，前者象征现代文明的压抑，后者象征人的自然本性，他的小说的主题是揭露现代工业文明对人性的扭曲和对人的自然本性的摧残以及对大自然的破坏。劳伦斯的小说因为对性的描写而受到批评和争议，1915年，劳伦斯最优秀的作品《虹》一出版就因淫秽而被禁，《查泰莱夫人的情人》一度被伦敦法庭定为"淫书"。但在劳伦斯看来，性爱是人类天性的一部分，他的作品中的性描写并不粗俗，很有象征意义和艺术性。劳伦斯小说的语言质朴、精炼，大量使用质朴的生活语言，在小说结构上不重视情节的发展，而重在对人物的内心世界的细腻刻画，探索人际关系，在姊妹篇小说《虹》和《恋爱中的女人》中，既描写了两性关系，同时也表现了同性恋关系。

劳伦斯是20世纪杰出的小说家，同时也是位出色的诗人。他的诗歌可大致分为早、中、晚三个阶段。他的早期诗歌大多带有自传性质。而到了中期，劳伦斯的目光转向了自然界，用生动的语言表达对鸟兽花草的热爱。在劳伦斯的晚期诗歌中，他主要表达了对死亡和重生的看法。

选读作品简介

主人公保罗的父母莫雷尔夫妇在一次舞会上结识，一见钟情。短暂的蜜月期后，由于出身不同，性格不合，追求迥异，两人便产生了隔阂和争吵。保罗父亲是一位浑浑噩噩的煤矿工人，贪杯粗俗。保罗母亲出身于中产阶级，受过良好教育，对下嫁给一个平凡的矿工耿耿于怀，对丈夫完全绝望。她把时间精力和全部感情转移到大儿子威廉和二儿子保罗身上。

莫雷尔太太竭力阻止儿子步父亲的后尘下井挖煤；她千方百计教促他们跳出底层人的圈子，出人头地，实现她未能实现的追求。她的言行不但增加了她和丈夫之间的隔阂，而且影响了儿子们，使他们与母亲结成牢固的统一战线，去共同对付身体依然健壮而精神日渐衰老的父亲。

大儿子肺炎死后，二儿子保罗就逐渐成了母亲唯一的感情和希望寄托，她鼓励督促保罗出人头地，跻身上流社会；保罗的母亲想方设法从精神上控制儿子，使他不移情他人，特别是别的女人，以便满足自己婚姻的缺憾。这种强烈的带占有性质的爱使儿子感到窒息，迫使他设法逃脱，但即使在短暂的逃离中，保罗也常常被母亲那无形的精神枷锁控制着，处于痛苦中。

保罗和女友米丽安的交往过程也是年轻的保罗经历精神痛苦的过程。他们兴趣相投，在频繁的接触中产生了感情，然而米丽安过分追求柏拉图式的精神满足,缺乏激情,而且米丽安像保罗的母亲一样,企图从精神上占有保罗,这使她与保罗的母亲成了情敌。保罗的另一个名叫克拉拉的女人同样是一个灵与肉相分离的畸形人,她生活在社会底层,与丈夫分居。保罗从她那里身上得到肉体上的满足,而这种纯肉体的关系注定是肤浅的、不能长久的。

成长主题解读

《儿子与情人》带有很大的自传性质,在很大程度上再现了劳伦斯自身的成长经历,同小说主人公保罗一样,劳伦斯出生在诺丁汉郡的一个矿工家庭,父亲文化程度低,性格暴躁;父母的婚姻生活充满着不幸。由于母亲对婚姻的失望,将情感全部倾注在儿子身上,劳伦斯受到其母亲的精神控制,他在心理上的困惑体现在小说主人公保罗的精神生活和成长历程上,小说反映了深刻的心理问题和社会问题,这是一部深入探索资本主义工业社会中青年人的心理障碍和精神困惑的现代主义成长小说。

一、疏离感

在《儿子与情人》中,疏离(英语中疏离和异化是同一个词 alienation)体现在三个方面:人与自然的疏离,人与人的疏离和人与自我的疏离即人性的扭曲。工业化大生产不仅破坏了美丽的自然环境,而且割断了人与自然的联系,它不仅使旧的农村经济破产,而且使人丧失了主体性,沦为机器的奴隶。劳动本是一种美德,一种乐趣,一种自发的活动,而在西方工业文明下却不再如此,人为了生活得更好而创造的"物"反过来支配人、排斥人、约束人、压抑人,人获得的物越多,却越来越为物所累,劳动压迫着人的精神和肉体,扼杀了人性使人成为"非人"。

19世纪中期以后,英国逐渐实现了全国规模的工业化,英格兰中部诺丁汉郡一带也深受影响发生了变化,一边依然是田园式的传统英格兰乡村,另一边却成为肮脏的工业化煤矿区。莫雷尔先生的热情洋溢、朝气蓬勃,吸引了葛楚德下嫁于他,他们新婚之后也曾有过一段短暂的幸福时光,但资本主义工业化的非人劳动条件和生活状况改变了一切,以莫雷尔为代表的矿工们冒着生命危险整天在黑暗肮脏的煤矿里做着苦工,无处宣泄,性格逐渐扭曲变形,他们借酒消愁,使用家庭暴力,他与人交往时的扭曲心理深刻地体现了现代机械力量对人性的摧残。莫雷尔太太把本应给丈夫的感情全部倾注到保罗的身上,对儿子产生了畸形的感情并在精神上占有控制孩子。保罗从小目睹父亲对母亲的粗暴行为,他憎恨父亲,和母亲互相倾吐心声,分享忧伤和欢乐,导致父在家里越来越孤立,这种扭曲的家庭关系的根源是非人性化的工业文明。莫雷尔太太对儿子扭曲的爱使他走入俄狄浦斯情结,并且在之后的成长中与其他女性的交往出现严重的心理障碍。当莫雷尔太太发现保罗与米丽安的交往越来越密切时,内心充满了嫉妒,同时保罗在与米丽安的交往中也渐渐发现了自己处于一种爱无能状态。每当与米丽安在一起时他会不由自主地想起母亲内心受到极大的煎熬,最终在母亲的干涉下,他中断了和米丽安的关系。米丽安是保罗的第一个情人,他们一直有着密切的心灵和思想上的交流,这逐渐使莫雷尔太太不能接受米丽安,她害怕儿子对她精神上的远离。保罗成长中形成的"俄狄浦斯情结"即恋母情结,以及他的恋爱失败的社会根源是扭曲人性的工业文明。

二、成长引路人和影响人

在成长小说的叙事结构中,成长的引路人是其中的一个重要构件。每个人在成长过程中或多或少地会受到一些人的影响,从而其思想和行为逐渐发生一系列的变化。小说中莫雷尔太太在家庭中占据着主导地位,这使得她在儿子们的成长过程中扮演着引路人的作用。保罗无论是在个性上,还是在事业和爱情上都潜移默化地受到母亲的影响。莫雷尔太太有着中产阶级的家庭背景,有一定的文化修养和情趣,她在对儿子的教育培养上付出了很大的努力。保罗从童年时起就展露出一种艺术家的气质,工厂的女孩们也都喜欢他,他在与人的交往中展现了个人的魅力,这所有个性上的闪光点都或多或少地源于他母亲的教诲。但同时从小和母亲的亲近也使得保罗成为一个情绪多变、多愁善感的男人,思想经常处于复杂的矛盾斗争之中。莫雷尔太太对于幸福生活的幻想已经破灭,但她不希望自己的孩子继续这种社会底层的生活,她尽量提供一切可能的条件让孩子受教育,使他们的才能得到最大限度的发挥,不断地给予他们积极向上的动力,鼓励他们努力摆脱矿工家庭的命运从而尽可能地跻身上流社会。

米丽安是保罗的第一个情人,是他青梅竹马的恋人。两人自从相识之后发现彼此志趣相投,交往越来越密切,并在懵懂中产生了爱情。米丽安是保罗才智的忠实崇拜者和支持者,她总是对保罗创作的作品大加赞赏,不断地给予他鼓励,而保罗也不断地从米丽安的身上获得灵感,从而激发他的创作。克拉拉是保罗的第二个情人,是一个有夫之妇。自从保罗第一眼看到她,就深深感受到她的成熟和性感。当保罗和米丽安的感情破裂之后,他转向了克拉拉。但是他们之间的关系走向了另一个极端,如果说保罗和米丽安的爱情是完全的精神层面的柏拉图式的爱情的话(见选读),那后来他与克拉拉的交往仅限于一种赤裸裸的性爱,没有任何精神上的交流,保罗从克拉拉的身上得不到心灵上的慰藉,这就注定了他们之间的关系是肤浅的,不堪一击的。保罗很快就意识到这一点,对克拉拉渐渐失去了兴趣,他意识到自己不能在她身上获得精神和肉体相统一的爱情,他们之间不会有幸福美满的婚姻生活。米丽安和克拉拉作为保罗成长中恋爱经历的重要人物,使他对爱情有了更好的理解,在爱情的道路上得到了成长。

选读选自第七章,描写了保罗母亲发现保罗与米丽安的交往越来越密切时内心充满了嫉妒,以及保罗和米丽安的恋爱细节。

Always when he went with Miriam, and it grew rather late, he knew his mother was fretting and getting angry about him—why, he could not understand. As he went into the house, flinging down his cap, his mother looked up at the clock. She had been sitting thinking, because a chill to her eyes prevented her reading. She could feel Paul being drawn away by this girl. And she did not care for Miriam. "She is one of those who will want to suck a man's soul out till he has none of his own left," she said to herself; "and he is just such a gaby[1] as to let himself be absorbed. She will never let him become a man; she never will." So, while he was away with Miriam, Mrs. Morel grew more and more worked up[2].

She glanced at the clock and said, coldly and rather tired:

"You have been far enough to-night."

His soul, warm and exposed from contact with the girl, shrank.

"You must have been right home with her," his mother continued.

He would not answer. Mrs. Morel, looking at him quickly, saw his hair was damp on his forehead with haste, saw him frowning in his heavy fashion, resentfully.

"She must be wonderfully fascinating, that you can't get away from her, but must go trailing eight miles at this time of night."

He was hurt between the past glamour with Miriam and the knowledge that his mother fretted. He had meant not to say anything, to refuse to answer. But he could not harden his heart to ignore his mother.

"I DO like to talk to her," he answered irritably.

"Is there nobody else to talk to?"

"You wouldn't say anything if I went with Edgar[3]."

"You know I should. You know, whoever you went with, I should say it was too far for you to go trailing, late at night, when you've been to Nottingham. Besides"—her voice suddenly flashed into anger and contempt—"it is disgusting—bits of lads and girls courting."

"It is NOT courting," he cried.

"I don't know what else you call it."

"It's not! Do you think we SPOON and do[4]? We only talk."

"Till goodness knows what time and distance," was the sarcastic rejoinder.

Paul snapped at the laces of his boots angrily.

"What are you so mad about?" he asked. "Because you don't like her."

"I don't say I don't like her. But I don't hold with children keeping company, and never did."

"But you don't mind our Annie[5] going out with Jim Inger."

"They've more sense than you two."

"Why?"

"Our Annie's not one of the deep sort."

He failed to see the meaning of this remark. But his mother looked tired. She was never so strong after William's[6] death; and her eyes hurt her.

"Well," he said, "it's so pretty in the country. Mr. Sleath asked about you. He said he'd missed you. Are you a bit better?"

"I ought to have been in bed a long time ago," she replied.

"Why, mother, you know you wouldn't have gone before quarter-past ten."

"Oh, yes, I should!"

"Oh, little woman, you'd say anything now you're disagreeable with me, wouldn't you?"

He kissed her forehead that he knew so well: the deep marks between the brows, the rising of the fine hair, greying now, and the proud setting of the temples. His hand lingered on her shoulder after his kiss. Then he went slowly to bed. He had forgotten Miriam; he only saw how his mother's hair was lifted back from her warm, broad brow. And somehow, she was hurt.

Then the next time he saw Miriam he said to her:

"Don't let me be late to-night—not later than ten o'clock. My mother gets so upset."

Miriam dropped her bead, brooding.

"Why does she get upset?" she asked.

"Because she says I oughtn't to be out late when I have to get up early."

"Very well!" said Miriam, rather quietly, with just a touch of a sneer.

He resented that. And he was usually late again.

That there was any love growing between him and Miriam neither of them would have acknowledged. He thought he was too sane for such sentimentality, and she thought herself too lofty. They both were late in coming to maturity, and psychical ripeness was much behind even the physical. Miriam was exceedingly sensitive, as her mother had always been. The slightest grossness made her recoil[7] almost in anguish. Her brothers were brutal, but never coarse in speech. The men did all the discussing of farm matters outside. But, perhaps, because of the continual business of birth and of begetting which goes on upon every farm, Miriam was the more hypersensitive to the matter, and her blood was chastened almost to disgust of the faintest suggestion of such intercourse. Paul took his pitch from her, and their intimacy went on in an utterly blanched and chaste fashion. It could never be mentioned that the mare was in foal[8].

······

He would not have it that they were lovers. The intimacy between them had been kept so abstract, such a matter of the soul, all thought and weary struggle into consciousness, that he saw it only as a platonic friendship. He stoutly denied there was anything else between them. Miriam was silent, or else she very quietly agreed. He was a fool who did not know what was happening to himself. By tacit agreement they ignored the remarks and insinuations of their acquaintances.

"We aren't lovers, we are friends," he said to her. "We know it. Let them talk. What does it matter what they say."

Sometimes, as they were walking together, she slipped her arm timidly into his. But he always resented it, and she knew it. It caused a violent conflict in him. With Miriam he was always on the high plane of abstraction, when his natural fire of love was transmitted into the fine stream of thought. She would have it so. If he were jolly and, as she put it, flippant, she waited till he came back to her, till the change had taken place in him again, and he was wrestling with his own soul, frowning, passionate in his desire for understanding. And in this passion for understanding her soul lay close to his; she had him all to herself. But he must be made abstract first.

Then, if she put her arm in his, it caused him almost torture. His consciousness seemed to split. The place where she was touching him ran hot with friction. He was one internecine battle, and he became cruel to her because of it.

One evening in midsummer Miriam called at the house, warm from climbing. Paul was alone in the kitchen; his mother could be heard moving about upstairs.

"Come and look at the sweet-peas," he said to the girl.

They went into the garden. The sky behind the townlet and the church was orange-red; the flower-garden was flooded with a strange warm light that lifted every leaf into significance. Paul passed along a fine row of sweet-peas, gathering a blossom here and there, all cream and pale blue. Miriam followed, breathing the fragrance. To her, flowers appealed with such strength she felt she must make them part of herself. When she bent and breathed a flower, it was as if she and the flower were loving each other. Paul hated her for it. There seemed a sort of exposure about the action, something too intimate.

When he had got a fair bunch, they returned to the house. He listened for a moment to his mother's quiet movement upstairs, then he said:

"Come here, and let me pin them in for you." He arranged them two or three at a time in the bosom of her dress, stepping back now and then to see the effect. "You know," he said, taking the pin out of his mouth, "a woman ought always to arrange her flowers before her glass."

Miriam laughed. She thought flowers ought to be pinned in one's dress without any care. That Paul should take pains to fix her flowers for her was his whim[9].

He was rather offended at her laughter.

"Some women do—those who look decent," he said.

Miriam laughed again, but mirthlessly, to hear him thus mix her up with women in a general way. From most men she would have ignored it. But from him it hurt her.

He had nearly finished arranging the flowers when he heard his mother's footstep on the stairs. Hurriedly he pushed in the last pin and turned away.

"Don't let mater know," he said.

Miriam picked up her books and stood in the doorway looking with chagrin at the beautiful sunset. She would call for Paul no more, she said.

"Good-evening, Mrs. Morel," she said, in a deferential way. She sounded as if she felt she had no right to be there.

"Oh, is it you, Miriam?" replied Mrs. Morel coolly.

But Paul insisted on everybody's accepting his friendship with the girl, and Mrs. Morel was too wise to have any open rupture.[10]

Notes:

1. gaby:傻瓜

2. worked up:激动不安的

3. Edgar:住在保罗家旁边的一家人

4. spoon and do:指男女间的拥抱做爱

5. Annie:保罗的姐姐

6. William:保罗最大的哥哥,莫雷尔太太最喜欢的儿子,后因病夭折

7. recoil:感到厌恶

8. in foal:怀孕

9. whim:心血来潮

10. open rupture:当面闹翻脸

Questions:

1. How did Paul's mother affect his relationship with Miriam?

2. What kind of relationship did Paul and Miriam have?

7

Of Human Bondage

作者及背景简介

威廉·萨默塞特·毛姆(William Somerset Maugham,1874—1965)出生于巴黎,父亲是律师,在英国驻法使馆供职。毛姆不满十岁父母就先后去世,他被送回英国由伯父抚养。毛姆进坎特伯雷皇家公学之后,由于身材矮小,且严重口吃,经常受到大孩子的欺凌和折磨,有时还遭到冬烘学究的无端羞辱。孤寂凄清的童年生  活,在他稚嫩的心灵上投下了痛苦的阴影,养成了他孤僻、敏感、内向的性格。幼年的经历对他的世界观和文学创作产生了深刻的影响。1892 年初,他去德国海德堡大学学习了一年。在那里,毛姆接触到德国哲学史家昆诺·费希尔的哲学思想和以易卜生为代表的新戏剧潮流。同年毛姆返回英国,在伦敦一家会计师事务所当了六个星期的见习生,随后进入伦敦圣托马斯医学院学医。为期五年的习医生涯,不仅使他有机会了解到底层人民的生活状况,而且使他学会用解剖刀一样冷峻、犀利的目光来剖析人生和社会。他的第一部小说《兰贝斯的丽莎》,即根据他作为见习医生在贫民区为产妇接生时的见闻用自然主义手法写成。从 1897 年起,毛姆弃医专门从事文学创作。1902 年,他转向戏剧创作,获得成功,成了红极一时的剧作家。1908 年,伦敦舞台竟同时上演他的四个剧本——《弗雷德里克夫人》《杰克·斯特劳》《杜特太太》《探险家》,其中《弗雷德里克夫人》连续上演达一年之久。1913 年起,毛姆决定暂时中断戏剧创作,用两年时间潜心写作酝酿已久的小说《人性的枷锁》。第一次世界大战期间,毛姆先在比利时火线救护伤员,后入英国情报部门工作,这一段间谍与密使的生活,后来写进了间谍小说《艾兴顿》(1928)中。1916 年,毛姆去南太平洋旅行,此后多次到远东。

1919年，长篇小说《月亮与六便士》问世。1920年到中国，写了游记《在中国的屏风上》(1922)，并以中国为背景写了一部长篇小说《面纱》(1925)。以后又去拉丁美洲与印度。1928年毛姆定居在地中海之滨的里维埃拉，直至1940年纳粹入侵时才仓促离去。两次世界大战的间隙，是毛姆创作精力最旺盛的时期。20世纪20年代及30年代初期，他写了一系列揭露上流社会尔虞我诈、钩心斗角、道德堕落的剧本，如《周而复始》《比我们高贵的人们》《坚贞的妻子》等。第二次世界大战期间，毛姆到了美国，在南卡罗来纳、纽约和罗德岛等地待了六年。1944年发表长篇小说《刀锋》。在这部作品里，作家试图通过一个青年人探求人生哲理的故事，揭示精神与实利主义之间的矛盾冲突。1946年，毛姆回到法国里维埃拉，设立了萨默塞特·毛姆奖，奖励优秀的年轻作家，鼓励并资助他们到各处旅游。1948年，他创作了最后一部小说《卡塔丽娜》，以16世纪的西班牙为背景。1954年，英国女王授予他"荣誉侍从"的称号，毛姆成为皇家文学会的会员。同年1月25日，英国嘉里克文学俱乐部特地设宴庆贺他的八十寿辰；在英国文学史上受到这种礼遇的，只有狄更斯、萨克雷、特罗洛普三位作家。1959年，毛姆作了最后一次远东之行。1965年12月15日，毛姆在法国里维埃拉去世，享年91岁。骨灰安葬在坎特伯雷皇家公学内。

作为一个有着独特个性的作家，毛姆一方面继承了英国小说的现实主义传统，另一方面又因为时代风气和个人经历等原因接受了自然主义的影响。因此，毛姆的小说从总体上可以归入现实主义的行列，但又具有较为明显的自然主义特征。自然主义文艺观的核心是对文学的真实性、客观性的极度强调，认为小说家最高的品格就是真实感，真实感就是如实地感受自然，如实地表现自然。主张在描写人物时，作家除了应关注人的社会、阶级性之外，为了能够更彻底地揭示人性的真实，还应重视对人的自然品性和生理本能的刻画。毛姆也将人作为自然人的情欲视为人性正常的组成部分，认为欲望不过是性的本能的天然结果，毛姆的多部小说中都不同程度地有对人物原始情欲的揭示和描写。在题材选择方面，他重视对人的生理本能和原始欲望的描写，以求更彻底地揭示人性的真实。同时，下层民众的生活环境和贫寒状态也在他的小说中得到了细致的展现，凸显了环境对人的深刻影响。在创作手法方面，毛姆常用近乎科学的眼光和客观的态度来描绘现实。

毛姆在20世纪英国短篇小说史中，占据了重要的地位。毛姆短篇小说的标志就是冷静、客观和深刻地剖析与解读人性的弱点，人世间的人情冷暖、苦与恶、尔虞我诈、道貌岸然。在作品中他无情地嘲弄、讽刺了当时西方社会中人与人之间的畸形关系、上流社会的荒淫无度以及下层人民的苦难生活，导致了人们对美好世界的幻想破灭,让人们从他的小说中亲身领略、目睹了社会的罪恶、人性的丑恶及命运的不公和多劫难。毛姆对新时代自我价值的追求充满渴望,同时又不忍彻底颠覆维多利亚传统文化。正是出于这种心理,毛姆选择了逃避,追求人性的自我完善与超然物外。他笔下的主人公对造成自身孤独的外在世界冷眼相看。在西方文化的樊笼中,他们无所适从,惶惶不可终日。毛姆笔下的主人公在放逐中寻求灵魂栖息之地。《刀锋》中的拉里和《月亮与六便士》中的斯特里克兰便是其中的典型。

毛姆的小说之所以能够引起不同国家不同阶层读者的兴趣,原因之一是他作品中浓郁的异国情调。这种异国情调既与当时的社会文化背景有关,也与作者本人的生活经历有关。科技带来的进步使得西方文明迅猛发展,不仅使得后起的欧洲迅速超过了古老的东方,而且促进了"欧洲中心主义"意识形态和霸权意识的增长。在疯狂的殖民扩张过程中,殖民者从"愚昧、野蛮"的东方人手中掠夺物质财富,人类学家和艺术家则看到了东方文化的独特魅力,将之视为人类灵魂的最终归属。作为一个敏感而极具才华的作家,毛姆深切地感受到了西方文明对人性的压抑和摧残,对东方文化则充满了无限的敬仰与向往,毛姆对处于非主流边缘地位的土著文化、印度文化、中国文化等倾注了自己高度的热情,寄予了无限的期望。在毛姆的小说中,"异质文化不再充当西方文化的配角,而一跃成为小说中真正的主宰"。

毛姆被称为英国的莫泊桑。他的众多作品涉及除诗歌以外的各个文学领域。他共写了长篇小说二十部,短篇小说一百多篇,剧本三十个,此外还著有游记、回忆录、文艺评论等作品。他的作品,特别是他的长、短篇小说,文笔质朴,脉络清晰,人物性格鲜明,情节跌宕有致,在各个阶层中都拥有相当数量的读者群。

选读作品简介

菲利普天生跛足,自幼失去双亲,自卑的心理深深植根在他的生活中。他在伯父凯里牧师和伯母路易莎的抚养下长大,伯父对其较为冷淡,但伯母悉心照料,给予他母亲般的温暖。菲利普自幼酷爱文学,在伯父的书房里找到寄托。伯父伯母希望菲利普到牛津学习神学,以后成为神父,把他送到一所宗教气氛浓厚的寄宿学校学习。在那里,虽然菲利普崭露了学习的天分,但生性腼腆的他并不能融入学校生活中,也因为跛足受尽嘲笑。

随后,菲利普不顾伯父的反对,远赴德国海德堡求学,在那里结识了英国人海沃德和美国人威克斯,开始对神学产生怀疑。在一个假期回到英国家中时,菲利普同威尔金森小姐互生情愫但并非真心相恋,在回到德国后便逐渐停止通信。

之后,菲利普到伦敦成为一名会计学徒,但他对枯燥的生活感到厌倦,很快就转而到巴黎学习艺术,在巴黎学了两年绘画。在巴黎,菲利普结交了一些朋友,其中有毫无天分、脾气怪异的普莱斯小姐。普莱斯小姐暗中喜欢菲利普,后来因为穷困无助和绝望而自杀。

菲利普最终意识到自己在艺术上资质平平,不会有所建树,而伯母的死讯传来,菲利普回到英国,并决定去伦敦学医。在伦敦,菲利普爱上了女招待米尔德,但米尔德并不喜欢菲利普,天性自私的米尔德拒绝了菲利普的追求,同他人发生关系并怀孕。在追求失败后,菲利普投向女作家诺拉的怀抱。之后米尔德被人抛弃,又找到了菲利普,菲利普同诺拉分手,努力接济米尔德的生活。但米尔德随后恋上了菲利普的朋友哈利并再次离开。

当菲利普再次遇到米尔德时,发现她再次被抛弃,成为妓女。此时的菲利普已不再爱她,但因为怜悯而收留了她。米尔德试图引诱菲利普未果,一怒之下逃走。后来菲利普知晓她的孩子病死,再次沦落风尘。

菲利普后来因投资南非矿山失败而破产,不得不在商店里打工。但最终因得到伯父死后留下的遗产而再次回到医学院,取得医生资质。后来菲利普同多次帮助过自己的公司职员阿瑟尔尼的女儿萨莉相恋,并得知她怀孕的消息。菲利普果断放弃之前游历的计划,同萨莉订婚。

《人性的枷锁》是毛姆的半自传体的作品。小说通过叙述主人公菲利普从童年时代起的三十年生活经历,反映了一个青年的痛苦、迷惘、失望、挫折和探索,以及逐步摆脱种种枷锁,寻找生命意义,走向成熟,获得精神解放的历程。作品文字简练通俗、意义深刻。有人说它是呼唤人性自由的一部最全面、彻底的宣言。这部小说的主要价值在于其揭示的深刻主题思想和蕴涵的丰富人生哲理。面临种种压抑人性的枷锁,主人公菲利普追求自由,寻找人生意义,他的不断成长的经历极具代表性,集中体现了资本主义社会令人窒息的社会制度。菲利普面临的人生枷锁包括不合理的教育制度及基督教虚伪教义的禁锢,对性爱的盲目狂热和沉溺,对伯父的经济依赖,生活的窘迫以及因跛足造成的心理压抑,这些枷锁主要来自情感枷锁、金钱枷锁及宗教枷锁三方面。小说用了很大篇幅描述了菲利普在感情上的纠葛及其所经历的矛盾挣扎。整部小说以菲利普的感情生活为主线,描写了菲利普大半生在感情上受到的折磨。菲利普一生爱过四位女性,其中同女招待米尔德和普通职员的女儿萨莉的爱情对他的生活产生了重大影响。小说通过对米尔德和菲利普之间关系的描述,描绘出了种种复杂的情感纠葛和情感与理智、欲望与自控、自由与束缚等矛盾。菲利普一次次克服了对米尔德的着魔,然而又一次次地陷入情网;同时,在与另一位女性诺拉的关系上,菲利普佩服诺拉助人为乐、顽强自立、理智聪慧的品格,但菲利普不爱她,只是利用她的可贵品质为自己服务,却给她带来痛苦,菲利普因此而感到良心不安。

成长主题解读

《人性的枷锁》从以下方面体现了成长小说的一些要素。

一、天真与迷惑

在《人性的枷锁》中,主人公菲利普先天跛足、父母早逝,伯父的抚养并没有使他感受到家庭的温暖,周遭的朋友嘲笑排斥,使他形成了敏感、忧郁、沉默的性格。在学校,他与罗斯的友谊及他对这种友谊的强烈的占有欲显示出孩童的天真:他妒忌罗斯与别人交往,后与罗斯决裂。他参加圣经联谊会,虔诚祈求上帝把他的跛足治好,这也体现了其不谙世事的天真。然而跛足依然如故,这使他对宗教产生迷茫。他开始怀疑宗教,怀疑自己的信仰。他在学校的遭遇以及在以伯父为代表的基督徒身上所看到的使他越发感到信徒们的自私、虚伪。菲利普不理解万能的上帝为什么不能帮他摆脱困境,为什么身边的人没有基督宣称的那种宽容博爱的精神。菲利普不再相信上帝了,这是他自我意识的初次觉醒,他希望能主宰自己的命运,开始新的生活,他变得大胆,敢于反驳伯父:"他们凭哪点可以这么想当然地认为年长必定智高睿深?"最终他抗争成功,退学去海德堡学习。

二、上路与考验

上路是成长小说情节发展模式的重要组成部分,主人公通过上路获得发现,发现自我,发现世界。在《人性的枷锁》中,菲利普多次上路。他在海德堡求学一年,遇到知识渊博的英国人海沃德,后者成为他的良师益友。他与美国人威克斯对于宗教的讨论,使菲利普最终抛弃上帝,进入了心明神清的不惑之境。他在伦敦会计师事务所的经历使他体会到身居大都市的孤寂感以及对会计事物感到枯燥无趣。在巴黎学习画画的两年里,他不再像旅居海德堡时那样少不更事,而是对周围的人产生了一种更为冷静而成熟的兴趣,这些上路经历促成了菲利普心智的成长,使他认识到现实的残酷。这一切促使菲利普思考人生的真谛,他试图从落魄诗人克朗肖的玩世不恭的奇谈怪论中寻找精神寄托,为自己勾画出一套所谓"尽可为所欲为,只是得留神街角处的警察"的处世准则。事实证明,这套准则在现实中根本行不通。菲利普饱尝人间艰辛,历经世态炎凉,这些残酷无情的经历使菲利普反思自己。当意识到他缺少"艺术家气质"时,便毅然决然地放弃了绘画,返回伦敦上医学院,继承了父业,从医当大夫。

三、顿悟与引路人

小说中主人公在其成长历程中经历数次顿悟,这种顿悟有些是其历经沧桑后的人生感悟,有些则是经成长的引路人点化而得。在菲利普的成长过程中,珀金斯校长和诗人克朗肖扮演了这样的引路人角色。当菲利普深受跛足这一身体枷锁困扰之时,珀金斯校长与他促膝谈心,解开了他跛足羞耻的情结。后来当菲利普再次回想校长所说的话,他突然间获得顿悟:"他能够愉快地接受这种耻辱了,他将这一缺陷看作是为上帝所做的奉献。"每个人都有缺陷,或为肉体,或为精神,顿悟使菲利普从身体的枷锁中摆脱出来。在小说的最后一章,面对淳朴善良、温柔坚强的姑娘萨莉,菲利普得到了对人生的顿悟,"他的理想是什么呢?他想起了他那个要从纷繁复杂、毫无意义的生活琐事中编织一种精巧、美丽的图案的愿望。一个男人来到世上,干活,结婚,生儿育女,最后悄然去世。这是一种最简单的然而却是最完美的人生格局。他有没有意识到这一点呢?"菲利普终于摆脱了情欲的枷锁,认识到了人生的真谛,经历了感情的折磨后最终找到了归宿。

菲利普成长道路上最重要的引路人就是诗人克朗肖。在他的引导下,菲利普获得了人生至关重要的一次顿悟。一天,菲利普忽然听闻海沃德的死讯,内心神伤,在大英博物馆细看那些雕像回首往事思索人生意义时,他忽然顿悟,想通了那条波斯地毯的秘密:"织工精心编织地毯的图案时,并没有什么目的,只不过是由于地毯的美而感到快乐罢了。一个人幻想着生活既无意义,又无重要性,就可以随意选择几股纬线来编织成图案,从而得到自我满足。有一种图案最明显,最完美,也最美丽,在这种图案中,一个人生下来,长大成人,然后结婚,生儿育女,为衣食而劳碌,最后死去。"他最后终于明白了诗人克朗肖送给他地毯时所说的人生的意义,你自己去找,就在这条地毯里的道理。这时候他已经完全打破了枷锁,人生的意义在于为自己树立目标,让人在追求的过程中不至于流于虚空,追求人生的目标时,去慢慢参悟人生的意义。菲利普的伯父凯里牧师则是反面引路人。凯里牧师自私、冷漠、虚伪,生活刻板,毫无情趣。当菲利普问他关于《圣经》中"如果拥有信念是否能搬动高山"时,他答道:"在上帝的仁慈之下,你可以搬动高山。"他的话使菲利普坚信只要虔诚地祈祷就能使上帝治愈他的跛足。

四、自我超越

　　成长小说中的主人公的成长往往伴随着自我超越。《人性的枷锁》中菲利普的自我超越体现在以下几个方面。

　　首先是宗教的超越。在菲利普的生存过程中,他朦胧地意识到宗教的虚伪,伯父满嘴仁爱慈善,实际上冷酷自私,爱财如命,菲利普看到了宗教的外衣下教会学校的学生之间老师之间的钩心斗角、互相陷害。菲利普的瘸腿受尽了同学的讥笑嘲弄,用真心结交的朋友背叛了他,菲利普认识到宗教教义的仁慈博爱和现实是两回事。这一切使菲利浦发出"人何必非要信上帝"的呐喊,最后毅然与宗教决裂,在家庭和学校安排他以宗教为一生的职业时,他拒绝了,尽管他也知道走这条路比较平坦,一生都可衣食无忧。但他对宗教的反感使他不可能把自己交给上帝,所以伯母的哭求也没有动摇他的决心。这表明菲利普已经从盲目迷信宗教中走了出来,世界上从来都没有一个宗教能满足所有人的精神需求,每个人都必须寻找到属于自己的宗教。

　　其次是情欲的超越。小说通过对米尔德和菲利普之间关系的描绘,展现出了种种复杂的情感纠葛和情感与理智、欲望与自控、自由与束缚等矛盾。菲利普一次次克服了对米尔德的着魔,然而,却又一次次地陷入情网;同时,在与另一位女性诺拉的关系上,他佩服诺拉助人为乐、顽强自立、理智聪慧,但他不爱她,只是利用她的可贵品质为自己服务。菲利普在经历了感情的折磨后最终找到了归宿。淳朴、善良、健康、坚强的姑娘萨莉默默地爱着他,关心他,帮助他。开始时菲利普忽略了她,相处久后,他为她的淳朴善良而感动,菲利普发现她才是那个能给他带来幸福的人。为了和萨莉结婚,菲利普放弃了酝酿已久的去西班牙的打算,决定和她结婚后到渔村当医生,为穷人治病,过上平静的生活。小说中两位女性米尔德和萨莉形成了鲜明对比:前者自私自利,放荡邪恶,对菲利普一味地索取、利用;而后者温柔善良,健康能干,在菲利普落魄失意的时候,给了菲利普温暖和家的感觉,她像天使一般、宁静、完美。菲利普摆脱了米尔德的阴影,决心和萨莉共度一生,这标志着菲利普在感情、心理上的成熟,也标志着他从对性爱的盲目狂热沉溺中解脱出来,能够运用理智去追求健康、美好的感情,寻找一个合适的伴侣,这是对人性弱点的一次重要的超越,也是他摆脱人生枷锁,寻求人生意义的关键一步。

　　最后是自卑心理的超越。因为自卑,菲利普对来之不易的友谊产生独占意识,不愿意朋友和其他人产生友谊,这正是内心极度不自信的表现。菲利普对自卑感的克服和超越体现在他在和威尔金森小姐的交往中,菲利普用手勾住了威尔金森小姐的腰,在她的嘴上亲了亲。面对威尔金森小姐的微笑,菲利普充满了征服的自豪感。菲利普幼年父母双亡的经历,让他对爱有超过常人的渴望,因此在成年后在与异性的交往上获得这种爱缺失的补偿,菲利普在征服威尔金森小姐的过程中获得了超越自卑的胜利感,菲利普一直处于这种自卑又要超越自卑的状态中。

选读出自小说最后一章,描写了菲利普终于克服了情欲的枷锁,最终找到了生活的归宿。

He had arranged to meet Sally[1] on Saturday in the National Gallery. She was to come there as soon as she was released from the shop and had agreed to lunch with him. Two days had passed since he had seen her, and his exultation had not left him for a moment. It was because he rejoiced in the feeling that he had not attempted to see her. He had repeated to himself exactly what he would say to her and how he should say it. Now his impatience was unbearable. He had written to Doctor South and had in his pocket a telegram from him received that morning: 'Sacking the mumpish fool. When will you come?' Philip walked along Parliament Street. It was a fine day, and there was a bright, frosty sun which made the light dance in the street. It was crowded. There was a tenuous mist in the distance, and it softened exquisitely the noble lines of the buildings. He crossed Trafalgar Square. Suddenly his heart gave a sort of twist in his body; he saw a woman in front of him who he thought was Mildred.[2] She had the same figure, and she walked with that slight dragging of the feet which was so characteristic of her. Without thinking, but with a beating heart, he hurried till he came alongside, and then, when the woman turned, he saw it was someone unknown to him. It was the face of a much older person, with a lined, yellow skin. He slackened his pace. He was infinitely relieved, but it was not only relief that he felt; it was disappointment too; he was seized with horror of himself. Would he never be free from that passion? At the bottom of his heart, notwithstanding everything, he felt that a strange, desperate thirst for that vile woman would always linger. That love had caused him so much suffering that he knew he would never, never quite be free of it. Only death could finally assuage his desire.

But he wrenched the pang from his heart. He thought of Sally, with her kind blue eyes; and his lips unconsciously formed themselves into a smile. He walked up the steps of the National Gallery and sat down in the first room, so that he should see her the moment she came in. It always comforted him to get among pictures. He looked at none in particular, but allowed the magnificence of their colour, the beauty of their lines, to work upon his soul. His imagination was busy with Sally. It would be pleasant to take her away from that London in which she seemed an unusual figure, like a cornflower in a shop among orchids and azaleas; he had learned in the Kentish hop-field that she did not belong to the town; and he was sure that she would blossom under the soft skies of Dorset to a rarer beauty. She came in, and he got up to meet her. She was in black, with white cuffs at her wrists and a lawn collar round her neck. They shook hands.

'Have you been waiting long?'

'No. Ten minutes. Are you hungry?'

'Not very.'

'Let's sit here for a bit, shall we?'

'If you like.'

They sat quietly, side by side, without speaking. Philip enjoyed having her near him. He was warmed by her radiant health. A glow of life seemed like an aureole to shine about her.

'Well, how have you been?' he said at last, with a little smile.

'Oh, it's all right. It was a false alarm.'

'Was it?'

'Aren't you glad?'

An extraordinary sensation filled him. He had felt certain that Sally's suspicion was well-founded; it had never occurred to him for an instant that there was a possibility of error. All his plans were suddenly overthrown, and the existence, so elaborately pictured, was no more than a dream which would never be realised. He was free once more. Free! He need give up none of his projects, and life still was in his hands for him to do what he liked with. He felt no exhilaration, but only dismay. His heart sank. The future stretched out before him in desolate emptiness. It was as though he had sailed for many years over a great waste of waters, with peril and privation, and at last had come upon a fair haven, but as he was about to enter, some contrary wind had arisen and drove him out again into the open sea; and because he had let his mind dwell on these soft meads and pleasant woods of the land, the vast deserts of the ocean filled him with anguish. He could not confront again the loneliness and the tempest. Sally looked at him with her clear eyes.

'Aren't you glad?' she asked again, 'I thought you'd be as pleased as Punch.'[3]

He met her gaze haggardly. 'I'm not sure,' he muttered.

'You are funny. Most men would.'

He realised that he had deceived himself; it was no self-sacrifice that had driven him to think of marrying, but the desire for a wife and a home and love; and now that it all seemed to slip through his fingers he was seized with despair. He wanted all that more than anything in the world. What did he care for Spain and its cities, Cordova, Toledo, Leon; what to him were the pagodas of Burmah and the lagoons of South Sea Islands? America was here and now. It seemed to him that all his life he had followed the ideals that other people, by their words or their writings, had instilled into him, and never the desires of his own heart. Always his course had been swayed by what he thought he should do and never by what he wanted with his whole soul to do. He put all that aside now with a gesture of impatience. He had lived always in the future, and the present always, always had slipped through his fingers. His ideals? He thought of his desire to make a design, intricate and beautiful, out of the myriad, meaningless facts of life: had he not seen also that the simplest pattern, that in which a man was born, worked, married, had children, and died, was likewise the most perfect? It might be that to surrender to happiness was to accept defeat, but it was a defeat better than many victories.

He glanced quickly at Sally, he wondered what she was thinking, and then looked away again.

'I was going to ask you to marry me,' he said.

'I thought perhaps you might, but I shouldn't have liked to stand in your way.'

'You wouldn't have done that.'

'How about your travels, Spain and all that?'

'How d'you know I want to travel?'

'I ought to know something about it. I've heard you and Dad talk about it till you were blue in the face.'

'I don't care a damn about all that.' He paused for an instant and then spoke in a low, hoarse whisper, 'I don't want to leave you! I can't leave you.'

She did not answer. He could not tell what she thought.

'I wonder if you'll marry me, Sally.'

She did not move and there was no flicker of emotion on her face, but she did not look at him when she answered.

'If you like.'

'Don't you want to?'

'Oh, of course I'd like to have a house of my own, and it's about time I was settling down.'

He smiled a little. He knew her pretty well by now, and her manner did not surprise him.

'But don't you want to marry ME?'

'There's no one else I would marry.'

'Then that settles it.'

'Mother and Dad will be surprised, won't they?'

'I'm so happy.'

'I want my lunch,' she said.

'Dear!'

He smiled and took her hand and pressed it. They got up and walked out of the gallery. They stood for a moment at the balustrade and looked at Trafalgar Square. Cabs and omnibuses hurried to and fro, and crowds passed, hastening in every direction, and the sun was shining.

Notes:

1. Sally:萨莉,一个淳朴、善良、温柔、坚强的姑娘,多次给予菲利普帮助

2. Mildred:米尔德,一个放荡自私的女招待,菲利普曾陷入她的情网中不能自拔

3. as pleased as Punch:得意扬扬

Questions:

1. What does Philip try to free himself from?

2. What is his epiphany about life?

8 Gone with the Wind

作者及背景简介

玛格丽特·米切尔(Margaret Mitchell, 1900—1949),美国现代著名女作家,曾获文学博士学位,担任过《亚特兰大新闻报》的记者。1937年玛格丽特获得普利策奖,1939年获纽约南方协会金质奖章。1949年,玛格丽特·米切尔在车祸中罹难。玛格丽特·米切尔短暂的一生并未留下太多的作品,但仅凭一部《飘》足以奠定她在世界文学史中不可动摇的地位。

玛格丽特·米切尔于1900年出生于美国南部的亚特兰大,三四岁时,她就喜欢听关于亚特兰大历史的故事。她的外祖母时常坐在房前的门廊上,给坐在自己膝上的玛格丽特指点着一条一直穿过后院的战壕。"大片大片的火焰吞没了整个城市,你无论朝哪儿看,都有一片奇怪而难以形容的亮光映彻天际。"这便是《飘》中亚特兰大沦陷的原型。菲茨塔拉德庄园是玛格丽特童年的乐园,玛格丽特在那里听家族的历史,战争的故事和母亲的童年,她想象着过去这里的豪华舞会和烤肉野餐。这些都为她创作《飘》带来了素材和灵感。一战的风波第一次让玛格丽特体验到了战争的真实与残酷,她意识到生命的可贵。1918年,即玛格丽特18岁时,她已经出落成一位南方美女。她结识了一名青年军官——克利福特·亨利少尉。玛格丽特很快坠入了情网,亨利有着英俊的外表,诗人般的气质,这便是《飘》中的艾希礼(Ashley)的原型,但战争夺去了这个年轻人的生命。母亲梅贝莉的去世,让玛格丽特成为她父亲和长兄生命中唯一的女人。像《飘》中的斯嘉丽一样,她代替不了母亲在父亲心中的位置。如同斯嘉丽一样,玛格丽特生来就有一种反叛的气质。她同狂放不羁的厄普肖结识,并凭着一时的冲动与一个冷酷无情、酗酒成性的恶棍结婚。这段婚姻不久便以失败告终,虽然她很快便重新振作,但这段婚姻带给她的痛苦和屈辱一直伴随着她。1944年,玛格丽特成为一名大牌记者,从事她所喜欢的写作。她与一直支持和深爱她的约翰·马什结合,没有马什,《飘》就不可能完成和发表。"她从未真正理解过她所爱的那两个男人中的任何一个,所以她把两个人都失去了。"这是《飘》中斯嘉丽对自己的爱情经历的总结,同时也是米切尔对自己的总结。

选读作品简介

小说的背景是美国南北战争。南北战争(American Civil War)即美国内战,是美国历史上唯一一次内战,参战双方为北的方美利坚合众国和南方的美利坚联盟国,最终以北方的胜利告终。战争之初北方为了维护国家统一而战,后来演变为一场消灭南方奴隶制的革命战争。

1861年美国南北战争爆发前夕,塔拉庄园的千金小姐斯嘉丽爱上了另一庄园主的儿子艾希礼,但艾希礼却选择了温柔善良的梅兰妮。斯嘉丽赌气嫁给梅兰妮的弟弟查尔斯。南北战争爆发后,查尔斯上前线死于战场。斯嘉丽成了寡妇,她内心却一直热恋着艾希礼。斯嘉丽和风度翩翩的商人白瑞德相识,但拒绝了他的追求。目睹战乱带来的惨状,任性的斯嘉丽成熟了许多。不少人家惊惶地开始逃离家园,但正巧梅兰妮要生孩子,斯嘉丽只好留下来照顾她。战后斯嘉丽在绝望中去找白瑞德借钱,但没借到,回来路上偶遇本来要迎娶她妹妹的暴发户弗兰克,为了让弗兰克出钱帮她保住塔拉庄园,斯嘉丽勾引弗兰克,和他结了婚。

弗兰克和艾希礼加入了反政府的秘密组织,在一次集会时遭北方军包围,弗兰克中弹身亡,艾希礼负伤逃亡,在白瑞德帮助下回到梅兰妮身边。斯嘉丽再次成为寡妇,此时,白瑞德前来向她求婚,她终于与一直爱她的靠私运军火和粮食发财的白瑞德结了婚。一年后,女儿邦妮出生,白瑞德把全部感情投注到邦妮身上,对白瑞德的感情却因斯嘉丽忘不了艾希礼而蒙上阴影。斯嘉丽再次怀孕,但在和白瑞德的争吵中滚下楼梯流产。白瑞德感到内疚,决心同斯嘉丽言归于好,不料就在这时,小女儿邦妮意外坠马摔死了。与此同时梅兰妮终因操劳过度卧病不起。临终前,她把自己的丈夫艾希礼和儿子托付给斯嘉丽,斯嘉丽不顾一切投向艾希礼的怀中,紧紧拥抱住他,站在一旁的白瑞德再也无法忍受下去,转身离去。面对伤心欲绝毫无反应的艾希礼,斯嘉丽终于明白,她爱的艾希礼其实是不存在的,她真正需要的是白瑞德。

当斯嘉丽赶回家里告诉白瑞德,她是真正爱他的时候,白瑞德已不再相信她。他决心离开斯嘉丽,返回老家去寻找美好的事物,被遗弃的斯嘉丽站在浓雾迷漫的院中,想起了父亲曾经对她说过的一句话:"世界上唯有土地与明天同在。"斯嘉丽决定守在她的土地上重新创造新的生活。"明天又是新的一天!"

成长主题解读

　　主人公斯嘉丽既是一个平凡的女子,她拥有许多少女共同的特征:热情、开朗、纯真、浪漫。但她又是一个不平凡的女子,面对环境变化,更多地表现出她的坚强、勇敢、拼搏、自强。斯嘉丽生长在一个富裕的家庭,拥有美丽的容貌和智慧,她有一般贵族小姐的缺点:骄傲、自大、虚荣、任性。斯嘉丽是一个鲜明、生动、丰富、复杂的人物形象,这一形象的魅力之所以经久不衰,在于作家对人物性格的成功塑造。

　　斯嘉丽的生活经历和复杂性格形成大致分为战前、战中和战后三个阶段。战前优越的生活造就了斯嘉丽骄傲、自大、虚荣、任性,作为一个南方大种植园主的女儿,斯嘉丽身上有一种温和的、过分讲究教养的贵族血统和精明而凡俗的爱尔兰贫民血统相混合的气质。她既沿袭了父亲豪爽、粗犷、不拘小节和脾气暴躁的性格,又从小受到母亲良好的道德观念的熏陶,她既想做个像母亲那样有着大家闺秀风范的淑女,骨子里又有背叛种种道德规范的意识,这使得她爱慕虚荣、单纯而又实际,却不乏狡黠,但不擅长缜密地思考问题,这一性格特征在战前表现得比较突出。战前,斯嘉丽作为拥有众多黑人奴隶的塔拉庄园主的女儿,拥有着财富和地位,生活安逸、富有魅力的外貌赋予她很强的虚荣心。她只热衷于舞会、引人注目的漂亮衣服,迷恋骑马及穿梭于众多男子之间,成为各种聚会的中心。战争中过多的磨难迫使斯嘉丽变得坚强、勇敢、拼搏、自强,战争中的经历同时也是这个女主角的转变过程。在这段时期,斯嘉丽从一个随心所欲、贪图享乐的少妇变成了一个精明强悍、敢想敢做,同时又吝啬贪婪、斤斤计较的当家人,表现出一种不畏艰难、艰苦创业的惊人毅力。她在前一个阶段的自私、任性到这个时候已被她对命运的顽强抗争精神掩盖得不那么明显了。战后残酷的现实促使斯嘉丽变得贪婪、倔强、自私。她清楚地认识到只有理智地面对这个新兴的功利主义世界,才能保全她自己、她的家人和她的塔拉庄园。在这种观念的支配下,金钱对她来说显得越来越重要了。为了能赚取更多的钱,她毫不顾忌那种以为女人应该是无知、不能有自己意见的上流社会的传统观念,自作主张买下锯木厂并抛头露面亲自经营。斯嘉丽根本不在乎别人对她的看法,她想的只是能让自己过得更好一些,不再贫穷挨饿。她一旦决定了的事就会全力以赴地按照自己的意愿行事。在爱情上,斯嘉丽终于明白,她以前一直爱着的艾希礼其实是不存在的,她真正需要的是正在爱着她的白瑞德,这表明斯嘉丽在爱情上的成熟。

　　选读选自小说《飘》的结尾,描写了斯嘉丽意识到了真正爱她的人以及白瑞德离去后的心理。

For years she had had her back against the stone wall of Rhett's love and had taken it as much for granted as she had taken Melanie's love, flattering herself that she drew her strength from herself alone. And even as she had realized earlier in the evening that Melanie[1] had been beside her in her bitter campaigns against life, now she knew that silent in the background, Rhett had stood, loving her, understanding her, ready to help. Rhett at the bazaar, reading her impatience in her eyes and leading her out in the reel, Rhett helping her out of the bondage of mourning, Rhett convoying her through the fire and explosions the night Atlanta fell, Rhett lending her the money that gave her her start, Rhett who comforted her when she woke in the nights crying with fright from her dreams—why, no man did such things without loving a woman to distraction!

The trees dripped dampness upon her but she did not feel it. The mist swirled about her and she paid it no heed. For when she thought of Rhett, with his swarthy face, flashing teeth and dark alert eyes, a trembling came over her.

"I love him," she thought and, as always, she accepted the truth with little wonder, as a child accepting a gift. "I don't know how long I've loved him but it's true. And if it hadn't been for Ashley, I'd have realized it long ago. I've never been able to see the world at all, because Ashley stood in the way."

She loved him, scamp, blackguard, without scruple or honor—at least honor as Ashley saw it "Damn Ashley's honor!" she thought. "Ashley's honor has always let me down. Yes, from the very beginning when he kept on coming to see me, even though he knew his family expected him to marry Melanie. Rhett has never let me down, even that dreadful night of Melly's reception[2] when he ought to have wrung my neck. Even when he left me on the road the night Atlanta fell, he knew I'd be safe. He knew I'd get through somehow. Even when he acted like he was going to make me pay to get that money from him at the Yankee camp. He wouldn't have taken me. He was just testing me. He's loved me all along and I've been so mean to him. Time and again, I've hurt him and he was too proud to show it. And when Bonnie died—Oh, how could I?"

She stood up straight and looked at the house on the hill. She had thought, half an hour ago, that she had lost everything in the world, except money, everything that made life desirable, Ellen, Gerald, Bonnie, Mammy, Melanie and Ashley. She had to lose them all to realize that she loved Rhett—loved him because he was strong and unscrupulous, passionate and earthy, like herself.

"I'll tell him everything," she thought. "He'll understand. He's always understood. I'll tell him what a fool I've been and how much I love him and I'll make it up to him."

Suddenly she felt strong and happy. She was not afraid of the darkness or the fog and she knew with a singing in her heart that she would never fear them again. No matter what mists might curl around her in the future, she knew her refuge. She started briskly up the street toward home and the blocks seemed very long. Far, far too long. She caught up her skirts to her knees and began torun lightly. But this time she was not running from fear. She was running because Rhett's arms were at the end of the street.

……

She silently watched him go up the stairs, feeling that she would strangle at the pain in her throat. With the sound of his feet dying away in the upper hall was dying the last thing in the world that mattered. She knew now that there was no appeal of emotion or reason which would turn that cool brain from its verdict. She knew now that he had meant every word he said, lightly though some of them had been spoken. She knew because she sensed in him something strong, unyielding, implacable—all the qualities she had looked for in Ashley and never found.

She had never understood either of the men she had loved and so she had lost them both. Now, she had a fumbling knowledge that, had she ever understood Ashley, she would never have loved him; had she ever understood Rhett, she would never have lost him. She wondered forlornly if she had ever really understood anyone in the world.

There was a merciful dullness in her mind now, a dullness that she knew from long experience would soon give way to sharp pain, even as severed tissues, shocked by the surgeon's knife, have a brief instant of insensibility before their agony begins.

"I won't think of it now," she thought grimly, summoning up her old charm. "I'll go crazy if I think about losing him now. I'll think of it tomorrow."

"But," cried her heart, casting aside the charm and beginning to ache, "I can't let him go! There must be some way!"

"I won't think of it now," she said again, aloud, trying to push her misery to the back of her mind, trying to find some bulwark against the rising tide of pain. "I'll—why, I'll go home to Tara tomorrow," and her spirits lifted faintly.

She had gone back to Tara once in fear and defeat and she had emerged from its sheltering walls strong and armed for victory. What she had done once, somehow—please God, she could do again!

How, she did not know. She did not want to think of that now. All she wanted was a breathing space in which to hurt, a quiet place to lick her wounds, a haven in which to plan her campaign.

She thought of Tara and it was as if a gentle cool hand were stealing over her heart. She could seethe white house gleaming welcome to her through the reddening autumn leaves, feel the quiet hush of the country twilight coming down over her like a benediction, feel the dews falling on the acres of green bushes starred with fleecy white, see the raw color of the red earth and the dismal dark beauty of the pines on the rolling hills.

She felt vaguely comforted, strengthened by the picture, and some of her hurt and frantic regret was pushed from the top of her mind. She stood for a moment remembering small things, the avenue of dark cedars leading to Tara, the banks of cape jessamine bushes, vivid green against the white walls, the fluttering white curtains. And Mammy would be there. Suddenly she wanted Mammy desperately, as she had wanted her when she was a little girl, wanted the broad bosom on which to lay her head, the gnarled black hand on her hair. Mammy, the last link with the old days.

With the spirit of her people who would not know defeat, even when it stared them in the face, she raised her chin. She could get Rhett back. She knew she could. There had never been a man she couldn't get, once she set her mind upon him.

"I'll think of it all tomorrow, at Tara. I can stand it then. Tomorrow, I'll think of some way to get him back. After all, tomorrow is another day."

Notes:

1. 梅兰妮,艾希礼的妻子,温柔善良,对斯嘉丽很好。

2. 艾希礼生日宴会上,斯嘉丽对艾希礼仍然旧情不忘,两人谈得很亲密。

Questions:

1. What was she thinking about at the end of the novel?

2. How did Scarlet grow up during the war?

9

Adventures of Huckleberry Finn

作者及背景简介

马克·吐温(Mark Twain, 1835—1910),原名塞姆·朗赫恩·克列门斯(Samuel Langhorne Clemens),马克·吐温出身于美国密苏里州佛罗里达的乡村贫穷律师家庭,是家中7个小孩中的第6个。他的父亲是当地的律师,收入微薄,家境拮据,马克·吐温上学时就不得不打工。马克·吐温11岁那年父亲去世,从此他开始了独立的劳动生活,先在印刷厂当学徒,当  过送报员和排字工,后来又在密西西比河上当水手和舵手。马克·吐温的笔名源自其早年水手术语,意思是水深3英尺(1英尺≈30.48厘米),这是轮船安全航行的必要条件。后来他试图靠经营木材业与矿业发财致富,均未成功,便转而以写文章为生。1862年在内华达弗吉尼亚城一家报馆工作,1863年开始使用"马克·吐温"的笔名,1865年在纽约一家杂志发表幽默故事《卡拉韦拉斯县驰名的跳蛙》而全国闻名。此后,马克·吐温经常为报刊撰写幽默文章。

马克·吐温是美国著名的幽默大师、小说家、作家、演说家。在40年的创作生涯中,马克·吐温写出了10多部长篇小说、几十部短篇小说及其他体裁的大量作品,其中著名的有短篇小说《竞选州长》《哥尔斯密的朋友再度出洋》《百万英镑》等,长篇小说《镀金时代》《汤姆·索亚历险记》《王子与贫儿》等。《汤姆·索亚历险记》中的主人公汤姆·索亚天真活泼,富于幻想和冒险精神,不堪忍受束缚个性、枯燥乏味的生活,幻想干一番英雄事业。小说通过主人公的冒险经历,对美国虚伪庸俗的社会习俗、伪善的宗教仪式和刻板陈腐的学校教育进行了讽刺和批判,以欢快的笔调描写了少年儿童自由活泼的心灵。《汤姆·索亚历险记》以其浓厚的深具地方特色的幽默和对人物的敏锐观察,一跃成为最伟大的儿童文学作品,也是一首美国"黄金时代"的田园牧歌。

马克·吐温是美国批判现实主义文学的奠基人,他经历了美国从初期资本主义到帝国主义的发展过程,其思想和创作也表现为从轻快搞笑到辛辣讽刺到悲观厌世的发展阶段。马克·吐温被誉为"美国文学史上的林肯"。马克·吐温作为美国批判现实主义文学的代表人物,其创作的触角扎根于社会现实的方方面面。随着生活阅历的加深,马克·吐温对美国表面繁荣掩盖下的社会现实有了更清醒的认识,他开始在作品中探讨一些深刻的社会问题,这一时期是马克·吐温创作的黄金时代,也是他在继续观察社会的基础上加深对美国的政治制度、生活方式、思想情操的思考和探索的时期,尖锐的讽刺和无情的揭露是这一时期作品的主要特点。其作品的基调也由早期的幽默乐观转为无情的揭露和辛辣的讽刺,笔锋更加犀利,讽刺更加尖锐,幽默讽刺中批判的成分增强了。马克·吐温是著名的幽默讽刺作家,但是马克·吐温自己则说:"不能一味逗乐,要有更高的理想。"马克·吐温的幽默讽刺不仅仅是嘲笑人类的弱点,而是以夸张手法,将它放大了给人看,希望人类变得更完美、更理想化。

马克·吐温是美国地方色彩文学的代表作家,地方色彩文学(local colorism)又被称为乡土文学或地域文学,是美国现实主义文学的一部分,美国作家加兰(Hamlin Garland,1860—1940)从质地和背景两个方面界定地方色彩小说:它的质地和背景独特,使得它不可能出自其他地方或外人之手。质地指的是组成地方文化的方言、传说、民谣、民俗的综合体。背景是指地理背景,也指此背景中影响人的思维和行为的地域特点和风貌。

马克·吐温的传世佳作《哈克贝利·费恩历险记》为美国小说的语言带来了意义深远的变化,奠定了美国文学口语化风格的基础。这种风格文笔清新,不事雕琢,词汇和句法简单朴素,语言直接,准确简明,长句很少,多为简单句或并列复合句,有时甚至不合语法规则。字句和结构的重复出现使文字生动活泼,获得回旋复沓、意蕴幽深的效果。马克·吐温的风格开创了美国小说语言口语化的先河,对后世作家产生了巨大的影响。海明威曾经说过"一切美国当代文学都起源于马克·吐温一本叫《哈克贝利·费恩历险记》的书"。

选读作品简介

《哈克贝利·费恩历险记》是《汤姆·索亚历险记》的姊妹篇,是马克·吐温最优秀的作品。哈克贝利是一个聪明、善良、勇敢的白人少年。哈克贝利为了追求自由的生活，逃离了酗酒的父亲，逃到密西西比河上。在逃亡途中，他遇到了黑奴吉姆。吉姆是一个勤劳朴实、热情诚实、忠心耿耿的黑奴，他为了逃脱被主人再次卖掉的命运，从主人家中出逃，两个人经历了种种奇遇。哈克贝利知道帮助黑奴逃跑是违法行为，可是现在两人都是逃亡者，也就是同病相怜，成了患难之交。他们乘木筏沿密西西比河漂流，希望逃离蓄奴州。由于夜晚看不清方向，他们反而越来越深入到了蓄奴区，只好听天由命。有两个被愤怒人群追赶着的人向哈克贝利求救，善良的哈克贝利收留了他们，却很快发现他们是狡猾的骗子"国王"和"公爵"。他们喧宾夺主，控制了木筏，一路上不断招摇撞骗，甚至背着哈克贝利卖掉了吉姆。哈克贝利前去费尔普斯农场拯救吉姆。他在那里发现买下吉姆的正是汤姆的姨夫，这一家人把哈克贝利错认作侄儿汤姆。机灵的哈克贝利将错就错，索性冒充起汤姆，哈克贝利截住半路上的汤姆，一起设计救出了吉姆。事后汤姆告诉哈克贝利：根据吉姆原主人华岑小姐的遗嘱，吉姆早已获得自由。费尔普斯太太热情地提出要收养哈克贝利，但被谢绝。哈克贝利要到印第安人居住的地方去过漂泊不定的自由生活。

小说赞扬了男孩哈克贝利的机智和善良，谴责了宗教的虚伪和信徒的愚昧，同时，塑造了一位富有尊严的黑奴形象。它是马克·吐温作品精选中最杰出的一部。海明威曾评价道："整个现代美国文学都来源于马克·吐温的著作《哈克贝利·费恩历险记》，这是我们最优秀的一本书，此后还没有哪本书能和它匹敌。"

成长主题解读

《哈克贝利·费恩历险记》是美国文学中的一部经典成长小说，哈克贝利在社会道德与人性的冲突中的成长经历展示了青少年从无知到有知的社会化过程。马克·吐温让哈克贝利到纷繁复杂的成人世界游历，经受各种磨难和考验，从最初的天真烂漫到之后的迷茫、痛苦、挣扎直到最后的认识和道德的成长，反映了处于成长期的青少年特有的叛逆和追求、痛苦和烦恼，也体现出人类成长过程中的共性。

马克·吐温选择流浪儿哈克贝利颇有深意。哈克贝利有父等于无父，整日与孩童为伍，游荡于山林之中，没有接受过什么教育，更谈不上什么教养，因而社会化程度很低，社会规范、传统文化的种种信条在他身上的影响很少，这种身份让他更多地保留了纯真的儿童本色，也使得他对文明社会产生了质疑、叛逆和反抗的心理。哈克贝利一开始就表现出对刻板的文明规矩的厌恶和反抗，朦胧而执着地追求自由和独立。道格拉斯寡妇这位体面的小市民努力要把哈克贝利这只"可怜的迷途羔羊"改造成遵守社会规范的文明人,而处在"自然人"阶段习惯无拘无束的哈克贝利对种种清规戒律感到压抑和束缚。"只要想想这寡妇为人处世有多古板,多正经,就能明白一天到晚待在她屋里真是活受罪。"酒鬼父亲的虐待让哈克贝利下定决心逃离,哈克贝利精心谋划了一起"谋杀案",将猪血泼洒在小屋里制造自己被谋杀的假象,让所有人都断了寻找自己的念头,借此挣脱文明社会的束缚,摆脱父亲的压制,去过一种自由的无拘无束的生活。然而这只是文化与人格、社会与个人冲突的开始。哈克贝利在小岛上巧遇吉姆,两人结伴沿密西西比河而下,开始了追寻自由的旅程。一路上,密西西比河两岸呈现在他眼前的是普遍存在的拜金狂热、家族之间的血腥械斗和骗子的无耻与贪婪,哈克贝利逐步认识到成人世界的无聊、冷酷、丑恶。其间社会道德规范与人性的矛盾多次在他内心引发激烈冲突,哈克贝利不得不在两者之间进行取舍,每一次的冲突与抉择都使他得到了成长,获得了人生知识、道德原则和价值观念。在杰克逊岛上,哈克贝利得知吉姆出逃之后,他发誓要为吉姆保守秘密,哪怕别人叫他"下流的废奴主义者",因为他"是不回那儿去了"。此时哈克贝利仅仅把吉姆看作一个黑人玩伴,在吉姆面前拥有一种天生的优越感。和吉姆在雾中失散重聚后,他天性使然作弄吉姆,而吉姆对他流露出深切的关爱,这使他对吉姆肃然起敬:"他说的使我觉得自己多么卑鄙,我恨不得吻他的脚。"这时,他对吉姆有了一种不知不觉的尊敬与认同,同时民主和平等的道德观和价值观也开始在他内心萌芽。同时,哈克贝利毕竟不是生活在真空中的人,社会环境的熏陶也让他继承了黑人奴隶的命运由白人主人任意支配的传统观念。当吉姆因临近废奴城镇凯劳而兴奋不已时,这种与当时社会规范相左的言行让哈克贝利心里感到愧疚,社会道德准则开始发挥作用,他决定到岸上去告发吉姆。而吉姆对他真情的表白又让他犹豫不决,他"自己也拿不定这次上岸去是高兴还是不高兴"。当他遇到那些猎奴人,哈克贝利在社会规范和天性之间犹疑不定,最终善良的天性和与吉姆的友情占了上风,他谎称船上有天花支走了猎奴人。然而,哈克贝利内心的冲突还在继续。成人社会的种种暴力和残忍让他困惑,但是内心的纯真和善良却能够给他指引方向。于是哈克贝利决定以后见机行事,因为他还不是个成年人,不用像成年人那样行事。在社会与个人的冲突中,哈克贝利最终选择了顺应自己的天性。而哈克贝利内心最激烈的冲突发生在他们遇到国王和公爵两个骗子后。起初为了吉姆,加之他那精灵鬼怪的性格,哈克贝利没有直接揭发两个骗子的行径还偶尔参与其中。然而,当两个骗子穷途末路卖掉了吉姆时,哈克贝利又一次陷入了激烈的思想斗争之中。一方面,社会道德再次抬头谴责他帮助黑奴逃跑,"是个卑鄙无耻的小人",要下地狱去受煎熬,于是他决定写信给华岑小姐告知她黑奴的下落以求内心的平静;另一方面,在大河上的漂流让哈克贝利和吉姆感情日渐浓厚,心理上更加接近,回想起吉姆对他的体贴、疼爱和由衷的感激,哈克贝利再次犯难,他"几乎屏住呼吸,琢磨了一阵",终于善良天性战胜了社会道德,他下定决心:"好吧,我就下地狱吧……一不做,二不休,要走就走到底。"(见选读)至此,纯真战胜了谬误,善良战胜了邪恶,人性战胜了社会规范和上帝,甘愿入地狱的人性发出夺目的光辉。经过艰难的挣扎,哈克贝利的社会化过程得以完成,树立了自我意识,获得了新生,从而有能力去完成更艰巨的任务。在此之后,哈克贝利撕掉信件,开始了营救吉姆的活动并想方设法去除他的奴隶身份。

  每个人的成长都需要经验丰富的成人的正确引导。黑人吉姆在小说中就扮演着哈克贝利的精神导师的角色,对他进行正面的道德教育。尽管吉姆大字不识,头脑简单,但是善良、正直、富有同情心。吉姆像父亲般照顾着哈克贝利,用他的善良和关爱赢得了哈克贝利的信任和尊重。起初,种族的偏见让哈克贝利仅仅把吉姆当作流浪的玩伴并且搞恶作剧戏弄吉姆。而吉姆的真情使哈克贝利羞愧难当并勇敢地道歉,一个白人向一个黑人道歉本身就说明了哈克贝利开始跨越种族偏见的樊篱。到后来两人几经离散重聚,吉姆身上的正直、善良、愿意为哈克贝利牺牲一切的美好品质感动影响着哈克贝利,哈克贝利也把吉姆当作朋友、亲人,直至最后当作自己的父亲,甚至不惜为救吉姆而甘愿下地狱。哈克贝利对吉姆的态度变化的过程正表现了哈克贝利从少年到成年、从无知到有知的转化,其自身道德价值观念不断健全和增进。生活不仅有美好善良的一面,同时也存在着虚伪和冷酷。"国王"和"公爵"的出现则为哈克贝利这个未成年人的成长提供了反面教育。这两个坏蛋是哈克贝利成长过程中的"阻碍者",他们的闯入搅乱了哈克贝利和吉姆木筏上平静惬意的生活,把哈克贝利从河上的天真的生活引到岸上纷繁复杂的成人世界。起初,"公爵"和"国王"刚来到木筏上的时候,哈克贝利一方面作为局外人冷眼旁观,一方面又不自觉地参与了他们的欺诈活动。这既与他精灵鬼怪、喜好恶作剧的性格有关;也反映出哈克贝利作为一个未成年人道德观念还不是很健全。正是在与这两个坏蛋打交道的过程中,哈克贝利的口才、智慧和责任感都经受了考验。善与恶的鲜明对比让哈克贝利深入了解成人社会的虚伪和欺诈,他的自我意识越来越明确,道德观念也越来越健全,并开始用自己的行动在善与恶、真诚与欺诈之间进行了选择。他不再是一个旁观者,而成为一个行动者;不再是欺骗行为的追随者,而成为一个反叛者。他把公爵骗来的金子藏进棺材里,又向曼丽·吉恩小姐揭穿了他的所谓的"主人"的真相,通过这些行为,哈克贝利的道德境界进一步提高。

选读出自第 31 章，描写了哈克贝利和黑奴吉姆一起逃跑时的矛盾犹豫心理。

Once I said to myself it would be a thousand times better for Jim to be a slave at home where his family was, as long as he'd got to be a slave, and so I'd better write a letter to Tom Sawyer and tell him to tell Miss Watson where he was. But I soon give up that notion for two things: she'd be mad and disgusted at his rascality and ungratefulness for leaving her, and so she'd sell him straight down the river again; and if she didn't, everybody naturally despises an ungrateful nigger, and they'd make Jim feel it all the time, and so he'd feel ornery and disgraced. And then think of me! It would get all around that Huck Finn helped a nigger to get his freedom; and if I was ever to see anybody from that town again I'd be ready to get down and lick his boots for shame. That's just the way: a person does a low-down thing, and then he don't want to take no consequences of it. Thinks as long as he can hide it, it ain't no disgrace. That was my fix exactly. The more I studied about this the more my conscience went to grinding me, and the more wicked and low-down and ornery I got to feeling. And at last, when it hit me all of a sudden that here was the plain hand of Providence slapping me in the face and letting me know my wickedness was being watched all the time from up there in heaven, whilst I was stealing a poor old woman's nigger that hadn't ever done me no harm, and now was showing me there's one that's always on the lookout, and ain't a-going to allow no such miserable doings to go only just so fur and no further, I most dropped in my tracks I was so scared. Well, I tried the best I could to kinder soften it up somehow for myself by saying I was brung[1] up wicked, and so I warn't[2] so much to blame; but something inside of me kept saying, "There was the Sunday-school, you could a gone to it; and if you'd a done it they'd a learnt you there that people that acts as I'd been acting about that nigger goes to everlasting fire."

It made me shiver. And I about made up my mind to pray, and see if I couldn't try to quit being the kind of a boy I was and be better. So I kneeled down. But the words wouldn't come. Why wouldn't they? It warn't no use[3] to try and hide it from Him. Nor from me, neither. I knowed very well why they wouldn't come. It was because my heart warn't right; it was because I warn't square; it was because I was playing double. I was letting on to give up sin, but away inside of me I was holding on to the biggest one of all. I was trying to make my mouth say I would do the right thing and the clean thing, and go and write to that nigger's owner and tell where he was; but deep down in me I knowed it was a lie, and He knowed it. You can't pray a lie—I found that out.

So I was full of trouble, full as I could be; and didn't know what to do. At last I had an idea; and I says, I'll go and write the letter—and then see if I can pray. Why, it was astonishing, the way I felt as light as a feather right straight off, and my troubles all gone. So I got a piece of paper and a pencil, all glad and excited, and set down and wrote:

Miss Watson, your runaway nigger Jim is down here two mile below Pikesville, and Mr. Phelps has got him and he will give him up for the reward if you send.

Huck Finn

I felt good and all washed clean of sin for the first time I had ever felt so in my life, and I knowed I could pray now. But I didn't do it straight off, but laid the paper down and set there thinking—thinking how good it was all this happened so, and how near I come to being lost and going to hell. And went on thinking. And got to thinking over our trip down the river; and I see Jim before me all the time: in the day and in the night-time, sometimes moonlight, sometimes storms, and we a-floating along, talking and singing and laughing. But somehow I couldn't seem to strike no places to harden me against him, but only the other kind. I'd see him standing my watch on top of his'n,' stead of calling me, so I could go on sleeping; and see him how glad he was when I come back out of the fog; and when I come to him again in the swamp, up there where the feud was; and such-like times; and would always call me honey, and pet me and do everything he could think of for me, and how good he always was; and at last I struck the time I saved him by telling the men we had small-pox aboard, and he was so grateful, and said I was the best friend old Jim ever had in the world, and the only one he's got now; and then I happened to look around and see that paper.

It was a close place. I took it up, and held it in my hand. I was a-trembling, because I'd got to decide, forever, betwixt two things, and I knowed it. I studied a minute, sort of holding my breath, and then says to myself:

"All right, then, I'll go to hell"—and tore it up.

It was awful thoughts and awful words, but they was said. And I let them stay said; and never thought no more about reforming. I shoved the whole thing out of my head, and said I would take up wickedness again, which was in my line, being brung up to it, and the other warn't. And for a starter I would go to work and steal Jim out of slavery again; and if I could think up anything worse, I would do that, too; because as long as I was in, and in for good, I might as well go the whole hog.

Notes:

1. brung:brought

2. warn't:wasn't

3. It warn't no use, 即 it was no use, 这里是 substandard English, 双重否定仍然表示否定。

Questions:

1. How did Huck hesitate between turning Jim in and helping him running away?

2. How is Huck thought affected by the conventional idea?

10

The Great Gatsby

作者及背景简介

弗朗西斯·斯科特·基·菲茨杰拉德（Francis Scott Key Fitzgerald，1896—1940），现代主义的代表作家，20世纪美国最杰出的作家之一。菲茨杰拉德出身于一个家具商家庭，年轻时尝试写过剧本。读完高中后考入普林斯顿大学，在校时曾自组剧团，并为校内文学刊物写稿，后因身体原因辍学。1917年入伍军训，未出国打仗，退伍后坚持业余写作。1920年出版了长篇小说《人间天堂》而成名。小说出版后他与泽尔达结婚，婚后携妻旅居巴黎，结识了安德逊、海明威等多位美国作家。1925年《了不起的盖茨比》问世，奠定了他在现代美国文学史上的地位，成了20世纪20年代"爵士时代"的代言人和"迷惘的一代"的代表作家之一。菲兹杰拉德成名后继续勤奋写作，但婚后妻子生活奢侈，讲究排场，挥霍无度，后来精神失常，给菲兹杰拉德带来了极大痛苦。菲茨杰拉德经济上入不敷出，一度去好莱坞写剧本挣钱维持生计。1936年菲兹杰拉德不幸染上肺病，使他几乎无法创作，精神濒于崩溃，终日酗酒。1940年12月21日心脏病发作，死于洛杉矶，年仅44岁，遗留一部未竟之作《最后的大亨》。他死前已破产，遗嘱中要求举办"最便宜的葬礼"。因在精神病院的妻子，最后相伴左右鼓励他写作的情人，均未能参加葬礼。仅有很少的亲友出席了葬礼，好友女诗人多罗茜·帕克失声痛哭："这家伙真可怜。"这与《了不起的盖茨比》中的主人公的命运结局惊人地相似。在20多年的创作生涯中，菲茨杰拉德发表了《了不起的盖茨比》《夜色温柔》等长篇小说，以及160多篇短篇小说。

菲茨杰拉德创造力最旺盛的时期是美国历史上的一个特殊年代，第一次世界大战结束了（1918），经济大萧条（1929）还没有到来，传统的清教徒道德已经土崩瓦解，享乐主义开始大行其道。菲茨杰拉德说："这是一个奇迹的时代，一个艺术的时代，一个挥金如土的时代，也是一个充满嘲讽的时代。"菲茨杰拉德称这个时代为"爵士乐时代"，他自己也因此被称为爵士乐时代的"编年史家"和"桂冠诗人"。菲茨杰拉德本人也热情洋溢地投身到这个时代的灯红酒绿之中，他敏锐地感觉到了这个时代对浪漫的渴求，以及表面的奢华背后的空虚和无奈，并在他的作品中把这些情绪传神地反映出来。在他的笔下，那些出入高尔夫球场、乡村俱乐部和豪华宅第的上流社会年轻人之间微妙的感情纠葛是一个永恒的主题，他们无法被金钱驱散的失意和惆怅更是无处不在。菲茨杰拉德的作品经常以年轻的渴望和理想主义为主题，因为他认为这是美国人的特征；他的作品经常涉及感情的变幻无常和失落感，因为这是那个时代的人们无法逃遁的命运。菲茨杰拉德是"迷惘的一代"（Lost Generation）的代表作家，是"爵士乐时代"（Jazz Age）的代言人。

选读作品简介

尼克从中西部故乡来到纽约，在他住所旁边是盖茨比的豪华宅第，这里每晚都在举行盛大的宴会。尼克了解到盖茨比内心深处有一段不了之情，年轻时的盖茨比是一个并不富有的少校军官。他爱上了一位叫黛茜的姑娘，黛茜对他也情有所钟。后来第一次世界大战爆发，盖茨比被调往欧洲，黛茜因此和他分手，转而与一个出身于富豪家庭的纨绔子弟汤姆结了婚。黛茜婚后的生活并不幸福，丈夫汤姆另有情妇。物欲的满足并不能填补黛茜精神上的空虚。失去黛茜的盖茨比坚信是金钱使黛茜背叛了自己的灵魂，立志要成为富翁，让黛茜重新回到他身边。几年后，盖茨比经过个人的奋斗成为当地的超级富豪，盖茨比在黛茜府邸的对面建造起了一幢大厦。在这幢大厦，盖茨比每天举行奢华无比的宴会，彻夜笙箫，一心想引起黛茜的注意，以夺回失去的爱情。

尼克为盖茨比的痴情所感动，去拜访久不联系的远房表妹黛茜，并向她转达盖茨比的心意。黛茜在与盖茨比相会中时时有意挑逗盖茨比，盖茨比天真地以为他们可以回到纯真的爱情。然而黛茜早已不是旧日的黛茜，黛茜不过将他俩的暧昧关系当作一种刺激。盖茨比坚信黛茜对他的爱，一次在酒店盖茨比要黛茜当着他的面告诉她丈夫她爱的不是汤姆而是他，从酒店回来的路上，黛茜在心绪烦乱的状态下开车，正好撞死了丈夫汤姆的情妇。盖茨比为保护黛茜，承担了车祸责任，但此时黛茜已打定主意离开盖茨比。在汤姆的唆使下，汤姆情妇的丈夫开枪打死了盖茨比，盖茨比最终彻底成为梦想的牺牲品。盖茨比的悲剧在于他把一切都献给了自己编织的美丽梦想，把黛茜作为理想的化身，固执地追求重温旧梦。人们在为盖茨比举行葬礼，黛茜和她丈夫此时却早已在欧洲旅行的路上。尼克目睹了人类现实的薄情寡义，深感厌恶，离开了喧嚣、冷漠、空洞、虚假的纽约，回到了西部。

1925年出版的《了不起的盖茨比》是菲茨杰拉德写作生涯的顶点，这部小说生动地描绘了财富和成功掩盖下的空虚和虚幻，反映了20世纪20年代"美国梦"的破灭。盖茨比所追求的黛茜是美国梦的象征，所谓的"美国梦"(American Dream)，广义上指美国的平等、自由、民主；狭义上指一种相信只要在美国经过努力不懈奋斗便能获得更好生活的理想，亦即人们必须通过自己的勤奋工作、勇气、创意和决心迈向繁荣，而非依赖于特定的社会阶层和他人的援助。许多欧洲移民都是抱持着美国梦的理想前往美国的。《独立宣言》是美国梦的根基，自由女神像是美国梦的象征。"人人生而平等，造物主赋予他们若干不可剥夺的权利，其中包括生命权、自由权和追求幸福的权利。"这句话吸引了世界各地的男男女女来到美国实现自己的梦想。在《独立宣言》之后制定的宪法等各种法律为美国梦提供了法制保障，法制确保每个人都有机会实现自己的梦想，一个国家如果没有好的制度，个人再好的梦也难以实现。

美国梦的普遍意义是不管出身如何，背景如何，个人只要努力就可以实现自己的梦想。正如美国作家托马斯·沃尔夫(Thomas Wolfe, 1900—1938)对美国梦解释的那样："任何人，不管他出身如何，也不管他有什么样的社会地位，更不管他有何种得天独厚的机遇……他有权生存，有权工作，有权活出自我，有权依自身先天和后天条件成为自己想成为的人。"

美国历史学家詹姆斯·特拉斯洛·亚当斯(James Truslow Adams, 1878—1949)在《美国史诗》(*Epic of America*)中写道："美国梦远远超过物质范畴，美国梦就是让个人才能得到充分发展，实现自我。"他认为："美国梦不是汽车，也不是高工资，而是一种社会秩序，在这种秩序下，所有男人和女人都能实现依据自身素质所能取得的最大成就，并得到社会的承认，而与他（她）的出身、社会背景和社会地位无关。"

成长主题解读

在《了不起的盖茨比》中，菲茨杰拉德通过叙述者尼克·卡络威，向读者呈献了一曲华丽的"爵士时代"的挽歌。尼克既是盖茨比追逐梦想的参与者、见证者和评论者，是一个特殊的叙述者，同时在这一过程中尼克得到了成长。

起初尼克认为盖茨比是他所鄙视的那一类人。在与盖茨比的接触中，尼克发现盖茨比没有受过良好的教育，尼克不理解盖茨比为什么要为了一个粗俗的、华而不实的女人而牺牲自己。对于这样的盖茨比，尼克流露出了鄙视之情。随着小说情节的发展，尼克发现在道德废都中，唯有盖茨比保持着高尚的道德感和人性的光辉。盖茨比死后，尼克感到他有责任为盖茨比举办葬礼，因为没有任何人关心他。在为盖茨比操办葬礼的过程中，他尽量让人们来参加。然而，除了盖茨比的仆人和他的父亲，没有人来参加葬礼。尼克对盖茨比的理解和同情来自于他对盖茨比的重新认识，在接触中他逐步认识到盖茨比的道德高尚，并且能够坚持不懈地追求自己的理想，尽管他的理想只是一个永远无法实现的幻想。与汤姆和黛茜无所事事和毫无目标的生活相比，盖茨比的生活充满了意义，这种追求和斗争让盖茨比的人生有了意义。而汤姆和黛茜是社会的寄生虫，对社会的发展毫无贡献。他们为追求财富而生活，他们唯一的想法是保护自己的财富和特权。因此，他们的人生不可避免地变得毫无目的、毫无意义、没有根基。

尼克和盖茨比一样也怀有美国梦，小说呈现了一个来自西部对生活充满向往的懵懂青年在经过不寻常的东部之旅后获得了道德认知上的成熟，尼克认清了被灯红酒绿纸醉金迷的外表所掩盖的普遍的精神危机，他的美国梦破灭了，带着极度的失望和厌倦回到了西部家乡，尼克对整个社会和人性的复杂有了深刻的认知和理解。尼克的东部之行使他对美国社会和自我有了新的认识，得到了成长。

以下选读选自第 3 章，描写了盖茨比的奢华宴会和那些去蹭吃蹭玩的人们对盖茨比的传言以及叙述者第一次见到盖茨比的印象。

There was music from my neighbor's house through the summer nights. In his blue gardens men and girls came and went like moths among the whisperings and the champagne and the stars. ...

Every Friday five crates of oranges and lemons arrived from a fruiterer in New York—every Monday these same oranges and lemons left his back door in a pyramid of pulpless halves. There was a machine in the kitchen which could extract the juice of two hundred oranges in half an hour, if a little button was pressed two hundred times by a butler's thumb.

......

The lights grow brighter as the earth lurches away from the sun and now the orchestra is playing yellow cocktail music and the opera of voices pitches a key higher. Laughter is easier, minute by minute, spilled with prodigality, tipped out at a cheerful word. The groups change more swiftly, swell with new arrivals, dissolve and form in the same breath—already there are wanderers, confident girls who weave here and there among the stouter and more stable, become for a sharp, joyous moment the center of a group and then excited with triumph glide on through the sea-change of faces and voices and color under the constantly changing light.

......

I believe that on the first night I went to Gatsby's house I was one of the few guests who had actually been invited. People were not invited—they went there. They got into automobiles which bore them out to Long Island and somehow they ended up at Gatsby's door. Once there they were introduced by somebody who knew Gatsby and after that they conducted themselves according to the rules of behavior associated with amusement parks. Sometimes they came and went without having met Gatsby at all, came for the party with a simplicity of heart that was its own ticket of admission.

I had been actually invited. A chauffeur in a uniform of robin's egg blue crossed my lawn early that Saturday morning with a surprisingly formal note from his employer—the honor would be entirely Gatsby's, it said, if I would attend his "little party" that night. He had seen me several times and had intended to call on me long before but a peculiar combination of circumstances had prevented it—signed Jay Gatsby in a majestic hand.

Dressed up in white flannels I went over to his lawn a little after seven and wandered around rather ill-at-ease among swirls and eddies of people I didn't know—though here and there was a face I had noticed on the commuting train. I was immediately struck by the number of young Englishmen dotted about; all well dressed, all looking a little hungry and all talking in low earnest voices to solid and prosperous Americans. I was sure that they were selling something: bonds or insurance or automobiles. They were, at least, agonizingly aware of the easy money in the vicinity and convinced that it was theirs for a few words in the right key.[1]

……

"Do you come to these parties often?" inquired Jordan[2] of the girl beside her.

"The last one was the one I met you at," answered the girl, in an alert, confident voice. She turned to her companion: "Wasn't it for you, Lucille?"

It was for Lucille, too.

"I like to come," Lucille said. "I never care what I do, so I always have a good time. When I was here last I tore my gown on a chair, and he asked me my name and address—inside of a week I got a package from Croirier's[3], with a new evening gown in it."

"Did you keep it?" asked Jordan.

"Sure I did. I was going to wear it tonight, but it was too big in the bust and had to be altered. It was gas blue with lavender beads. Two hundred and sixty-five dollars."

"There's something funny about a fellow that'll do a thing like that," said the other girl eagerly. "He doesn't want any trouble with ANYbody."

"Who doesn't?" I inquired.

"Gatsby. Somebody told me— —"

The two girls and Jordan leaned together confidentially.

"Somebody told me they thought he killed a man once."

A thrill passed over all of us. The three Mr. Mumbles[4] bent forward and listened eagerly.

"I don't think it's so much THAT," argued Lucille skeptically; "it's more that he was a German spy during the war."

One of the men nodded in confirmation.

"I heard that from a man who knew all about him, grew up with him in Germany," he assured us positively.

"Oh, no," said the first girl, "it couldn't be that, because he was in the American army during the war." As our credulity switched back to her she leaned forward with enthusiasm. "You look at him sometimes when he thinks nobody's looking at him. I'll bet he killed a man."

She narrowed her eyes and shivered. Lucille shivered. We all turned and looked around for Gatsby. It was testimony to the romantic speculation he inspired that there were whispers about him from those who found little that it was necessary to whisper about in this world.

The first supper—there would be another one after midnight—was now being served, and Jordan invited me to join her own party who were spread around a table on the other side of the garden. There were three married couples and Jordan's escort, a persistent undergraduate given to violent innuendo and obviously under the impression that sooner or later Jordan was going to yield him up her person to a greater or lesser degree. Instead of rambling this party had preserved a dignified homogeneity, and assumed to itself the function of representing the staid nobility of the countryside—East Egg condescending to West Egg, and carefully on guard against its spectroscopic gayety.[5]

"Let's get out," whispered Jordan, after a somehow wasteful and inappropriate half hour. "This is much too polite for me."[6]

We got up, and she explained that we were going to find the host—I had never met him, she said, and it was making me uneasy. The undergraduate nodded in a cynical, melancholy way.

The bar, where we glanced first, was crowded but Gatsby was not there.
......

I was still with Jordan Baker. We were sitting at a table with a man of about my age and a rowdy little girl who gave way upon the slightest provocation to uncontrollable laughter. I was enjoying myself now. I had taken two finger bowls of champagne and the scene had changed before my eyes into something significant, elemental and profound.

At a lull in the entertainment the man looked at me and smiled.

· 117 ·

"Your face is familiar," he said, politely. "Weren't you in the Third Division during the war?"

"Why, yes. I was in the Ninth Machine-Gun Battalion."

"I was in the Seventh Infantry until June nineteen-eighteen. I knew I'd seen you somewhere before."

We talked for a moment about some wet, grey little villages in France. Evidently he lived in this vicinity for he told me that he had just bought a hydroplane and was going to try it out in the morning.

"Want to go with me, old sport?⁷ Just near the shore along the Sound."

"What time?"

"Any time that suits you best."

It was on the tip of my tongue to ask his name when Jordan looked around and smiled.

"Having a gay time now?" she inquired.

"Much better." I turned again to my new acquaintance. "This is an unusual party for me. I haven't even seen the host. I live over there—" I waved my hand at the invisible hedge in the distance, "and this man Gatsby sent over his chauffeur with an invitation."

For a moment he looked at me as if he failed to understand.

"I'm Gatsby," he said suddenly.

"What!" I exclaimed. "Oh, I beg your pardon."

"I thought you knew, old sport. I'm afraid I'm not a very good host."

He smiled understandingly—much more than understandingly. It was one of those rare smiles with a quality of eternal reassurance in it, that you may come across four or five times in life. It faced—or seemed to face—the whole external world for an instant, and then concentrated on YOU with an irresistible prejudice in your favor. It understood you just so far as you wanted to be understood, believed in you as you would like to believe in yourself and assured you that it had precisely the impression of you that, at your best, you hoped to convey. Precisely at that point it vanished—and I was looking at an elegant young rough-neck, a year or two over thirty, whose elaborate formality of speech just missed being absurd.⁸ Some time before he introduced himself I'd got a strong impression that he was picking his words with care.

Almost at the moment when Mr. Gatsby identified himself a butler hurried toward him with the information that Chicago was calling him on the wire. He excused himself with a small bow that included each of us in turn.

"If you want anything just ask for it, old sport," he urged me.

"Excuse me. I will rejoin you later."

When he was gone I turned immediately to Jordan—constrained to assure her of my surprise. I had expected that Mr. Gatsby would be a florid and corpulent person in his middle years.[9]

"Who is he?" I demanded. "Do you know?"

"He's just a man named Gatsby."

"Where is he from, I mean? And what does he do?"

"Now YOU're started on the subject," she answered with a wan smile. "Well, he told me once he was an Oxford man."

A dim background started to take shape behind him but at her next remark it faded away.

"However, I don't believe it."

"Why not?"

"I don't know," she insisted, "I just don't think he went there."

Something in her tone reminded me of the other girl's "I think he killed a man," and had the effect of stimulating my curiosity. I would have accepted without question the information that Gatsby sprang from the swamps of Louisiana or from the lower East Side of New York.

……

The caterwauling horns had reached a crescendo and I turned away and cut across the lawn toward home. I glanced back once. A wafer of a moon was shining over Gatsby's house, making the night fine as before and surviving the laughter and the sound of his still glowing garden. A sudden emptiness seemed to flow now from the windows and the great doors, endowing with complete isolation the figure of the host who stood on the porch, his hand up in a formal gesture of farewell.

Notes:

1. it was theirs for a few words in the right key: 只要几句话说得投机, 钱就到手了

2. Jordan:乔丹,黛茜的闺蜜,一个高尔夫选手,据说比赛作弊

3. Croirier's:纽约高级服装店

4. Mr. Mumbles：在晚会上,因人多吵闹,听不清名字,所以把对方称为"呼噜先生"

5. Instead of rambling this party had preserved a dignified homogeneity, and assumed to itself the function of representing the staid nobility of the countryside—East Egg condescending to West Egg, and carefully on guard against its spectroscopic gayety. 这伙人不到处转悠,而是正襟危坐,自成一体,并且俨然自封为庄重的农村贵族的代表——东卵人屈尊光临西卵人,而又小心翼翼提防它那灯红酒绿的欢乐。

6. This is much too polite for me. 过于讲究礼貌了,太拘礼了。这反映了出身世族的"东卵人"的矫揉造作,也表现了乔丹的性格特点。

7. old sport:老朋友、老兄,这是典型的英国上流社会的口头用语,出自暴发户盖茨比之口,盖茨比自称是牛津大学毕业生

8. Precisely at that point it vanished—and I was looking at an elegant young rough-neck, a year or two over thirty, whose elaborate formality of speech just missed being absurd. 于是我看到的不过是一个风度翩翩的年轻男子,三十一二岁,说起话来文质彬彬,几乎有点可笑。

9. I had expected that Mr. Gatsby would be a florid and corpulent person in his middle years. 我本以为盖茨比是一个红光满面、肥头大耳的中年人。

Questions：

1. Why did the narrator tell so much about the rumors about Gatsby?

2. How did the narrator's first impression of Gatsby differ from his expectation?

以下选读的是小说结尾，是尼克对盖茨比和汤姆等人的评论和感想。

"Look here, this is a book he had when he was a boy. It just shows you."

He[1] opened it at the back cover and turned it around for me to see.

On the last fly-leaf was printed the word SCHEDULE, and the date September 12th,1906. And underneath:

Rise from bed... 6.00 A.M.

Dumbbell exercise and wall-scaling... 6.15-6.30 A.M.

Study electricity, etc... 7.15-8.15 A.M.

Work... 8.30-4.30 P.M.

Baseball and sports... 4.30-5.00 P.M.

Practice elocution, poise and how to attain it 5.00-6.00 P.M.

Study needed inventions... 7.00-9.00 P.M.

GENERAL RESOLVES

No wasting time at Shafters or a name, indecipherable

No more smoking or chewing

Bath every other day

Read one improving book or magazine per week

Save $5.00 crossed out $3.00 per week

Be better to parents[2]

"I come across this book by accident," said the old man. "It just shows you, don't it?"

"It just shows you."

"Jimmy was bound to get ahead. He always had some resolves like this or something. Do you notice what he's got about improving his mind? He was always great for that. He told me I ate like a hog once and I beat him for it."

He was reluctant to close the book, reading each item aloud and then looking eagerly at me. I think he rather expected me to copy down the list for my own use.

......

They were careless people, Tom and Daisy—they smashed up things and creatures and then retreated back into their money or their vast carelessness or whatever it was that kept them together, and let other people clean up the mess they had made... I shook hands with him; it seemed silly not to, for I felt suddenly as though I were talking to a child. Then he went into the jewelry store to buy a pearl necklace—or perhaps only a pair of cuff buttons—rid of my provincial squeamishness forever.³ Gatsby's house was still empty when I left—the grass on his lawn had grown as long as mine. One of the taxi drivers in the village never took a fare past the entrance gate without stopping for a minute and pointing inside; perhaps it was he who drove Daisy and Gatsby over to East Egg⁴ the night of the accident and perhaps he had made a story about it all his own. I didn't want to hear it and I avoided him when I got off the train.

I spent my Saturday nights in New York because those gleaming, dazzling parties of his were with me so vividly that I could still hear the music and the laughter faint and incessant from his garden and the cars going up and down his drive. One night I did hear a material⁵ car there and saw its lights stop at his front steps. But I didn't investigate. Probably it was some final guest who had been away at the ends of the earth and didn't know that the party was over.⁶

On the last night, with my trunk packed and my car sold to the grocer, I went over and looked at that huge incoherent failure of a house⁷ once more. On the white steps an obscene word, scrawled by some boy with a piece of brick, stood out clearly in the moonlight and I erased it, drawing my shoe raspingly along the stone. ⁸ Then I wandered down to the beach and sprawled out on the sand.

Most of the big shore places were closed now and there were hardly any lights except the shadowy, moving glow of a ferryboat across the Sound⁹.

And as the moon rose higher the inessential houses began to melt away until gradually I became aware of the old island here that flowered once for Dutch sailors' eyes—a fresh, green breast of the new world.

Its vanished trees, the trees that had made way for Gatsby's house, had once pandered in whispers to the last and greatest of all human dreams; for a transitory enchanted moment man must have held his breath in the presence of this continent, compelled into an aesthetic contemplation he neither understood nor desired, face to face for the last time in history with something commensurate to his capacity for wonder.

And as I sat there brooding on the old, unknown world, I thought of Gatsby's wonder when he first picked out the green light at the end of Daisy's dock. He had come a long way to this blue lawn and his dream must have seemed so close that he could hardly fail to grasp it. He did not know that it was already behind him, somewhere back in that vast obscurity beyond the city, where the dark fields of the republic rolled on under the night.

Gatsby believed in the green light, the orgastic future that year by year recedes before us. It eluded us then, but that's no matter—tomorrow we will run faster, stretch out our arms farther… And one fine morning— —So we beat on, boats against the current, borne back ceaselessly into the past.

Notes:
1. he:他是指盖茨比的父亲,他来处理后事
2. 这个作息时间表及后面的个人原则与本杰明·富兰克林《自传》中所谈的修身自律极为相似。富兰克林认为艰苦劳动、节约和诚实,普通人可以实现自己的梦想。然而时过境迁,富兰克林所体现的"美国梦"到盖茨比的时代已经破灭。
3. 在这里,作者的自贬中蕴含着虚伪、自私、金钱至上的现代文明的讽刺。
4. East Egg:东卵镇,汤姆和黛茜住过的地方,象征着传统的上流社会
5. material:真的,实质性的
6. 宴席已散。同第三章的"宴会已开始"。尼克回首往事,百感交集,感叹人生的荣枯沉浮。
7. house:被遗弃的房子成为盖茨比的生涯的象征——离奇、矛盾、失败的一生
8. 这个动作说明尼克在维护盖茨比的名誉。尼克虽然说他"鄙夷"盖茨比所代表的一切,但他推崇他对人生前景的敏感和对未来充满希望。
9. the Sound:指长岛海峡(Long Island Sound)

Questions:
1. What did Gatsby's schedule reveal about his character?
2. What's the symbolic meaning of the landscape description at the end of the novel?
3. How did the Nick, the narrator of the story, grow in the novel?

The Catcher in the Rye

作者及背景简介

杰罗姆·大卫·塞林格（Jerome David Salinger,1919—2010）美国现代主义作家,塞林格出生于纽约的一个犹太中产家庭,年幼时拘谨好静,13岁入曼哈顿一所很好的中学学习,一年后因成绩不及格而离开。少年时期塞林格不好交际,喜欢独自做出一些奇怪的事情。15岁时塞林格被父亲送到宾夕法尼亚州的一所军事学校,在这里他感到自己不能适应环境。《麦田里的守望者》中关于寄宿学校的描写,很大部分是以那所学校为背景的。1936年,塞林格从军事学校毕业,取得了他毕生唯一的一张文凭。二战中断了塞林格的写作,1942年塞林格从军,1944年他前往欧洲战场从事反间谍工作。塞林格亲历了战争的可怕,之后写了多部以战争为题材的小说。

1946年塞林格退伍,回到纽约开始专心创作。他的第一部长篇小说《麦田里的守望者》1951年出版,获得了很大的成功,塞林格一举成名。他之后的作品包括了《弗兰尼与卓埃》(1961)、《木匠们,把屋梁升高》和《西摩:一个介绍》(1963)和收录了他的短篇故事的《九故事》(1953),但都不像《麦田里的守望者》那么成功。塞林格擅长塑造早熟、出众的青少年的形象。

《麦田里的守望者》获得成功之后,塞林格变得更孤僻。他在新罕布什尔州乡间的河边小山附近买下了90多英亩(1英亩≈4046.86平方米)的土地,在山顶上建了一座小屋,过起了隐居的生活。虽然他从未放弃写作,但在1951年之后,就很少公开出版自己的作品。他后期的作品也越来越倾向于东方哲学和禅宗。

《麦田里的守望者》之所以受到重视,不仅是由于作者创造了一种新颖的艺术风格,通过第一人称以青少年的说话口吻叙述,说明了人活着除了物质生活外,还要有精神生活,而且在一个比较富裕的社会里,精神生活往往比物质生活更为重要。美国在二战中发了横财,战后物质生产发展得很快,生活水平迅速提高,中产阶级的人数也在激增。但广大人民的精神生活却越来越贫乏空虚。20世纪50年代初美国政府奉行杜鲁门主义和麦卡锡主义,遏制共产主义,国际上冷战加剧,国内镇压进步力量,核战争的恐怖笼罩着每个人的心灵,有些人粉饰太平,过着浑浑噩噩的日子;另有些人看不惯庸俗、虚伪的世道,想要反抗,却又缺乏光辉的理想,找不到一条光明的出路。因此美国有的当代史家把美国的20世纪50年代称为"静寂的50年代"或"怯懦的50年代"。

有些青年人以消极的方式(主要通过酗酒、吸毒、群居等颓废的方式)对现实进行反抗,他们后来被称为"垮掉的一代"或"垮掉分子"。本书作者塞林格和他笔下的人物如本书主人公霍尔顿·考尔菲德一样也是垮掉分子的代表,但还不到吸毒群居的地步,霍尔顿还想探索和追求理想(包括爱情理想),他向往东方哲学,提出长大成人后想当一个"麦田里的守望者"。

塞林格的作品以短篇和中篇居多,他以现实主义的手法客观地描写了人物的内心世界和外部世界的矛盾,他的作品一般以第一人称和内心独白来叙述,语言诙谐,讥讽中透出幽默,伤感中流露出同情。他的许多作品显示出东方禅宗的影响。

塞林格的作品大多数主要描写美国中产阶级出身的子弟,反映出这些少年在成长过程中所遇到的困难和挫折以及内心的矛盾和痛苦。他理想中的人物是儿童和少年,透过他们的眼睛,塞林格刻画了成人世界的虚伪、腐化和堕落及战后美国青年一代的迷茫、不知所措和渴望自由、友爱、帮助和理解的苦闷心情以及他们内心深处的反叛精神。

选读作品简介

小说以主人公霍尔顿·考尔菲德(Holden Caulfield)第一人称口吻讲述自己被学校开除后在纽约城游荡将近两个昼夜,企图逃出虚伪的成人世界去寻求纯洁与真理的经历与感受。该书在1951年出版之后,立刻引起巨大的轰动,受到读者特别是青年人的热烈欢迎,被翻译为多国语言。有的评论家说它大大地影响了几代美国青年,并且有学者认为霍尔顿是当代美国文学中最早出现的反英雄形象之一。

主人公霍尔顿是个中学生,出身于富裕的中产阶级家庭。他虽只有16岁,但比常人高出一头,整日穿着风雨衣,戴着鸭舌帽,游游荡荡,不愿读书。

他对学校里的一切——老师、同学、功课、球赛等,全都烦透了,3次被学校开除。又一个学期结束了,他又因5门功课中4门不及格被校方开除。霍尔顿丝毫不感觉到难受,在和同房间的同学打了一架后,霍尔顿深夜离开学校,回到纽约城,但他不敢回家,住进了一家小旅馆,在旅馆里看到的都是些不三不四的人,有穿着女装的男人,有相互喷水洒酒的男女,他们寻欢作乐,忸怩作态,霍尔顿感到惊讶,感到无聊,去夜总会混了一阵,回到旅馆,心里仍觉得十分烦闷,糊里糊涂答应拉皮条客,叫来一个妓女,妓女一到他又紧张害怕,最后按讲定的价格给了5块钱,把她打发走了。

　　第二天是星期天,霍尔顿上街游荡,遇见两个修女,捐了10块钱。后来和他的女友萨利去看了场戏,又去溜冰。看到萨利那假情假义的样子,霍尔顿很不痛快,两人吵了一场分了手。接着霍尔顿独自去看了场电影,又到酒吧里和一个老同学喝得酩酊大醉。他走进厕所,把头伸进盥洗盆里用冷水浸了一阵,才清醒过来。走出酒吧后,被冷风一吹,他的头发都结了冰,霍尔顿想到自己也许会因此患肺炎死去,永远见不着妹妹菲比了,决定冒险回家和她诀别。

　　霍尔顿偷偷回到家里,幸好父母都出去了。他叫醒菲比,向她诉说了自己的苦闷和理想。他对妹妹说,他将来要当一名"麦田里的守望者":"有那么一群小孩子在一大块麦田里做游戏。几千几万个小孩子,附近没有一个人——没有一个大人,我是说——除了我。我呢,就在那混账的悬崖边。我的职责是在那儿守望,要是有哪个孩子往悬崖边奔来,我就把他捉住——我是说孩子们都在狂奔,也不知道自己是在往哪儿跑,我得从什么地方出来,把他们捉住。我整天就干这样的事。我只想当个麦田里的守望者。"后来父母回来了,霍尔顿吓得躲进壁橱。等父母去卧室,他急忙溜出家门,到一个他尊敬的老师家中借宿。睡到半夜,他发觉这个老师有可能是个同性恋者,于是只好偷偷逃出来,到车站候车室过夜。

　　霍尔顿不想再回家,也不想再念书了,决定去西部谋生,做一个又聋又哑的人,但他想在临走前再见妹妹一面,于是托人给她带去一张便条,约她到博物馆的艺术馆门边见面,菲比拖着一只装满自己衣服的大箱子来了,她一定要跟哥哥一起去西部。最后,因对妹妹劝说无效,霍尔顿只好放弃西部之行,带她去动物园和公园玩了一阵,然后一起回家。回家后不久,霍尔顿就生了一场大病。整部小说是以回忆的方式写的。

　　本书在艺术上颇具特色,心理描写细致入微,可以说开当代美国文学中心理现实主义的先河。从表面上看,霍尔顿不求上进,抽烟、喝酒,甚至找妓女,简直是个十足的"坏孩子"。从家庭和学校环境来看,成年人往往用简单、粗暴、主观的方法去对待青少年(包括自己的子女),从而造成或加深两代人的隔阂；从大的社会背景看，霍尔顿的叛逆的生活方式是垮掉的一代对社会发泄不满、反抗的方式。

全书用青少年的口吻平铺直叙，使用了大量的俚语和口语。本书作者以敏锐的洞察力剖析青少年的复杂心理，透过现象观察精神实质，栩栩如生地描绘了霍尔顿的精神世界的各个方面，既揭示了他受环境影响颓废、没落的一面，也写出了他纯朴、敏感、善良的一面，在某种程度上确实反映了青春期青少年的特点，在西方社会里引起了广大青少年的强烈反响，不少成年人也把它看作启发自己理解年轻一代的钥匙。

成长主题解读

二战后的美国，伴随经济繁荣而来的是人们精神生活的空虚和传统价值观的崩溃。政府对内实行麦卡锡主义，镇压异己；对外发动朝鲜战争，卷入越南事件之中。一方面科技迅猛发展，人们的物质生活水平有了极大提高；另一方面科技大发展使得大量的劳动力被机器代替，在节省大量劳动力的同时，人们的创造性劳动减少，人们变得缺乏理想、意志消沉，生活中充满欺骗虚伪铜臭味，但人们还若无其事地沉浸在物欲横流的社会。一些人粉饰太平，过着浑浑噩噩的日子；而另外一些人则对现实不满，看透了虚伪、庸俗、丑陋的社会，但又缺乏光辉的理想，只能保持沉默，作消极的反抗。这一时期被称为"静寂的一代"或"怯懦的一代"，《麦田里的守望者》中的霍尔顿正是这一时期的代表人物。霍尔顿的成长经历了以下四个阶段。

一、逃离——对现实世界的强烈不满

在霍尔顿看来，成人世界充斥着商业化，物质主义泛滥，既丑陋又荒谬。他对社会中的邪恶、欺骗、人与人之间的疏离和周围的"假模假式"深恶痛绝。霍尔顿无法接受父母、兄长、师长、同学等身边人的生存状态，想追求一种更有意义的生活。作为一个16岁的孩子，他只能用逃跑这种最有效的方式来表达不满和反抗。霍尔顿从一所学校逃到另一所学校，又从潘西中学逃到纽约，最后幻想从纽约逃到西部一个不为人知的地方，霍尔顿总是"在路上"。随着他的逃离，他的环境更加恶化，霍尔顿看到了一个不讲道德、完全堕落的社会。霍尔顿在纽约一天两夜的流浪生活，彻底粉碎了他寻找真善美的梦想。他已无处可逃，于是只能从现实逃避到想象，去西部当个聋哑人。在一次又一次的逃离中，霍尔顿苦苦挣扎，以期在理想和现实之间找到栖身之所。然而在一次次的挫折之后，他终于意识到自己的努力是徒劳无益的。霍尔顿逃离的过程

就是他逐渐成熟的过程。

二、反抗——离经叛道的言行举止

霍尔顿是当代美国文学中最早出现的反英雄形象之一，其个性化的穿着打扮、叛逆的行为和粗俗的言语淋漓尽致地表现出了他对社会的反抗。反抗首先表现在他的穿着打扮上。霍尔顿喜欢戴一顶红色的猎人帽，帽子的样子很怪，有一个很长的鸭舌，虽然并不时尚，但霍尔顿对它非常钟爱，戴的方式也与众不同："我戴的时候，把鸭舌转到脑后——这样戴十分粗俗，我承认，可我喜欢这样戴。我这么戴了看上去挺美的。"其次表现在他的行为上。霍尔顿憎恶成人世界，拒绝物质至上的价值观和物质上的成功，蔑视这个充满妥协、丧失了纯真、缺乏正义和真实感的成人世界。霍尔顿违反规定甚至法律、旷课、抽烟、酗酒、召妓……表面上他自暴自弃，不可救药，实际上是在表明自己对身边"假模假式"的反抗。再次表现在他的语言上。霍尔顿有意误用了许多词语来表达自己的反抗，霍尔顿的语言是对标准语言和传统文化的有意反叛。

三、幻想——对纯真世界的热切向往

霍尔顿既不能挽救丑恶的现实世界，又不愿生活在这样的世界里，因此就退回到幻想的世界中，这也反映了霍尔顿在现实世界的失败。当菲比要求霍尔顿说一件长大后最想干的事，他说自己喜欢罗伯特·彭斯的一首诗——《你要是在麦田里捉到了我》。他要像诗里写的那样，当一名麦田里的守望者。霍尔顿幻想自己站在悬崖边的麦田里，一大群孩子在麦田里游戏玩耍，如果有哪个孩子要掉下去，自己会一把抓住："我老是在想象，有那么一群小孩子在一大块麦田里做游戏。几千几万个小孩子，附近没有一个人——没有一个大人，我是说——除了我。我呢，就站在那混账的悬崖边。我的职责是在那儿守望，要是有哪个孩子往悬崖边奔来，我就把他捉住——我是说孩子们都在狂奔，也不知道自己是在往哪儿跑，我得从什么地方出来，把他们捉住。我整天就干这样的事。我只想当个麦田里的守望者。"（见选读）

除了幻想"当一名麦田里的守望者"，霍尔顿还为未来编织了一个幻想。霍尔顿拜访了老师安多里尼先生后，他对周围的"假模假式"感到绝望，他幻想去西部当个聋哑人，远离所有的"伪君子"，他想在加油站里找份工作，娶一个聋哑姑娘一起生活，生了孩子就教他们读书写字。然而，这只不过是他充满孩子气的想法。当妹妹菲比提出要和他一起到西部去，霍尔顿拒绝了，作为哥哥，他要对妹妹的成长负责，霍尔顿的幻想并不能解决他在成人世界遇到的折磨和痛苦。

四、顿悟——融入社会走向成熟的标志

"顿悟"一词早先是一个宗教术语,指上帝在人间显灵。在文学中,"顿悟"指一种突发的精神现象,当某个事物触发了以前不曾获得的认识时,主人公就会油然而生一种"顿悟感"。霍尔顿的一次顿悟发生在博物馆,博物馆代表了霍尔顿与童年的联系,代表了稳定与不变。霍尔顿多次回忆起小时候和同学去博物馆参观,他认为"博物馆里最好的一点是一切东西总待在原来的地方不动。谁也不挪移一下位置……谁也不会改变样儿。"但是当霍尔顿站在埃及人的坟墓里发现了游客涂画的"fuck you"时,不由感叹说:"你永远找不到一个舒服、宁静的地方,因为这样的地方并不存在。"霍尔顿绝望地认识到甚至在古代人的墓室里,他都逃不出这些下流的东西,自己不可能擦掉世界上所有下流的字眼。在观看菲比乘旋转木马时,霍尔顿又一次顿悟,他认识到孩子们的成长是一个自然过程,是无法阻止的。霍尔顿知道不可能用自己编织的梦想之网捉住孩子们,他们最终会落下悬崖长大,这是成长的必经之路。

选读选自第 22 章,霍尔顿向妹妹描述了他在学校的经历和见闻及自己喜欢做的事情。

"Oh, God, Phoebe, don't ask me. I'm sick of everybody asking me that," I said. "A million reasons why. It was one of the worst schools I ever went to. It was full of phonies.[1] And mean guys. You never saw so many mean guys in your life. For instance, if you were having a bull session in somebody's room, and somebody wanted to come in, nobody'd let them in if they were some dopey, pimply guy. Everybody was always locking their door when somebody wanted to come in. And they had this goddam secret fraternity that I was too yellow not to join. There was this one pimply, boring guy, Robert Ackley,[2] that wanted to get in. He kept trying to join, and they wouldn't let him. Just because he was boring and pimply. I don't even feel like talking about it. It was a stinking school. Take my word."

Old Phoebe didn't say anything, but she was listening. I could tell by the back of her neck that she was listening. She always listens when you tell her something. And the funny part is she knows, half the time, what the hell you're talking about. She really does.

I kept talking about old Pencey.[3] I sort of felt like it.

"Even the couple of nice teachers on the faculty, they were phonies, too," I said. "There was this one old guy, Mr. Spencer. His wife was always giving you hot chocolate and all that stuff, and they were really pretty nice. But you should've seen him when the headmaster, old Thurmer, came in the history class and sat down in the back of the room. He was always coming in and sitting down in the back of the room for about a half an hour. He was supposed to be incognito[4] or something. After a while, he'd be sitting back there and then he'd start interrupting what old Spencer was saying to crack a lot of corny jokes. Old Spencer'd practically kill himself chuckling and smiling and all, like as if Thurmer was a goddam prince or something."

"Don't swear so much."

"It would've made you puke, I swear it would," I said. "Then, on Veterans' Day. They have this day, Veterans' Day, that all the jerks that graduated from Pencey around 1776 come back and walk all over the place, with their wives and children and everybody. You should've seen this one old guy that was about fifty. What he did was, he came in our room and knocked on the door and asked us if we'd mind if he used the bathroom. The bathroom was at the end of the corridor—I don't know why the hell he asked us. You know what he said? He said he wanted to see if his initials were still in one of the can doors. What he did, he carved his goddam stupid sad old initials in one of the can doors about ninety years ago, and he wanted to see if they were still there. So my roommate and I walked him down to the bathroom and all, and we had to stand there while he looked for his initials in all the can doors. He kept talking to us the whole time, telling us how when he was at Pencey they were the happiest days of his life, and giving us a lot of advice for the future and all. Boy, did he depress me! I don't mean he was a bad guy—he wasn't. But you don't have to be a bad guy to depress somebody—you can be a good guy and do it. All you have to do to depress somebody is give them a lot of phony advice while you're looking for your initials in some can door—that's all you have to do. I don't know. Maybe it wouldn't have been so bad if he hadn't been all out of breath. He was all out of breath from just climbing up the stairs, and the whole time he was looking for his initials he kept breathing hard, with his nostrils all funny and sad, while he kept telling Stradlater[5] and I to get all we could out of Pencey. God, Phoebe! I can't explain. I just didn't like anything that was happening at Pencey. I can't explain."

Old Phoebe said something then, but I couldn't hear her. She had the side of her mouth right smack on the pillow, and I couldn't hear her.

"What?" I said. "Take your mouth away. I can't hear you with your mouth that way."

"You don't like anything that's happening."

It made me even more depressed when she said that.

"Yes I do. Yes I do. Sure I do. Don't say that. Why the hell do you say that?"

"Because you don't. You don't like any schools. You don't like a million things. You don't."

"I do! That's where you're wrong—that's exactly where you're wrong! Why the hell do you have to say that?" I said. Boy, was she depressing me.

"Because you don't," she said. "Name one thing."

"One thing? One thing I like?" I said. "Okay."

The trouble was, I couldn't concentrate too hot. Sometimes it's hard to concentrate.

"One thing I like a lot you mean?" I asked her.

She didn't answer me, though. She was in a cockeyed position way the hell over the other side of the bed. She was about a thousand miles away. "C'mon answer me," I said. "One thing I like a lot, or one thing I just like?"

"You like a lot."

"All right," I said. But the trouble was, I couldn't concentrate. About all I could think of were those two nuns that went around collecting dough[6] in those beatup old straw baskets. Especially the one with the glasses with those iron rims. And this boy I knew at Elkton Hills. There was this one boy at Elkton Hills, named James Castle, that wouldn't take back something he said about this very conceited boy, Phil Stabile. James Castle called him a very conceited guy, and one of Stabile's lousy friends went and squealed on him to Stabile. So Stabile, with about six other dirty bastards, went down to James Castle's room and went in and locked the goddam door and tried to make him take back what he said, but he wouldn't do it. So they started in on him. I won't even tell you what they did to him—it's too repulsive—but he still wouldn't take it back, old James Castle. And you should've seen him. He was a skinny little weak-looking guy, with wrists about as big as pencils. Finally, what he did, instead of taking back what he said, he jumped out the window. I was in the shower and all, and even I could hear him land outside. But I just thought something fell out the window, a radio or a desk or something, not a boy or anything. Then I heard everybody running through the corridor and down the stairs, so I put on my bathrobe and I ran downstairs too, and there was old James Castle laying right on the stone steps and all. He was dead, and his teeth, and blood, were all over the place, and nobody would even go near him. He had on this turtleneck sweater I'd lent him. All they did with the guys that were in the room with him was expel them. They didn't even go to jail.

That was about all I could think of, though. Those two nuns I saw at breakfast and this boy James Castle I knew at Elkton Hills. The funny part is, I hardly even know James Castle, if you want to know the truth. He was one of these very quiet guys. He was in my math class, but he was way over on the other side of the room, and he hardly ever got up to recite or go to the blackboard or anything. Some guys in school hardly ever get up to recite or go to the blackboard. I think the only time I ever even had a conversation with him was that time he asked me if he could borrow this turtleneck sweater I had. I damn near dropped dead when he asked me, I was so surprised and all. I remember I was brushing my teeth, in the can, when he asked me. He said his cousin was coming in to take him for a drive and all. I didn't even know he knew I had a turtleneck sweater. All I knew about him was that his name was always right ahead of me at roll call. Cabel, R. , Cabel, W. , Castle, Caulfield—I can still remember it. If you want to know the truth, I almost didn't lend him my sweater. Just because I didn't know him too well.

"What?" I said to old Phoebe. She said something to me, but I didn't hear her.

"You can't even think of one thing."

"Yes, I can. Yes, I can."

"Well, do it, then."

"I like Allie,"[7] I said. "And I like doing what I'm doing right now. Sitting here with you, and talking, and thinking about stuff, and—"

"Allie's dead—You always say that! If somebody's dead and everything, and in Heaven, then it isn't really—"

"I know he's dead! Don't you think I know that? I can still like him, though, can't I? Just because somebody's dead, you don't just stop liking them, for God's sake—especially if they were about a thousand times nicer than the people you know that're alive and all."

Old Phoebe didn't say anything. When she can't think of anything to say, she doesn't say a goddam word.

"Anyway, I like it now," I said. "I mean right now. Sitting here with you and just chewing the fat and horsing—"

"That isn't anything really!"

"It is so something really! Certainly it is! Why the hell isn't it? People never think anything is anything really. I'm getting goddam sick of it."

"Stop swearing. All right, name something else. Name something you'd like to be. Like a scientist. Or a lawyer or something."

"I couldn't be a scientist. I'm no good in science."

"Well, a lawyer—like Daddy and all."

"Lawyers are all right, I guess—but it doesn't appeal to me," I said. "I mean they're all right if they go around saving innocent guys' lives all the time, and like that, but you don't do that kind of stuff if you're a lawyer. All you do is make a lot of dough and play golf and play bridge and buy cars and drink Martinis and look like a hot-shot. And besides. Even if you did go around saving guys' lives and all, how would you know if you did it because you really wanted to save guys' lives, or because you did it because what you really wanted to do was be a terrific lawyer, with everybody slapping you on the back and congratulating you in court when the goddam trial was over, the reporters and everybody, the way it is in the dirty movies? How would you know you weren't being a phony? The trouble is, you wouldn't."

I'm not too sure old Phoebe knew what the hell I was talking about. I mean she's only a little child and all. But she was listening, at least. If somebody at least listens, it's not too bad.

"Daddy's going to kill you. He's going to kill you," she said.

I wasn't listening, though. I was thinking about something else—something crazy. "You know what I'd like to be?" I said. "You know what I'd like to be? I mean if I had my goddam choice?"

"What? Stop swearing."

"You know that song 'If a body catch a body comin' through the rye'? I'd like—"

"It's 'If a body meet a body coming through the rye'!" old Phoebe said. "It's a poem. By Robert Burns."

"I know it's a poem by Robert Burns[8]."

She was right, though. It is "If a body meet a body coming through the rye." I didn't know it then, though.

"I thought it was 'If a body catch a body,'" I said. "Anyway, I keep picturing all these little kids playing some game in this big field of rye and all. Thousands of little kids, and nobody's around—nobody big, I mean—except me. And I'm standing on the edge of some crazy cliff. What I have to do, I have to catch everybody if they start to go over the cliff—I mean if they're running and they don't look where they're going I have to come out from somewhere and catch them. That's all I'd do all day. I'd just be the catcher in the rye and all. I know it's crazy, but that's the only thing I'd really like to be. I know it's crazy."

Notes：

1. phony：虚假，赝品

2. Robert Ackley：霍尔顿隔壁寝室的同学

3. Pencey：霍尔顿就读的第四个学校

4. incognito：隐瞒身份的人

5. Stradlater：霍尔顿的室友，外表比较帅，穿着体面，在同学中很有人气，但在寝室很邋遢，有很多性经历

6. dough：金钱，后面提到律师的目的不是拯救无辜的人，而是挣钱

7. Allie：霍尔顿的弟弟，小说情节开始前死于白血病，Allie 聪明热情，霍尔顿经常想念他

8. Robert Burns：罗伯特·彭斯，英国浪漫主义诗人，生活在苏格兰高地，他的很多诗歌表现了纯朴的农民的生活

Questions：

1. How did Holden Caulfield feel about the world around him?

2. What was his ideal?

12 Beloved

作者及背景简介

托妮·莫里森(Toni Morrison, 1931—)美国黑人女作家,魔幻现实主义作家。生于俄亥俄州(美国中西部)钢城洛里恩,父亲是船厂焊接工,母亲是忠实的教徒并且参加教会歌咏队,在白人家庭做帮佣。为了逃避种族歧视,父母从俄亥俄州迁徙到美国南方,又为了工作迁移到北方。父母都为黑人文化感到骄傲,托妮·莫里森
从小在家里学会无数的黑人歌曲,听过许多南方黑人的民间传说。在黑人文化的影响和熏陶下,她读遍与此相关的书籍,尤其对文学有兴趣。

托妮·莫里森小学一年级时是班上唯一的黑人,她很会与白人同学交朋友,直到开始交男朋友时才感觉到种族歧视。1949年,托妮·莫里森以优异的成绩考入当时专为黑人开设的大学,攻读英语和古典文学。大学毕业后,又入康奈尔大学研究福克纳和伍尔芙的小说,并以此获得硕士学位。此后,她在得克萨斯南方大学和霍德华大学任教。1966年,托妮·莫里森在纽约兰登书屋担任高级编辑,曾努力帮助出版拳王穆罕默德·阿里自传和一些青年黑人作家的作品。她所主编的《黑人之书》,记叙了美国黑人三百年历史,被称为美国黑人史的百科全书。1969年,托妮·莫里森的处女作《最蓝的眼睛》发表,此后,她经常应邀撰写社会评论,为黑人的利益而呼吁。20世纪70年代起,托妮·莫里森先后在纽约州立大学、耶鲁大学和巴尔德学院讲授美国黑人文学。20世纪70年代初,也是美国第二波女权运动轰轰烈烈进行之时,托妮·莫里森曾在一篇名为《黑人女性对女权运动的态度》的文章中公开发表过自己对当时女权运动的看法。1988年起,托妮·莫里森出任普林斯顿大学教授,讲授文学创作。同年获美国普利策文学奖。1993年,她的作品由于被认为具有极其丰富的想象力和诗意的表达方式获诺贝尔文学奖，托妮·莫里森是文学史上第一位获得诺贝尔文学奖的黑人女作家。2003年，托妮·莫里森出版新书《爱》，再一次引起评论界的广泛关注。2015年4月，面对美国社会又一次变得日益严峻的种族问题，在接受《每日电讯报》的专访时，她再一次公开对种族歧视提出批评，并为种族平等做出呼吁。

托妮·莫里森的作品以美国的黑人生活为主要内容，人物、语言及故事情节生动逼真，笔触细腻，想象丰富。托妮·莫里森自觉地将小说创作与民族解放使命联系起来，淋漓尽致地描绘了当今黑人民众的生存境遇，从中揭示出霸权文化对少数族裔文化的破坏。托妮·莫里森力图通过文学话语呼吁转向黑人民族文化本身，从过去那些被白人主流文化鄙弃的传统中重新建构民族意识。同时，托妮·莫里森凭借她独特的女性视角，依托其特殊的女性经历，把黑人女性寻求自我的历程和重构黑人民族意识的进程结合起来。

1865年美国内战结束，黑奴制度在全国范围内废除，大约400万黑奴获得了自由。然而，废奴后的美国黑人贫困无助，在社会上孤立无援。"他们从以前的庄园中获得解放，但除了脚下尘土飞扬的路，他们一无所有……"因此，托妮·莫里森的作品更多地关注黑奴制度废除后非裔美国人尴尬的生活状态，以及种族隔离对美国黑人身心的严酷摧残。在小说《秀拉》中，托妮·莫里森描绘了黑人社区的原貌，虽然有了法律保护黑人的权利，但黑人未获得真正的平等自由；虽然黑人被解放了，但却是极度贫困中的自由。黑人被种族隔离，黑人社区被边缘化，他们被迫居住在偏远的地区，进入城市只能当廉价劳工。

在探索黑人民族振兴之路的问题上，托妮·莫里森提出了重拾黑人文化遗产的思想。托妮·莫里森的作品中的黑人往往因自我否定而迷失了自我身份。由于美国白人长期的精神压迫，黑人逐渐失去斗志并忘记了自己的文化身份。托妮·莫里森揭示出在充满种族歧视的美国社会里，黑人如果抛弃了自己的民族文化和传统，就意味着丧失了民族本性，导致自我灭亡。例如在《最蓝的眼睛》中，黑人母亲波莉羡慕白人生活与文化，逐渐觉得自己的丈夫与亲生女儿的黑色皮肤丑陋，不值得去关爱和为之付出；相反倒觉得主人家的金发碧眼的小女孩显得非常可爱，值得她经常爱抚和悉心照顾。波莉在假想中抛弃了自己的黑人身份，成为托妮·莫里森作品中因自我否定而异化的典型。同时，小说的主人公女孩佩科拉最希望拥有一双"蓝色的眼睛"，透过这双眼睛，她可以看到一个没有罪恶，也不会受到歧视的美好世界。拥有一双蓝眼睛意味着摆脱黑人身份，小女孩的这一愿望其实反映了很多当时美国黑人的心理状态：不幸的命运来自于低等的肤色和基因。这种自我否定甚至是自欺的心理，正是美国白人对其长期进行心理奴役的产物。

托妮·莫里森认为,黑人民族要生存下去,除了拥有政治权利和经济独立以外,必须回归传承黑人文化,摆脱白人文化的精神桎梏。托妮·莫里森的第三部小说《所罗门之歌》诠释了回归黑人文化的主题。托妮·莫里森在小说中塑造了一个在黑人文化洗礼下最终返璞归真的黑人少年奶娃。黑人吟唱的所罗门之歌以及所罗门飞翔的传说贯穿整部小说,是黑人文化的象征也是黑人向往自由、回归自我的精神寄托。小说主人公奶娃受到白人文化价值观的影响,逐渐向白人文化价值观靠拢,这时童年时的所罗门之歌指引着他走向黑人文化的守护者——奶娃的姑妈,最后奶娃在所罗门之歌中得到启示,找到了自己的祖先,完成了自己的寻根之旅。从最初的象征白人文化价值观的"寻金之旅"到后来象征着黑人文化回归的"寻根之旅",这表明了黑人文化对黑人回归自我所产生的巨大力量。

　　黑人女性所遭受的压迫和歧视是格外突出的,她们受到来自黑人男性、白人男性和白人女性的压迫和歧视。作为一名黑人女性,托妮·莫里森试图通过文学作品的创作来唤醒人们对于黑人女性辛酸史的同情,并鼓励黑人女性站起来进行勇敢的抗争。托妮·莫里森的作品关注黑人女性,同时也上升到了关怀人类命运的高度。托妮·莫里森的作品将自然环境和女性完美地融合起来,其中最具代表性的作品有《最蓝的眼睛》《所罗门之歌》《柏油娃》《宠儿》。在《最蓝的眼睛》中,作者表达了对女性命运的关注同时表现了工业文明对大自然的破坏;在《所罗门之歌》中,托妮·莫里森表现了女性与自然界的完美融合;在《宠儿》中,树、花草等植物成为女性的精神安慰和力量来源。

选读作品简介

　　母爱和自由并不矛盾,然而在美国黑人历史中,二者之间却是对立甚至是水火不相容的。一个母亲为了自由,被逼无奈下只能剥夺孩子的生命。《宠儿》讲述一个叫塞丝的黑奴为了获取自由,带着两个女儿逃离了一个名为"甜蜜之家"的种植园,逃亡的船上只能坐两个人,为了让自己的孩子摆脱做奴隶的悲惨命运,她毅然将其中的小女儿割喉杀死。通过一次肉体交易,塞丝才把女儿下葬。这个惨死在亲生母亲手里的还没取名的孩子被称为"宠儿"(beloved)。塞丝也因为亲手杀死了自己的孩子,后来一直受到社区人们的仇视和排斥,忍受着良知的折磨和巨大的孤独。被母亲杀死的宠儿阴魂不散,十八年后化作少女重返人间,无休止地向塞丝索取母爱,还用身体引诱母亲的伴侣曾经的工友保罗,将母亲刚刚稳定和回暖的生活摧毁。

　　托妮·莫里森运用魔幻现实主义描述一个还魂人间的少女有其深刻的寓

意。这里的宠儿已不仅仅是塞丝朝思暮想的女儿,更是美国奴隶社会里千千万万个被剥夺了母爱的不幸的黑奴孩子的代表。宠儿既是塞丝死去的女儿,也是在运奴船上经历了非人折磨的非洲女性。在小说的第二部分有三大段独白,其中一段是宠儿的独白,整个独白没有标点符号,语无伦次,倾诉了宠儿在地狱中所遭受的煎熬,这一描写象征着黑奴被运往美洲时在船舱中的悲惨经历,宠儿也是无数被贩卖到美洲的非洲女儿的化身,她们在非洲的生活艰苦但自由快乐,失去自由的生活对她们来说如同地狱。

从更广义的角度来看,宠儿还代表了塞丝被压抑的过去,代表了她那挥之不去的记忆,可以说是塞丝的另一个自我。那些已经获得自由的黑奴,依然无法摆脱过去苦难生活的阴影。对他们来说,曾经的精神及肉体折磨如鬼魅般萦绕在心头,挥之不去。塞丝竭尽全力使自己不受过去的侵扰,但宠儿的到来证明,一个人很难或根本不可能抑制过去的回忆。面对宠儿,塞丝最终选择了讲述自己过去的经历,这也就意味着塞丝开始真正面对并接纳自己。直到塞丝最终懂得如何去直面自己惨淡的记忆时,她才与过去的自我合二为一,和平相处,面对未来。

成长主题解读

《宠儿》中主要刻画了三个黑人妇女的形象,三位女性代表了黑奴制度从兴盛到瓦解的不同时代里黑人妇女所扮演的不同角色以及黑人女性的成长。贝比·萨格斯是麻木和屈服黑奴的代表,她做了近一生的奴隶,直到七十多岁才被儿子赎得了自由。她从没想过逃跑,唯一的愿望是不被主人当着她孩子的面打倒在地。黑奴制度下的黑人妇女,除了要做和男黑奴同量的工作,还要承担生育孩子的义务,因为黑奴孩子对主人来说是一笔不小的收入。贝比自己都记不得一共生了多少个孩子和他们的名字,她也拒绝去记,因为每个孩子最终都是要被卖掉的。塞丝是抗争的代表,她选择了逃跑,因为她饱受了黑奴制度的所有折磨,她必须让她的孩子脱离那个地狱。她之所以狠心杀掉自己的女儿,是因为她不愿意女儿成为奴隶,她知道女黑奴的苦难生活。

奴隶主之所以允许黑奴婚姻的存在,不是因为尊重他们的感情,而是为了用妻子和孩子的牵挂阻止黑奴逃跑,而且黑奴家庭的存在可以保持黑人下一代的稳定生育和增长。但是一旦有需要,主人会不顾黑奴的哀求把夫妻、母子拆开卖掉。同时,女黑奴还会遭受各种惨绝人寰的鞭挞、火烙等酷刑,塞丝后背像枯树一样的伤痕就是最好的证明。丹芙是新一代美国黑人希望的代表。

她没有当过奴隶,但黑奴制度同样在她身上套上了枷锁。因为接受不了母亲杀害她姐姐的事实,她的耳朵失聪,心理上下意识地断绝了与外界的一切联系。丹芙康复之后也养成了孤僻的性格。和母亲塞丝一样,丹芙也在间接地逃避过去。由于缺乏与外界的交往,丹芙对外面的世界怀有恐惧。宠儿出现后,丹芙对她的照料给了丹芙被需要的感觉。丹芙对宠儿讲述和母亲逃亡的经历,一方面,满足了宠儿内心的渴望,另一方面,借助宠儿,丹芙构建了自我历史。但是当宠儿无止境地索取母爱,把母亲折磨得不成人形时,丹芙意识到了宠儿变本加厉的肆意妄为以及她母亲的节节屈服会使她们无法生活下去,她毅然鼓起了勇气走出门到社区中求助,从害怕和外界交往到主动寻求外界的帮助,这标志着丹芙社会人格的形成和追求自立的开始。面对黑奴制度的罪恶,丹芙不再逃避,而是正视它并击败它。保罗·D.是和塞丝一起遭受过非人的虐待的黑奴,和塞丝一起逃跑后成了塞丝的伴侣,过去梦魇般的记忆始终在他们心头挥之不去,宠儿的出现也促进了保罗·D.的成长。虽然保罗·D.对宠儿的憎恨一天也没有停止过,但他们之间所发生的梦魇般奇特的性关系,却开启了他那"烟盒"般的心扉。宠儿的出现使保罗·D.正确地面对过去,找回了一个完整真实、背负沉重历史的自我,这就促使保罗·D.最终回到塞丝的身边,得以和塞丝一起共同面对未来,去记忆,去感受,去爱。宠儿在小说中表现出的破坏性推开了丹芙和保罗·D.的那扇封闭心灵的门,使他们走出过去的阴影,面向未来,回归到社会当中。

　　新奴隶叙述旨在以解构主义消解中心的方法解析主流文化对少数族裔文化所造成的内在伤害,撕破历史的虚假性面纱以恢复民族的历史记忆。托妮·莫里森曾说:"我的工作已成为如何揭开那层面纱,发现那些曾被遗忘于脑后的东西,并在它们的启示中重建世界。"她试图在《宠儿》中叙述"那些不曾诉诸文字的人们的内心世界",去填补有关奴隶叙述的历史空白,引导黑人民众重新认识被种种伪装掩盖的历史。塞丝认清黑奴制度的罪恶成功地逃出"甜蜜之家",这一叙述模式与原奴隶叙述有类似之处。但不同的是,原来的奴隶逃亡的叙述往往以大团圆作为结局,这是因为他们不希望冒犯听众,尤其是废奴运动的支持者。为了更好地揭示殖民统治在黑人心理造成的历史创伤,托妮·莫里森改写了原奴隶叙述,在《宠儿》中一再使用 rememory 一词。在黑人的方言中,rememory 既可用作名词,表示"记忆",也可用作动词,表示"回想"。托妮·莫里森以 rememory 一词表示"记忆作为一种自觉的活动和情感,相对于单纯地回忆往事"。原奴隶叙述主要是以行动和时间为主轴的线性叙述,而《宠儿》的叙述却是非线性的、破碎的。对于塞丝而言,外在的时间是停滞的,她的心灵状况正如蓝石路124号一样，被苦不堪言的创伤记忆囚禁着。曾经的工友保罗·D.的介入，塞丝才开始倾诉衷肠，以话语治疗疾病；当丹芙迈出家门，向黑人社群求救，丹芙才开启了族群与个体对话的大门。托妮·莫里森拓展奴隶叙述的用意在于通过这种叙述话语修正"殖民化"的历史记忆。

选读选自小说第三部分，描写了塞丝无法摆脱宠儿所象征的过去的痛苦记忆的折磨。

Beloved sat around, ate, went from bed to bed.[1] Sometimes she screamed,"Rain! Rain!" and clawed her throat until rubies of blood opened there, made brighter by her midnight skin. Then Sethe shouted,"No!" and knocked over chairs to get to her and wipe the jewels away. Other times Beloved curled up on the floor, her wrists between her knees, and stayed there for hours. Or she would go to the creek, stick her feet in the water and whoosh it up her legs. Afterward she would go to Sethe, run her fingers over the woman's teeth while tears slid from her wide black eyes. Then it seemed to Denver the thing was done: Beloved bending over Sethe looked the mother, Sethe the teething child, for other than those times when Beloved needed her, Sethe confined herself to a corner chair. The bigger Beloved got, the smaller Sethe became; the brighter Beloved's eyes, the more those eyes that used never to look away became slits of sleeplessness. Sethe no longer combed her hair or splashed her face with water. She sat in the chair licking her lips like a chastised child while Beloved ate up her life, took it, swelled up with it, grew taller on it. And the older woman yielded it up without a murmur. Denver served them both. Washing, cooking, forcing, cajoling her mother to eat a little now and then, providing sweet things for Beloved as often as she could to calm her down. It was hard to know what she would do from minute to minute. When the heat got hot, she might walk around the house naked or wrapped in a sheet, her belly protruding like a winning watermelon.

Denver thought she understood the connection between her mother and Beloved: Sethe was trying to make up for the handsaw; Beloved was making her pay for it. But there would never be an end to that, and seeing her mother diminished shamed and infuriated her. Yet she knew Sethe's greatest fear was the same one Denver had in the beginning—that Beloved might leave. That before Sethe could make her understand what it meant—what it took to drag the teeth of that saw under the little chin; to feel the baby blood pump like oil in her hands; to hold her face so her head would stay on; to squeeze her so she could absorb, still, the death spasms that shot through that adored body, plump and sweet with life[2]—Beloved might leave. Leave before Sethe could make her realize that worse than that—far worse—was what Baby Suggs died of, what Ella knew, what Stamp saw and what made Paul D tremble. That anybody white could take your whole self for anything that came to mind. Not just work, kill, or maim you, but dirty you. Dirty you so bad you couldn't like yourself anymore. Dirty you so bad you forgot who you were and couldn't think it up.

Notes：

1. 这一段描写了被塞丝在逃跑路上杀死的小女儿重返人间，向塞丝无止境地索求母爱折磨塞丝。

2. 这里塞丝在回忆杀死女儿的情景。

Questions：

1. What does Beloved symbolize? How does she affect Sethe's present life?

2. How does Denver grow up?

13 The Kite Runner

作者及背景简介

卡勒德·胡赛尼（Khaled Hosseini, 1965—）生于阿富汗喀布尔市，后随父亲迁往美国。胡赛尼毕业于加州大学圣地亚哥医学系，现居加州。著有小说《追风筝的人》(*The Kite Runner*, 2003)、《灿烂千阳》(*A Thousand Splendid Suns*, 2007)、《群山回唱》(*And the Mountains Echoed*, 2013)，作品全球销量超过 4000 万册。

2006 年，因其作品巨大的国际影响力，胡赛尼获得联合国人道主义奖，并受邀担任联合国难民署亲善大使。

胡赛尼的父亲为外交官，母亲是喀布尔女子学校的教师。1970 年，全家随父亲外派到伊朗德黑兰，在 1973 年，全家搬回喀布尔，这一年是阿富汗政权维持稳定的最后一年。之后政变与外侵不断，也结束了胡赛尼在阿富汗美好的童年。1976 年，胡赛尼的父亲在法国巴黎找到了工作，于是全家搬迁到巴黎居住，由于阿富汗政权极不稳定，全家就再也没有回国了。1980 年，苏联入侵阿富汗，他父亲决定向美国申请政治庇护，之后就举家移民到美国加州的圣荷塞。初到时经济困难，曾向美国政府领取福利金与食物券。1984 年，胡赛尼高中毕业，申请到圣塔克拉拉大学读生物专业，毕业后在加州大学圣地亚哥分校的医学系就读。1993 年取得了 MD（行医执照）后，1996 年在加州洛城的锡安山医学院完成实习工作。

胡赛尼的第一部小说《追风筝的人》问世后大获成功，成为近年来国际文坛最大黑马，获得各项新人奖，全球热销 600 万册，创下了出版奇迹。因为小说的巨大影响力，胡赛尼于 2006 年获得联合国人道主义奖，受邀担任联合国难民署亲善大使，促进难民救援工作。该书于 2006 年 5 月在中国出版。

《灿烂千阳》是胡赛尼四年之后出版的第二部小说，出版之前即获得极大关注，2007年5月22日在美国首发，赢得评论界一致好评，胡赛尼由新人作家一跃成为受到广泛认同的成熟作家。2007年9月，该书在中国出版。

六年后，他的第三部小说《群山回唱》于2013年5月21日在美国出版，再次大获好评，被称为是作者迄今最具野心的小说，笔法较前两本也更为娴熟。《群山回唱》被评选为美国亚马逊书店2013年上半年最佳图书、巴诺书店上半年度最佳小说、美国国家公共电台夏季最佳图书、ABC《早安美国》读书俱乐部夏季最佳图书，并居于诸多畅销榜榜首。该书于2013年8月14日在中国出版。

卡勒德·胡赛尼说他的小说"立志拂去蒙在阿富汗普通民众面孔的尘灰，将背后灵魂的悸动展示给世人"。他的小说以历经战乱的多民族的伊斯兰教国家阿富汗为背景，以细腻温情深沉的笔触展现了阿富汗人民的生存状态及人性的弱点和光辉。

选读作品简介

小说以第一人称的角度讲述了阿米尔从童年到青年的故事。阿米尔生于1963年喀布尔的一个富人社区中的一个富裕家庭，父亲是普什图人，一名法官的儿子，成功的地毯商人。阿米尔家的仆人阿里的儿子哈桑则是哈扎拉人。哈桑是阿米尔的童年玩伴，对阿米尔无限忠诚，"为了你，千千万万遍！"爸爸对两个孩子都很喜爱，觉得阿米尔过于怯懦，两个孩子和外人打架时总是哈桑挺身而出。阿米尔展露出写作的才华，但爸爸并不看重。爸爸的朋友拉辛汗成了阿米尔的忘年知己。1973年，穆罕默德·达乌德·汗等发动政变，在阿富汗推翻帝制，建立共和国。

社区中一个仰慕纳粹的普什图族孩子阿塞夫与阿米尔和哈桑发生冲突，哈桑用弹弓保护了阿米尔。1975年，在一次风筝比赛中，阿米尔为了赢得爸爸的好感而勇夺冠军，哈桑去追到风筝以证明阿米尔的战绩，哈桑在回来时被阿塞夫等人拦截住。阿塞夫要哈桑把风筝给他，对阿米尔完全忠实的哈桑拒绝了，哈桑遭到阿塞夫的强暴。这一切被阿米尔看到，但怯懦的阿米尔没有挺身而出。

阿米尔由于无法面对哈桑而希望爸爸解雇阿里和哈桑，被爸爸严词拒绝。为了赶走哈桑，阿米尔陷害哈桑偷了自己的生日礼物。阿里和哈桑不顾阿米尔爸爸的挽留搬到了哈扎拉族聚居的哈扎拉贾特山区。

1979年苏联入侵阿富汗,1981年爸爸带着阿米尔历经艰辛逃往到巴基斯坦白沙瓦,把家留给拉辛汗照看。后来阿米尔父子又迁到美国旧金山湾区的费利蒙居住。阿米尔在美国上大学,毕业之后成了作家,阿米尔在圣何塞的跳蚤市场认识了同样来自阿富汗的一个将军塔赫里的女儿索拉雅并爱上了她,但索拉雅的父母看不上阿米尔,此时阿米尔的父亲已患肺癌,父亲看出了儿子的心思,去将军家说媒,张罗完儿子的婚事后不久去世,阿米尔和索拉雅搬到了旧金山。他们想有一个孩子,但始终没能如愿。

2001年,罹患绝症的拉辛汗给阿米尔打电话,告诉他后来发生的事情。哈桑后来结婚有了一个儿子索拉博。1996年塔利班占领喀布尔之后,强占了他们的房子,哈桑和妻子由于种族歧视被当街枪杀,索拉博进了孤儿院。拉辛汗希望阿米尔回喀布尔救索拉博,并告诉阿米尔哈桑其实是阿米尔爸爸的私生子,哈桑和阿米尔是同父异母的兄弟。

阿米尔找到了索拉博所在的孤儿院之后,发现索拉博已经被一个塔利班头目带走,这个塔利班头目就是阿塞夫,索拉博已经成了一个被性侵犯的舞童。阿塞夫告诉阿米尔可以带走索拉博,但必须和他了却以前的恩怨。阿米尔在被阿塞夫击打的过程中感到了一种赎罪,关键时刻又是索拉博的弹弓打瞎了其阿塞夫左眼,阿米尔和索拉博趁机逃出。

在巴基斯坦首都伊斯兰堡,因为阿米尔无法证明索拉博是孤儿,而无法取得美国签证,从而收养索拉博。索拉博需要暂时入住孤儿院。出于对孤儿院的惧怕,索拉博割腕自杀被救。在阿米尔带着索拉博回到美国之后,索拉博因为感情受到伤害不再和任何人交流。在2001年"9·11事件"之后的一个周末,在一个公园里,阿米尔带索拉博放风筝,阿米尔追风筝时对索拉博说:"为了你,千千万万遍!"

成长主题解读

《追风筝的人》不仅仅展现了一个人的心灵成长史,也展现了一个民族的灵魂史,一个国家的苦难史。小说里蕴含着阿富汗这个古老国家深厚的文化,激荡着善与恶的潜流撞击。这本书让世界了解了一个遭受战火蹂躏的阿富汗,讨论了关于人性和拯救人性的问题,这是现代人类面临的共同话题,成长和人性的救赎是这部小说的核心主题。从整体上来说,《追风筝的人》是一部成长小说,其主人公的成长是通过其完成自我救赎来实现的。

一、在成长中得到救赎

1. 外在成长

小说中主人公外在成长过程经历了童年生活、流亡美国、重返祖国等阶段。从成长救赎这一主题来看,其外在成长又分为放下过错、获知真相、完成救赎这几个阶段。尽管家境殷实,而且深受玩伴哈桑的崇拜,但小阿米尔始终认为自己得不到父爱,这时期幼小的心灵受到某种程度上的扭曲,这种扭曲心理使他看到忠诚的哈桑在被强暴时选择逃跑(见选读),从此阿米尔的内心笼罩在愧疚的阴影中,阿米尔要成长,就必须解开这个愧疚的心结。阿米尔逼走哈桑之后不久,苏联入侵阿富汗,阿米尔和父亲流亡美国。在异国他乡,阿米尔经过自己的努力,克服了因为流亡带来的很多困难和挫折,得到了锻炼。阿米尔在美国获得了自己的幸福和事业,从某种意义上来说,他的外在成长正在完成。然而,在读者眼里,包括阿米尔自己内心深处,阿米尔始终"做不回一个好人"。哈桑身世真相的揭露促成了阿米尔面对自己的过错完成救赎的决心。为了实现自己最后的成长仪式,阿米尔冒着生命危险回到阿富汗,从残暴的塔利班恐怖分子手中救出哈桑的儿子索拉博,但阿米尔的成长还没有完成,回到美国,阿米尔肩负起了对索拉博抚养的责任。阿米尔承担自己过错的责任,同时也用自己的努力和勇气完成了救赎,最终实现了其成长和成熟。

2. 内在成长

在小说中,阿米尔的外在成长可以通过作者的叙述表现出来。然而,在主人公外在成长的背后隐藏着其由天真到背叛,由心理煎熬到勇敢救赎的内在成长历程。在童年阶段,阿米尔在树上刻下"阿米尔和哈桑,喀布尔的苏丹",这说明在童年,阿米尔与哈桑还是有纯真的友谊。由于天性怯弱,不被父亲赏识,而勇敢的哈桑反而更受到阿米尔父亲的欣赏,阿米尔的内心从小就蒙上了阴影,风筝大赛上阿米尔内心的阴暗面完全展露出来后,看到哈桑为了替他保住风筝而遭受强暴,阿米尔不但选择了逃走,而且还陷害哈桑,撵走了他。从此阿米尔也因深深的愧疚饱受煎熬。18岁的阿米尔随父亲来到美国,"对我来说,美国是个埋葬往事的地方"。然而后来拉辛汗的电话还是将那段埋在心底的往事挖掘出来,阿米尔意识到必须经历一次勇敢的救赎才能真正完成成长的洗礼。最后阿米尔冒死救出了哈桑的儿子,也在内心走完了一段自我救赎的历程。

二、在救赎中实现成长

在《追风筝的人》中,阿米尔在营救索拉博,同时也在救赎自己灵魂的过程中。此外，其救赎是冒着生命危险完成的，同时在救赎的高潮，阿米尔被击倒流血的场景意味着其救赎过程中的牺牲，阿米尔通过以此流血的救赎仪式来实现自己的成长，通过流血抚平自己曾经的伤疤，同时也治愈着被掏空的灵魂。在这场流血的救赎过程中，当阿米尔被阿塞夫击中流血之后，阿米尔竟然开心笑了，这是其"自1975年冬天以来，第一次感到心安理得。我大笑，因为我知道，在我大脑深处某个隐蔽的角落，我甚至一直在期待这样的事情"。鲜血流出的那刻，阿米尔用鲜血抚平了自己心灵上的伤疤，他终于有勇气用身体上的疼痛去治愈其心灵上的创伤。阿米尔用鲜血实现了自己的救赎，同时也拯救了拉博尔（见选读）。

尽管阿米尔曾犯下过错，但他也对自己的错误一直深深自责，这说明在主人公内心深处还是有道义感，这种道义感使得他在犯下错误之后经受着内心的煎熬，即使流亡美国也没有使其在良心上安宁，他时时反省自己内心的罪孽。当阿辛汗打来电话得知哈桑生死真相之后，一直潜伏于主人公内心的道义感完全爆发出来，支撑他在阿富汗的血雨腥风中追寻救赎的希望，给予他救赎的动力。

成长过程中伴随着挫折和困难，要克服和正视这些挫折和困难必然要求主人公有莫大的勇气。在得知哈桑的悲剧之后，阿米尔又只身回到喀布尔，尽管在各种场合都充斥着暴力和血腥，但他仍然勇敢地选择单独面对残暴的阿塞夫，接受意味着死亡的挑战。此时此刻的阿米尔勇敢地正视自己多年前造成的罪孽，那个曾经胆怯、逃避的男孩终于鼓起了勇气完成了救赎，为死去的哈桑将自己的生死置之度外。

在道义感和勇气的指引下，阿米尔实现了自我的救赎。阿米尔将拉博尔带回美国的生活则是作者刻意赋予了主人公精神上的超越，同时也使得主题进一步深化。因为哈桑是主人公的父亲和仆人生的儿子，其父亲为了自己的名声一直将事实掩盖了，这间接地造成了后来哈桑的悲剧。回到美国后，当主人公不仅能够坦诚地面对自己的过错，而且能正视父亲留下来的过失，愿意为此承担责任时，主人公实现了精神上的成长。

以下选读出自小说第 7 章和第 8 章,描写了童年阿米尔目睹哈桑被强暴却由于怯懦不敢去救以及后来阿米尔对待哈桑的心理。

I had one last chance to make a decision. One final opportunity to decide who I was going to be. I could step into that alley, stand up for Hassan—the way he'd stood up for me all those times in the past—and accept whatever would happen to me. Or I could run.

In the end, I ran.

I ran because I was a coward. I was afraid of Assef and what he would do to me. I was afraid of getting hurt. That's what I told myself as I turned my back to the alley, to Hassan. That's what I made myself believe. I actually aspired to cowardice, because the alternative, the real reason I was running, was that Assef was right: Nothing was free in this world. Maybe Hassan was the price I had to pay, the lamb I had to slay, to win Baba. Was it a fair price? The answer floated to my conscious mind before I could thwart it: He was just a Hazara[1], wasn't he?

……

Later, well past midnight, after a few hours of poker between Baba and his cousins, the men lay down to sleep on parallel mattresses in the same room where we'd dined. The women went upstairs. An hour later, I still couldn't sleep. I kept tossing and turning as my relatives grunted, sighed, and snored in their sleep. I sat up. A wedge of moonlight streamed in through the window.

"I watched Hassan get raped," I said to no one. Baba stirred in his sleep. A part of me was hoping someone would wake up and hear, so I wouldn't have to live with this lie anymore. But no one woke up and in the silence that followed, I understood the nature of my new curse: I was going to get away with it.

I thought about Hassan's dream, the one about us swimming in the lake. There is no monster, he'd said, just water. Except he'd been wrong about that. There was a monster in the lake. It had grabbed Hassan by the ankles, dragged him to the murky bottom. I was that monster.

That was the night I became an insomniac.

I DIDN't SPEAK TO HASSAN until the middle of the next week. I had just half-eaten my lunch and Hassan was doing the dishes. I was walking upstairs, going to my room, when Hassan asked if I wanted to hike up the hill. I said I was tired. Hassan looked tired too—he'd lost weight and gray circles had formed under his puffed-up eyes. But when he asked again, I reluctantly agreed.

We trekked up the hill, our boots squishing in the muddy snow. Neither one of us said anything. We sat under our pomegranate tree and I knew I'd made a mistake. I shouldn't have come up the hill. The words I'd carved on the tree trunk with Ali's kitchen knife, Amir and Hassan: The Sultans of Kabul... I couldn't stand looking at them now.

He asked me to read to him from the Shahnamah and I told him I'd changed my mind. Told him I just wanted to go back to my room. He looked away and shrugged. We walked back down the way we'd gone up in silence. And for the first time in my life, I couldn't wait for spring.

MY MEMORY OF THE REST of that winter of 1975 is pretty hazy. I remember I was fairly happy when Baba was Home. We'd eat together, go to see a film, visit Kaka Homayoun or Kaka Faruq. Sometimes Rahim Khan came over and Baba let me sit in his study and sip tea with them. He'd even have me read him some of my stories. It was good and I even believed it would last. And Baba believed it too, I think. We both should have known better. For at least a few months after the kite tournament, Baba and I immersed ourselves in a sweet illusion, saw each other in a way that we never had before. We'd actually deceived ourselves into thinking that a toy made of tissue paper, glue, and bamboo could somehow close the chasm between us.

But when Baba was out—and he was out a lot—I closed myself in my room. I read a book every couple of days, wrote stories, learned to draw horses. I'd hear Hassan shuffling around the kitchen in the morning, hear the clinking of silverware, the whistle of the teapot. I'd wait to hear the door shut and only then I would walk down to eat. On my calendar, I circled the date of the first day of school and began a countdown.

To my dismay, Hassan kept trying to rekindle things between us. I remember the last time. I was in my room, reading an abbreviated Farsi translation of Ivanhoe, when he knocked on my door.

"What is it?"

"I'm going to the baker" he said from the other side. "I was wondering if you…if you wanted to come along."

"I think I'm just going to read," I said, rubbing my temples. Lately, every time Hassan was around, I was getting a headache.

"It's a sunny day," he said.

"I can see that."

"Might be fun to go for a walk."

"You go."

"I wish you'd come along," he said. Paused. Something thumped against the door, maybe his forehead. "I don't know what I've done, Amir agha. I wish you'd tell me. I don't know why we don't play anymore."

"You haven't done anything, Hassan. Just go."

"You can tell me, I'll stop doing it."

I buried my head in my lap, squeezed my temples with my knees, like a vice. "I'll tell you what I want you to stop doing," I said, eyes pressed shut.

"Anything?"

"I want you to stop harassing me. I want you to go away," I snapped. I wished he would give it right back to me, break the door open and tell me off—it would have made things easier, better. But he didn't do anything like that, and when I opened the door minutes later, he wasn't there. I fell on my bed, buried my head under the pillow, and cried.

HASSAN MILLED ABOUT the periphery of my life after that. I made sure our paths crossed as little as possible, planned my day that way. Because when he was around, the oxygen seeped out of the room. My chest tightened and I couldn't draw enough air; I'd stand there, gasping in my own little airless bubble of atmosphere. But even when he wasn't around, he was. He was there in the hand-washed and ironed clothes on the cane-seat chair, in the warm slippers left outside my door, in the wood already burning in the stove when I came down for breakfast. Everywhere I turned, I saw signs of his loyalty, his goddamn unwavering loyalty.

Early that spring, a few days before the new school year started, Baba and I were planting tulips in the garden. Most of the snow had melted and the hills in the north were already dotted with patches of green grass. It was a cool, gray morning, and Baba was squatting next to me, digging the soil and planting the bulbs I handed to him. He was telling me how most people thought it was better to plant tulips in the fall and how that wasn't true, when I came right out and said it. "Baba, have you ever thought about getting new servants?"

He dropped the tulip bulb and buried the trowel in the dirt. Took off his gardening gloves. I'd startled him. "Chi? What did you say?"

"I was just wondering, that's all."

"Why would I ever want to do that? Baba said curtly."

"You wouldn't, I guess. It was just a question," I said, my voice fading to a murmur. I was already sorry I'd said it.

"Is this about you and Hassan? I know there's something going on between you two, but whatever it is, you have to deal with it, not me. I'm staying out of it."

"I'm sorry, Baba."

He put on his gloves again. "I grew up with Ali," he said through clenched teeth. My father took him in, he loved Ali like his own son. Forty years Ali's been with my family. Forty goddamn years. And you think I'm just going to throw him out? He turned to me now, his face as red as a tulip. "I've never laid a hand on you, Amir, but you ever say that again ... " He looked away, shaking his head. "You bring me shame. And Hassan ... Hassan's not going anywhere, do you understand?"

I looked down and picked up a fistful of cool soil. Let it pour between my fingers.

"I said, Do you understand?" Baba roared.

I flinched. "Yes, Baba."

"Hassan's not going anywhere," Baba snapped. He dug a new hole with the trowel, striking the dirt harder than he had to. "He's staying right here with us, where he belongs. This is his Home and we're his family. Don't you ever ask me that question again!"

"I won't, Baba. I'm sorry."

We planted the rest of the tulips in silence.

I was relieved when school started that next week. Students with new notebooks and sharpened pencils in hand ambled about the courtyard, kicking up dust, chatting in groups, waiting for the class captains? Whistles. Baba drove down the dirt lane that led to the entrance. The school was an old two-story building with broken windows and dim, cobblestone hallways, patches of its original dull yellow paint still showing between sloughing chunks of plaster. Most of the boys walked to school, and Baba's black Mustang drew more than one envious look. I should have been beaming with pride when he dropped me off—the old me would have—but all I could muster was a mild form of embarrassment. That and emptiness. Baba drove away without saying good-bye.

I bypassed the customary comparing of kite-fighting scars and stood in line. The bell rang and we marched to our assigned class, filed in pairs. I sat in the back row. As the Farsi teacher handed out our textbooks, I prayed for a heavy load of Homework.

School gave me an excuse to stay in my room for long hours. And, for a while, it took my mind off what had happened that winter, what I had let happen. For a few weeks, I preoccupied myself with gravity and momentum, atoms and cells, the Anglo-Afghan wars, instead of thinking about Hassan and what had happened to him. But, always, my mind returned to the alley. To Hassan's brown corduroy pants lying on the bricks. To the droplets of blood staining the snow dark red, almost black. One sluggish, hazy afternoon early that summer, I asked Hassan to go up the hill with me. Told him I wanted to read him a new story I'd written. He was hanging clothes to dry in the yard and I saw his eagerness in the harried way he finished the job. We climbed the hill, making small talk. He asked about school, what I was learning, and I talked about my teachers, especially the mean math teacher who punished talkative students by sticking a metal rod between their fingers and then squeezing them together. Hassan winced at that, said he hoped I'd never have to experience it. I said I'd been lucky so far, knowing that luck had nothing to do with it. I had done my share of talking in class too. But my father was rich and everyone knew him, so I was spared the metal rod treatment.

We sat against the low cemetery wall under the shade thrown by the pomegranate tree. In another month or two, crops of scorched yellow weeds would blanket the hillside, but that year the spring showers had lasted longer than usual, nudging their way into early summer, and the grass was still green, peppered with tangles of wildflowers. Below us, Wazir Akbar Khan's white walled, flat-topped houses gleamed in the sunshine, the laundry hanging on clotheslines in their yards stirred by the breeze to dance like butterflies.

We had picked a dozen pomegranates from the tree. I unfolded the story I'd brought along, turned to the first page, then put it down. I stood up and picked up an overripe pomegranate that had fallen to the ground.

"What would you do if I hit you with this?" I said, tossing the fruit up and down.

Hassan's smile wilted. He looked older than I'd remembered. No, not older, old. Was that possible? Lines had etched into his tanned face and creases framed his eyes, his mouth. I might as well have taken a knife and carved those lines myself.

"What would you do?" I repeated.

The color fell from his face. Next to him, the stapled pages of the story I'd promised to read him fluttered in the breeze. I hurled the pomegranate at him. It struck him in the chest, exploded in a spray of red pulp. Hassan's cry was pregnant with surprise and pain.

"Hit me back!" I snapped. Hassan looked from the stain on his chest to me.

"Get up! Hit me!" I said. Hassan did get up, but he just stood there, looking dazed like a man dragged into the ocean by a riptide when, just a moment ago, he was enjoying a nice stroll on the beach.

I hit him with another pomegranate, in the shoulder this time. The juice splattered his face. "Hit me back! I spat. "Hit me back, goddamn you! I wished he would. I wished he'd give me the punishment I craved, so maybe I'd finally sleep at night. Maybe then things could return to how they used to be between us. But Hassan did nothing as I pelted him again and again. "You're a coward!" I said. Nothing but a goddamn coward!

I don't know how many times I hit him. All I know is that, when I finally stopped, exhausted and panting, Hassan was smeared in red like he'd been shot by a firing squad. I fell to my knees, tired, spent, frustrated.

Then Hassan did pick up a pomegranate. He walked toward me. He opened it and crushed it against his own forehead. "There," he croaked, red dripping down his face like blood. "Are you satisfied? Do you feel better?" He turned around and started down the hill.

I let the tears break free, rocked back and forth on my knees.

"What am I going to do with you, Hassan? What am I going to do with you?" But by the time the tears dried up and I trudged down the hill, I knew the answer to that question.

Note:

1. 哈扎拉人是蒙古族的后裔,有很多学者认为他们是成吉思汗西征后留下来的驻屯兵的后裔,普什图人是土生土长的原住民,早期哈扎拉人是讲蒙语而非波斯语,而且面貌着装与普什图人也是一眼就能区分的,比如塌鼻梁,这在哈桑的外貌描写中有体现。哈扎拉人与普什图人很早就有矛盾,受到歧视。

Questions:

1. How did Amir feel toward Hassan after Hassan was violated by Assef?
2. How was Amir's character at that time?

下面选读选自小说的第 22 章,是故事的高潮,描写了阿米尔解救哈桑的儿子索拉博(Sohrab)的过程,此时索拉博已被已加入塔利班的阿瑟夫作为童妓和舞童囚禁。

"I'll ask you something: What are you doing with that whore? Why aren't you here, with your Muslim brothers, serving your country?"[1]

"I've been away a long time," was all I could think of saying. My head felt so hot. I pressed my knees together, held my bladder.[2]

I thought about Soraya[3]. It calmed me. I thought of her sickle-shaped birthmark, the elegant curve of her neck, her luminous eyes. I thought of our wedding night, gazing at each other's reflection in the mirror under the green veil, and how her cheeks blushed when I whispered that I loved her. I remembered the two of us dancing to an old Afghan song, round and round, everyone watching and clapping, the world a blur of flowers, dresses, tuxedos[4], and smiling faces.

The Talib was saying something.

"Pardon?"

"I said would you like to see him? Would you like to see my boy?" His upper lip curled up in a sneer when he said those last two words.

……

The boy had his father's round moon face, his pointy stub of a chin, his twisted, seashell ears, and the same slight frame. It was the Chinese doll face of my childhood, the face peering above fanned-out playing cards[5] all those winter days, the face behind the mosquito net when we slept on the roof of my father's house in the summer. His head was shaved, his eyes darkened with mascara[6], and his cheeks glowed with an unnatural red. When he stopped in the middle of the room, the bells strapped around his anklets stopped jingling. His eyes fell on me. Lingered. Then he looked away. Looked down at his naked feet.

One of the guards pressed a button and Pashtu music filled the room. The three men began to clap.

Sohrab raised his arms and turned slowly. He stood on tiptoes, spun gracefully, dipped to his knees, straightened, and spun again. His little hands swiveled at the wrists, his fingers snapped, and his head swung side to side like a pendulum. His feet pounded the floor, the bells jingling in perfect harmony with the beat of the tabla. He kept his eyes closed.

......

Sohrab danced in a circle, eyes closed, danced until the music stopped. The bells jingled one final time when he stomped his foot with the song's last note. He froze in mid-spin.

......

"What mission is that?" I heard myself say. "Stoning adulterers?[7] Raping children? Flogging women for wearing high heels? Massacring Hazaras? All in the name of Islam?" The words spilled suddenly and unexpectedly, came out before I could yank the leash. I wished I could take them back. Swallow them. But they were out. I had crossed a line, and whatever little hope I had of getting out alive had vanished with those words.

A look of surprise passed across Assef's face, briefly, and disappeared. "I see this may turn out to be enjoyable after all," he said, snickering. "But there are things traitors like you don't understand."

"Like what?"

Assef's brow twitched. "Like pride in your people, your customs, your language. Afghanistan is like a beautiful mansion littered with garbage, and someone has to take out the garbage."

"That's what you were doing in Mazar[8], going door-to-door? Taking out the garbage?"

......

"I want the boy," I said again. Sohrab's eyes flicked to me. They were slaughter sheep's eyes. They even had the mascara, I remembered how, on the day of Eid of corban[9], the mullah in our backyard used to apply mascara to the eyes of the sheep and feed it a cube of sugar before slicing its throat. I thought I saw pleading in Sohrab's eyes.

......

"I want to take him to a better place."

"Tell me why."

"That's my business," I said. I didn't know what had emboldened me to be so curt, maybe the fact that I thought I was going to die anyway.

"I wonder," Assef said, "I wonder why you've come all this way, Amir, come all this way for a Hazara? Why are you here? Why are you really here?"

"I have my reasons," I said.

"Very well then," Assef said, sneering. He shoved Sohrab in the back, pushed him right into the table. Sohrab's hips struck the table, knocking it upside down and spilling the grapes. He fell on them, face first, and stained his shirt purple with grape juice. The table's legs, crossing through the ring of brass balls, were now pointing to the ceiling.

"Take him, then," Assef said. I helped Sohrab to his feet, swatted the bits of crushed grape that had stuck to his pants like barnacles[10] to a pier. "Go, take him," Assef said, pointing to the door.

......

We made it as far as the door.

"Of course," Assef said behind us, "I didn't say you could take him for free."

I turned. "What do you want?"

"You have to earn him."

"What do you want?"

"We have some unfinished business, you and I," Assef said, "You remember, don't you?"

He needn't have worried. I would never forget the day after Daoud Khan[11] overthrew the king. My entire adult life, whenever I heard Daoud Khan's name, what I saw was Hassan with his sling shot pointed at Assef's face, Hassan saying that they'd have to start calling him One-Eyed Assef instead of Assef Goshkhor. I remember how envious I'd been of Hassan's bravery. Assef had backed down, promised that in the end he'd get us both. He'd kept that promise with Hassan. Now it was my turn.

"All right," I said, not knowing what else there was to say. I wasn't about to beg; that would have only sweetened the moment for him.

Assef called the guards back into the room. "I want you to listen to me," he said to them, "In a moment, I'm going to close the door. Then he and I are going to finish an old bit of business. No matter what you hear, don't come in! Do you hear me? Don't come in."

The guards nodded. Looked from Assef to me. "Yes, Agha sahib."[12]

"When it's all done, only one of us will walk out of this room alive," Assef said. "If it's him, then he's earned his freedom and you let him pass, do you understand?"

The older guard shifted on his feet. "But Agha sahib—"

"If it's him, you let him pass!" Assef screamed. The two men flinched but nodded again. They turned to go. One of them reached for Sohrab.

"Let him stay," Assef said. He grinned. "Let him watch. Lessons are good things for boys."

......

Lying on the floor, blood from my split upper lip staining the mauve carpet, pain ripping through my belly, and wondering when I'd be able to breathe again. The sound of my ribs snapping like the tree branches Hassan and I used to break to sword fight like Sinbad[13] in those old movies. Sohrab screaming. The side of my face slamming against the corner of the television stand.

......

Biting down in pain, noticing how my teeth didn't align like they used to. Getting kicked. Sohrab screaming. I don't know at what point I started laughing, but I did. It hurt to laugh, hurt my jaws, my ribs, my throat. But I was laughing and laughing. And the harder I laughed, the harder he kicked me, punched me, scratched me.

"WHAT'S SO FUNNY?" Assef kept roaring with each blow. His spittle landed in my eye. Sohrab screamed.

"WHAT'S SO FUNNY?" Assef bellowed. Another rib snapped, this time left lower. What was so funny was that, for the first time since the winter of 1975, I felt at peace. I laughed because I saw that, in some hidden nook in a corner of my mind, I'd even been looking forward to this. I remembered the day on the hill I had pelted Hassan with pomegranates and tried to provoke him. He'd just stood there, doing nothing, red juice soaking through his shirt like blood. Then he'd taken the pomegranate from my hand, crushed it against his forehead. Are you satisfied now? He'd hissed. Do you feel better? I hadn't been happy and I hadn't felt better, not at all. But I did now. My body was broken—just how badly I wouldn't find out until later—but I felt healed. Healed at last. I laughed.

Then the end. That, I'll take to my grave:

I was on the ground laughing, Assef straddling my chest, his face a mask of lunacy, framed by snarls of his hair swaying inches from my face. His free hand was locked around my throat. The other, the one with the brass knuckles, cocked above his shoulder. He raised his fist higher, raised it for another blow.

Then, "Bas."[14] A thin voice.

We both looked.

"Please, no more."

I remembered something the orphanage director had said when he'd opened the door to me and Farid[15]. What had been his name? Zaman? He's inseparable from that thing[16], he had said. He tucks it in the waist of his pants everywhere he goes.

"No more."

Twin trails of black mascara, mixed with tears, had rolled down his cheeks, smeared the rouge. His lower lip trembled. Mucus seeped from his nose. "Bas," he croaked.

His hand was cocked above his shoulder, holding the cup of the slingshot at the end of the elastic band which was pulled all the way back. There was something in the cup, something shiny and yellow. I blinked the blood from my eyes and saw it was one of the brass balls from the ring in the table base. Sohrab had the slingshot pointed to Assef's face.

"No more, Agha, Please," he said, his voice husky and trembling. "Stop hurting him."

Assef's mouth moved wordlessly. He began to say something, stopped. "What do you think you're you doing?" he finally said.

"Please stop," Sohrab said, fresh tears pooling in his green eyes, mixing with mascara.

"Put it down, Hazara," Assef hissed. "Put it down or what I'm doing to him will be a gentle ear twisting compared to what I'll do to you."

The tears broke free. Sohrab shook his head. "Please, Agha," he said, "Stop."

"Put it down."

"Don't hurt him anymore."

Assef let go of my throat. Lunged at Sohrab.

The slingshot made a thwiiiiit sound when Sohrab released the cup. Then

Assef was screaming. He put his hand where his left eye had been just a moment ago. Blood oozed between his fingers. Blood and something else, something white and gel-like. That's called vitreous fluid, I thought with clarity. I've read that somewhere. Vitreous fluid.

Assef rolled on the carpet. Rolled side to side, shrieking, his hand still cupped over the bloody socket.

"Let's go!" Sohrab said. He took my hand. Helped me to my feet. Every inch of my battered body wailed with pain. Behind us, Assef kept shrieking.

"OUT! GET IT OUT!" he screamed.

Teetering, I opened the door. The guards' eyes widened when they saw me and I wondered what I looked like. My stomach hurt with each breath. One of the guards said something in Pashtu and then they blew past us, running into the room where Assef was still screaming…

I stumbled down the hallway, Sohrab's little hand in mine. I took a final look over my shoulder. The guards were huddled over Assef, doing something to his face. Then I understood: The brass ball was still stuck in his empty eye socket.

The whole world rocking up and down, swooping side to side, I hobbled down the steps, leaning on Sohrab. From above, Assef's screams went on and on, the cries of a wounded animal. We made it outside, into daylight, my arm around Sohrab's shoulder, and I saw Farid running toward us.

"Bismillah![17] Bismillah!" he said, eyes bulging at the sight of me.

He slung my arm around his shoulder and lifted me. Carried me to the truck, running. I think I screamed. I watched the way his sandals pounded the pavement, slapped his black, calloused heels. It hurt to breathe. Then I was looking up at the roof of the Land Cruiser,[18] in the backseat, the upholstery beige and ripped, listening to the ding-ding-ding signaling an open door. Running foot steps around the truck. Farid and Sohrab exchanging quick words. The truck's doors slammed shut and the engine roared to life. The car jerked forward and I felt a tiny hand on my forehead. I heard voices on the street, some shouting, and saw trees blurring past in the window Sohrab was sobbing. Farid was still repeating, "Bismillah! Bismillah!"

It was about then that I passed out.

Notes：

1. 此处是曾经强暴过哈桑，现已加入塔利班的阿瑟夫对阿米尔说的话。
2. bladder：膀胱，此处的身体反应表现了阿米尔的紧张害怕心理，与上一段选读中哈桑受到凌辱时阿米尔表现出的懦弱相呼应
3. Soraya：索拉雅，阿米尔在美国的阿富汗裔妻子，此处是阿米尔的回忆
4. tuxedos：男子无尾晚礼服
5. fanned-out playing cards：分成扇状的扑克牌
6. mascara：睫毛膏，此处的外貌描写表现了索拉博被塔利班作为性奴和舞童
7. stoning adulterers：指塔利班把私通者用乱石砸死的惩罚，以下列举了塔利班的暴行
8. Mazar：阿富汗城市马扎尔沙里夫（Mazar-e Sharif）
9. on the day of Eid of Corban：伊斯兰教开斋节那天
10. barnacles：藤壶（附在岩石、船底的甲壳类动物）
11. Daoud Khan：达乌德·汗（1909—1978），阿富汗首相及总统，他推翻了君主制，建立了共和国，致力于提高妇女地位，推动现代化，后被刺杀
12. Agha sahib：老爷
13. Sinbad：辛巴达（《天方夜谭》里的人物）
14. Bas：够了
15. Farid：带阿米尔去孤儿院找索拉博的司机
16. that thing：指弹弓
17. Bismillah：以真主的名义
18. Land Cruiser：丰田汽车公司生产的陆地巡洋舰汽车

Questions：

1. What details in his rescue reveal Amir's growing up?
2. Why did Amir laugh when he was being beaten?

14

A Thousand Splendid Suns

作者及背景简介(同 Unit 13)

选读作品简介

《灿烂千阳》以阿富汗近三十年的动荡历史为背景,用细腻温柔的笔触,着力刻画了两个不同家庭背景的女子历经磨难,相互扶持,虽饱受战火摧残和男权制的压迫,却不放弃对幸福和希望的追求。她们是生活在阿富汗最底层的普通女性,也是千千万万阿富汗妇女(灿烂千阳的含义)为了自由和爱而不懈奋斗的典型代表。如果说《追风筝的人》以男性的视角,探讨了男性世界或父子兄弟之间的情谊,那么《灿烂千阳》则以女性的视角,描写了女性世界或母女姐妹之间的生死情谊。该部小说以苏联入侵、塔利班专政的动荡年月为背景,讲述了两名阿富汗妇女凄婉动人的一生。

小说共由四部分组成。第一部分讲述的是玛丽雅姆的故事。玛丽雅姆是赫拉特市一个电影放映商和其女仆的私生女,与母亲相依为命在城外的一处窝棚居住。电影放映商偶尔会为母女二人送来一些日用品和小礼物,向玛丽雅姆一边讲述外面的世界。十五岁时,玛丽雅姆不顾母亲的反对逃离了窝棚,来到城里父亲的家,遭到父亲与其家人的拒绝。玛丽雅姆的母亲因为失去玛丽雅姆上吊自尽。走投无路的玛丽雅姆被迫接受父亲一家的安排,嫁给了比自己年长三倍的修鞋匠拉希德。拉希德视玛丽雅姆为自己的私有财产,让她穿上黑色罩袍,从头到脚把她包裹得严严实实。玛丽雅姆仅仅能透过眼前一小块网纱看到外面的世界。玛丽雅姆在第一次怀孕期间,也曾得到拉希德短暂的呵护。由于多次流产,玛丽雅姆失去了生育能力,拉希德对她的态度也逐渐变得冷漠粗暴,玛丽雅姆经常遭到殴打。

小说第二部分讲述的是另一位女性人物莱拉的故事。莱拉父母都是受过良好教育的开明人士,莱拉得以像男孩子一样受到教育。莱拉与邻家男孩塔里格是青梅竹马的恋人,塔里格在一次爆炸中失去了一条腿,但他依然保护着莱拉,不让她受到坏孩子的欺负。不久莱拉快乐的童年因为战争的到来戛然而止。莱拉十四岁的时候,随着共产党人与苏杰哈德之间斗争的不断升级,莱拉的两个哥哥在战争中不幸丧生。恋人塔里格因为战争和父亲病情恶化,举家逃往巴基斯坦。正当莱拉与她父母也准备逃亡的时候,一枚火箭弹袭来,莱拉的父母双双被炸死。

在小说第三部分,战争和苦难让玛丽雅姆和莱拉这两个不幸的女人走到了一起,成为"一家人"。被炸弹炸昏的莱拉数日后醒来,发现自己躺在邻居拉希德的家里。拉希德为了让莱拉成为自己的小老婆,谎称莱拉男友的塔里格已经在巴基斯坦的难民营中不幸病死。莱拉所面临的选择与众多的阿富汗女孩一样:不是沦落为街头妓女,就是饿死。为了腹中她与塔里格的胎儿,莱拉嫁给了拉希德,新婚之夜,莱拉刺破手指制造了处女的假象。一开始玛丽雅姆对莱拉充满敌意,莱拉的女儿出生后,失去生育能力的玛丽雅姆把莱拉的女儿当作自己的女儿,孩子成为她与莱拉之间情感的纽带,两个命途多舛历经苦难的女人走到了一起,她们结成同盟共同对付拉希德的压迫。

数年后,已是两个孩子母亲的莱拉在喀布尔遇见了来找寻她的塔里格。拉希德的谎言也真相大白。在得知莱拉与初恋情人碰面后,拉希德怒不可遏,对莱拉大打出手。看着莱拉几乎要被打死,玛丽雅姆挺身而出,从背后用铁锹杀死了拉希德,救下莱拉。玛丽雅姆让莱拉和塔里格带着孩子们离开阿富汗,独自一人承担了所有的罪名,走上了刑场。

小说的第四部分首先讲述了莱拉和塔里格在巴基斯坦穆里的生活。他们在抵达穆里的当天晚上就结了婚,远离战乱硝烟,生活恬静而幸福。在得知塔利班政府倒台,阿富汗战争结束之后,莱拉耳边不禁回响起父亲生前所说的话:"战争结束时,阿富汗会需要你。"莱拉决定回到阿富汗参与重建。回国后,莱拉去玛丽雅姆的出生地看了玛丽雅姆童年生活的窝棚,莱拉后来去孤儿院当了老师。

《灿烂千阳》通过对两位普通阿富汗女性坎坷的命运的述说,反映了在男权制和极端宗教主义的国度里女性的生活现状。在这个痛苦悲伤的故事中,胡塞尼用温情细腻的笔触讲述了爱与付出的感人故事。从成长的角度来观察主人公玛丽雅姆的人生历程,更能体会出残酷现实对人性的摧残以及阿富汗女性坚韧隐忍追求光明的伟大品格。而这种人性的光辉就像那"灿烂千阳",即使曾经深埋,仍然会顽强成长,闪耀着璀璨的光芒。

成长主题解读

《灿烂千阳》中玛丽雅姆从幼年到中年的年龄跨度超出了传统意义上成长小说的主人公 13～20 岁的年龄范围,玛丽雅姆经历了一系列磨难后发生了巨大的心理变化,在动态的发展过程中实现了女性意识的觉醒和精神的成熟。

一、童年的伊甸园

成长的结构大致为 U 型叙事模式,即离家出走—遭受困境—挣扎—回归,这种结构的原型来自《圣经》里的伊甸园的故事。亚当和夏娃在伊甸园里无忧无虑地生活,夏娃在蛇的诱惑下偷吃了禁果,天神动怒将他们打入人间,从此两人过上了终生劳累的生活。在《灿烂千阳》中,玛丽雅姆 15 岁之前一直过着幸福的童年生活,简陋的窝棚和质朴的村落对玛丽雅姆来说相当于伊甸园。虽然被别人称作"哈拉米"(私生子),但玛丽雅姆感到自己很幸福,有着自己最喜欢的人的陪伴——毛拉法苏拉赫和父亲扎里勒。作为村里的阿訇,这个总是面带微笑的老者,每个星期都会来教玛丽雅姆朝拜仪式,教她背诵《古兰经》,教她识字,在功课结束后陪她在泥屋外面吃松子,喝绿茶,给她讲故事。在玛丽雅姆说话的时候,他全神贯注地听着,这样玛丽雅姆总是能够轻松地把不敢跟妈妈娜娜说的话告诉毛拉法苏拉赫。作为娜娜和扎里勒的私生女,她每个星期最期待的就是星期四,因为这一天她最喜爱的父亲会来看望她,每当见到他踏着石块穿过溪流来到她们在山上的小屋的时候,玛丽雅姆会一下子跳起来,露出灿烂的笑容,兴奋地挥舞着手臂,投入父亲的怀抱。被抱着悬在半空的玛丽雅姆能够见到父亲仰起的脸,弯弯的微笑和酒窝,在父亲的眼中看到她带着兴奋光芒的脸庞,那时的玛丽雅姆无法用和妈妈一样的眼光去看世界。父亲会给她讲外面发生的许多好玩的事情,会陪她爬山、钓鱼、画画,跟父亲在一起,她觉得自己是世界上最幸福的人。尽管妈妈总是告诫她,对于她父亲来说,她们只是像野草一样无足轻重的人,但那时的玛丽雅姆还不能理解母亲对父亲的指责,她坚信父亲会带她回家,她会和父亲以及其他的兄弟姐妹们一起幸福地生活。

二、迷茫与困惑

成长小说大致遵循"天真—诱惑—出走流浪—迷惘困惑—考验—顿悟—失去天真—认识自我"这一叙事结构,讲述 13～20 岁的主人公成长经历的叙事,反映出人物的思想和心理从幼稚走向成熟的变化过程,呈现成长主体的道德和精神发展。成长小说中一个必不可少的环节是童真的幻灭,即主人公大多要经历从天真到受挫的转折。在《灿烂千阳》中,玛丽雅姆幻想的幸福在她15岁生日那年戛然而止,天真任性的她不顾妈妈的劝阻独自一人离开她和妈妈住的小屋来到了父亲的住处,以为父亲会接纳她,结果却是被拒之门外,回到窝棚时,以为失去了女儿的母亲已吊死在树上。玛丽雅姆被父亲和他的太太们打发掉,嫁给了大她30多岁的男人,从此受尽了压迫和虐待。从对父亲充满期待到后来沦为生育工具和遭受家庭暴力,玛丽雅姆陷入了对人生的迷惘。在婚姻之初,玛丽雅姆似乎感受到了"幸福",觉得丈夫对她还不错,拉希德会称赞她的厨艺,带她去市区,给她买喜欢的礼物,带她吃从没吃过的美食。当她得知拉希德的前妻和唯一的儿子死于10年前时,她对丈夫的遭遇充满了同情,玛丽雅姆也憧憬着休戚与共的婚姻生活。当她发现自己怀孕时,她对自己的未来充满了希望,已经做好了准备去迎接新的生活。然而,这种虚假的幸福并没有持续多久,在多次流产失去生育能力后,玛丽雅姆被丈夫看作是一种负担,丈夫对她百般刁难、动辄打骂,面对这种非人的折磨和虐待,玛丽雅姆选择了妥协和沉默。她渐渐接受了自己作为女人的命运,在玛丽雅姆看来,她唯一能做的事情就是忍受,玛丽雅姆失去了自尊,放弃了对美好生活的追求。

三、玛丽雅姆的顿悟

"顿悟"来自宗教术语,被詹姆斯·乔伊斯用来指"一种突发的精神现象"。通过顿悟,主人公对自己或者对某种事物的本质有了深刻的理解和认识。"顿悟"是成长小说的一个重要的内容要素。《灿烂千阳》中,在莱拉走入玛丽雅姆的生命之前,玛丽雅姆的精神处于休眠状态,她用内化的男权思想来麻痹自己,无声地承受着丈夫的暴虐。这样的状态一直持续到十几年后一个14岁的女孩走进了她的生活。最初玛丽雅姆本能地认为莱拉"偷走了她的丈夫",后来这两个命途多舛的女人在一起生活以及莱拉的孩子的出生给玛丽雅姆的生活带来幸福和希望,玛丽雅姆顿悟到自己是被尊重、被需要的人,没有人比莱拉更能理解她的恐惧和痛苦,在很大程度上是莱拉的鼓励让玛丽雅姆恢复了自信,同时也带给了她新的思想。随着与莱拉的共同生活,她们的关系也从敌视对立到相互理解同情,逐渐两个身受苦难的女人产生了姐妹般的亲情。"和莱拉在院子里分享三杯茶,听到阿兹莎欢快的咯咯笑声"成了玛丽雅姆生活中的快乐。在小说的高潮,为了保护莱拉一家顺利出逃,玛丽雅姆举起了铁锹,奋力砍向拉希德,这是她第一次用实际行动决定自己的人生轨迹。当玛丽雅姆被关进监狱后,她不后悔自己谋杀了拉希德,因为她所希望得到的一切,莱拉和她的孩子已经给了她。临死前,玛丽雅姆想到:自己来到这个世界时,自己是一个卑贱的村民的私生子,是一个没人照料的东西,自己的出生是一件可怜而遗憾的事情,而当她离开这个世界时,是作为一个懂得爱与被爱的人、一个朋友、一个伴侣、一个看护人、一个有价值的人。这种顿悟使玛丽雅姆以一种释然平静的心情面对死亡。"这样死去并不坏,这是一个不合法出生的生命的合法结局。"

四、成长引路人

成长引路人是美国成长小说的一个重要构件,成长的引路在一定程度上起到丰富主人公生活经验,引导主人公形成某种人生观、价值观的作用,大致可以归纳为正面、反面和自然神灵这三种引路人。

玛丽雅姆的第一个引路人是毛拉法苏拉赫,法苏拉赫是村里的阿訇,他是一个让所有村民都爱戴的老者。他每周都会来教玛丽雅姆背诵《古兰经》,教她识字,像爷爷一样关心着玛丽雅姆的生活。在功课结束后,法苏拉赫会给她讲故事,陪她散步,耐心地听她讲那些不敢跟母亲说的话。娜娜自杀后,玛丽雅姆充满了自责,毛拉法苏拉赫是唯一一个来家里探望玛丽雅姆的人,给了玛丽雅姆极大的心灵安慰。

玛丽雅姆的第二个引路人是莱拉和情人的孩子——阿兹莎。在玛丽雅姆心灰意冷想要放弃生命的时候,是孩子给了她生存的动力。在孩子出生前,玛丽雅姆认为自己是一个从小被人嫌弃的"哈拉米",一个被丈夫视为生育和发泄兽欲的工具;孩子的出生使玛丽雅姆感受到了人间的真情,她感到了自己被需要的价值,看到了一个人对她如此天真的、毫无保留的爱意。当阿兹莎"脸上流露出爱慕而又紧张得发抖的神情,两只小手焦急地张开合上"要求玛丽雅姆抱她时,孩子的纯真和对她的依恋,唤醒了她人性中最柔弱的情感与最深沉的母性。玛丽雅姆在这个小小的生灵身上找到了人世间的真情,找回了她生命中缺失的那份爱与希望,也唤醒了玛丽雅姆沉睡的自我意识,激起了她对幸福的希冀与追求,在她看似柔弱的身躯里激发了巨大的能量,支撑着玛丽雅姆顽强生存下去,在莱拉即将被她们的丈夫掐死的关键时刻,这种爱激起玛丽雅姆奋起反抗,举起铁锹击倒拉希德,救出了莱拉,击倒了摧残了她一生的男权制,第一次决定了自己的生活轨迹。作者让孩子阿兹莎作玛丽雅姆的领路人,更贴近人性,引起情感的共鸣。在男权制下,女人的卑微地位已经让她们忘却了自己,默默忍受,成为男人的附属品,然而孩子所激起的这份无私的、毫无保留的爱唤醒了玛丽雅姆内心深处的觉醒和反抗。

五、成长仪式

仪式是人类生活中一个不可缺少的组成部分。有些仪式甚至可以追溯到远古时代,并在现代生活中以各种变体再现。"死亡"与"再生"源自于神话故事中象征蜕变和成长的仪式。除了这些共同的仪式外,每个人的成长过程中,往往还有独特的只属于小说主人公的成长事件,对于成长仪式的叙述也是成长小说中一个具有独特表现力的叙事方式。成长小说中通过某种具体或具有象征意义的仪式凸显出主人公在成长道路上的蜕变。《灿烂千阳》中有多处具有成长仪式特征的成长事件的描写。对莱拉的女儿阿兹莎的描述可以看作是玛丽雅姆的成长仪式。阿兹莎的出生唤醒了玛丽雅姆的母性,标志着玛丽雅姆从女孩到母亲的成长,"玛丽雅姆发现自己每天都盼望听到阿兹莎的笑声,闻到她身上的奶香,看到她刚长出的乳牙"。看到孩子张开的双臂,玛丽雅姆感到一种被需要的幸福和无私的爱。玛丽雅姆被执行死刑也是她的成长仪式。为了保护莱拉一家能够顺利逃走,玛丽雅姆选择了留下来独自承担杀人的罪行。在生命的最后一刻,玛丽雅姆回顾自己苦难卑贱的一生,"心中再也没有懊悔,而是充满了一阵安宁的感觉",因为"她是一个付出了爱,也得到了爱的女人"。(见选读一)玛丽雅姆牺牲自己实现了对爱的承诺,也用自己的生命证明了其伟大的人格,实现了最终的精神救赎,玛丽雅姆的受刑仪式也是其精神成长仪式,死亡并不是生命的终结,而是精神的升华。小说的结尾,当莱拉带着对玛丽雅姆的怀念,来到玛丽雅姆童年生活的窝棚,窝棚里布满蜘蛛网,地面是腐烂开裂的木板、散落着枯叶、破瓶子、糖纸、野蘑菇、烟头,四周是恣意生长的杂乱的野草,从中莱拉仿佛看到了童年的玛丽雅姆,"她们对生活的要求很低,不会成为别人的负担,不会让别人知道她们也有悲伤、失望、被嘲弄的梦想。她们就像河床里的岩石,毫无怨言地承受着,上面冲刷而过的湍流侵蚀着她们,却不能玷污她们的美丽。"莱拉看到了"藏在她灵魂深处的品质,那是拉希德或者塔利班都无法将之摧毁的信念"。(见选读二)正是玛丽雅姆的善良、宽容和自我牺牲精神保护了莱拉幸福的明天,这种伟大的品质像那一千个太阳照耀着那些虽饱受摧残,但依然保持人性,勇敢追求幸福的阿富汗女性。也正是带着这种信念,莱拉与千千万万的阿富汗人开始重建自己的家园。小说的结尾莱拉去瞻仰玛丽雅姆童年生活的窝棚可以看作是莱拉的心灵成长仪式,莱拉回顾玛丽雅姆苦难顽强无私的一生,内心受到强烈的冲击和感染,精神上得到了成长,莱拉决定去孤儿院当老师,将玛丽雅姆的自我牺牲毫无保留无私的爱延续下去。

下面选读为小说第47章,描写了玛丽雅姆为了救莱拉而杀死了拉希德后被关进监狱以及被塔利班处死的情景及临死时玛丽雅姆的内心。

Back in a kolba, it seemed, after all these years.

The Walayat women's prison was a drab, square shaped building in Shar-e-Nau near Chicken Street. It sat in the center of a larger complex that housed male inmates. A padlocked door separated Mariam and the other women from the surrounding men. Mariam counted five working cells. They were unfurnished rooms, with dirty, peeling walls, and small windows that looked into the courtyard. The windows were barred, even though the doors to the cells were unlocked and the women were free to come and go to the courtyard as they pleased. The windows had no glass. There were no curtains either, which meant the Talib guards who roamed the courtyard had an eyeful of the interior of the cells. Some of the women complained that the guards smoked outside the window and leered in, with their inflamed eyes and wolfish smiles, that they muttered indecent jokes to each other about them. Because of this, most of the women wore burqas all day and lifted them only after sundown, after the main gate was locked and the guards had gone to their posts.

At night, the cell Mariam shared with five women and four children was dark. On those nights when there was electrical power, they hoisted Naghma, a short, flat chested girl with black frizzy hair, up to the ceiling. There was a wire there from which the coating had been stripped. Naghma would hand wrap the live wire around the base of the lightbulb then to make a circuit.

The toilets were closet sized, the cement floor cracked. There was a small, rectangular hole in the ground, at the bottom of which was a heap of feces. Flies buzzed in and out of the hole.

In the middle of the prison was an open, rectangular courtyard, and, in the middle of that, a well. The well had no drainage, meaning the courtyard was often a swamp and the water tasted rotten. Laundry lines, loaded with hand washed socks and diapers, slashed across each other in the courtyard. This was where inmates met visitors, where they boiled the rice their families brought them. The prison provided no food. The courtyard was also the children's playground. Mariam had learned that many of the children had been born in Walayat, had never seen the world outside these walls. Mariam watched them chase each other around, watched their shoeless feet sling mud. All day, they ran around, making up lively games, unaware of the stench of feces and urine that permeated Walayat and their own bodies, unmindful of the Talib guards until one smacked them.

Mariam had no visitors. That was the first and only thing she had asked the Talib officials here. No visitors.

None of the women in Mariam's cell were serving time for violent crime. They were all there for the common offense of "running away from home." As a result, Mariam gained some notoriety among them, became a kind of celebrity. The women eyed her with a reverent, almost awestruck expression. They offered her their blankets. They competed to share their food with her. The most avid was Naghma, who was always hugging her elbows and following Mariam everywhere she went. Naghma was the sort of person who found it entertaining to dispense news of misfortune, whether others' or her own. She said her father had promised her to a tailor some thirty years older than her.

"He smells like goh,[1] and has fewer teeth than fingers," Naghma said of the tailor.

She'd tried to elope to Gardez with a young man she'd fallen in love with, the son of a local mullah. They'd barely made it out of Kabul. When they were caught and sent back, the mullah's son was flogged before he repented and said that Naghma had seduced him with her feminine charms. She'd cast a spell on him, he said. He promised he would rededicate himself to the study of the Koran. The mullah's son was freed. Naghma was sentenced to five years.

It was just as well, she said, her being here in prison. Her father had sworn that the day she was released he would take a knife to her throat.

Listening to Naghma, Mariam remembered the dim glimmer of cold stars and the stringy pink clouds streaking over the Safid-koh mountains that long ago morning when Nana had said to her, *Like a compass needle that points north, a man's accusing finger always finds a woman. Always. You remember that, Mariam.*

Mariam's trial had taken place the week before. There was no legal council, no public hearing, no cross examining of evidence, no appeals. Mariam declined her right to witnesses. The entire thing lasted less than fifteen minutes.

The middle judge, a brittle-looking Talib, was the leader. He was strikingly gaunt, with yellow, leathery skin and a curly red beard. He wore eyeglasses that magnified his eyes and revealed how yellow the whites were. His neck looked too thin to support the intricately wrapped turban on his head.

"You admit to this, hamshira?[2]" He asked again in a tired voice.

"I do," Mariam said.

The man nodded. Or maybe he didn't. It was hard to tell; he had a pronounced shaking of his hands and head that reminded Mariam of Mullah Faizullah's tremor. When he sipped tea, he did not reach for his cup. He motioned to the square-shouldered man to his left, who respectfully brought it to his lips. After, the Talib closed his eyes gently, a muted and elegant gesture of gratitude.

Mariam found a disarming quality about him. When he spoke, it was with a tinge of guile and tenderness. His smile was patient. He did not look at Mariam despisingly. He did not address her with spite or accusation but with a soft tone of apology.

"Do you fully understand what you're saying?" the bony faced Talib to the judge's right, not the tea giver, said. This one was the youngest of the three. He spoke quickly and with emphatic, arrogant confidence. He'd been irritated that Mariam could not speak Pashto. He struck Mariam as the sort of quarrelsome young man who relished his authority, who saw offenses everywhere, thought it his birthright to pass judgment.

"I do understand," Mariam said.

"I wonder," the young Talib said, "God has made us differently, you women and us men. Our brains are different. You are not able to think like we can. Western doctors and their science have proven this. This is why we require only one male witness but two female ones."

"I admit to what I did, brother," Mariam said, "But, if I hadn't, he would have killed her. He was strangling her."

"So you say. But, then, women swear to all sorts of things all the time."

"It's the truth."

"Do you have witnesses? Other than your ambagh[3]?"

"I do not," said Mariam.

"Well, then." He threw up his hands and snickered.

It was the sickly Talib who spoke next. "I have a doctor in Peshawar," he said, "A fine, young Pakistani fellow. I saw him a month ago, and then again last week. I said, tell me the truth, friend, and he said to me, three months, Mullah sahib[4], maybe six at most all God's will, of course." He nodded discreetly at the square shouldered man on his left and took another sip of the tea he was offered. He wiped his mouth with the back of his tremulous hand. "It does not frighten me to leave this life that my only son left five years ago, this life that insists we bear sorrow upon sorrow long after we can bear no more. No, I believe I shall gladly take my leave when the time comes."What frightens me, hamshira, is the day God summons me before Him and asks, Why did you not do as I said, Mullah? Why did you not obey my laws? How shall I explain myself to Him, hamshira? What will be my defense for not heeding His commands? All I can do, all any of us can do, in the time we are granted, is to go on abiding by the laws He has set for us. The clearer I see my end, hamshira, the nearer I am to my day of reckoning, the more determined I grow to carry out His word. However painful it may prove."

He shifted on his cushion and winced.

"I believe you when you say that your husband was a man of disagreeable temperament," he resumed, fixing Mariam with his bespectacled eyes, his gaze both stern and compassionate. "But I cannot help but be disturbed by the brutality of your action, hamshira. I am troubled by what you have done; I am troubled that his little boy was crying for him upstairs when you did it."

"I am tired and dying, and I want to be merciful. I want to forgive you. But when God summons me and says, But it wasn't for you to forgive, Mullah, what shall I say?"

His companions nodded and looked at him with admiration.

"Something tells me you are not a wicked woman, hamshira. But you have done a wicked thing. And you must pay for this thing you have done. Shari'a is not vague on this matter. It says I must send you where I will soon join you myself."

"Do you understand, hamshira?"

Mariam looked down at her hands. She said she did.

"May Allah forgive you."

Before they led her out, Mariam was given a document, told to sign beneath her statement and the mullah's sentence. As the three Taliban watched, Mariam wrote it out, her name the meem, the reh, the yah, and the meem remembering the last time she'd signed her name to a document, twenty-seven years before, at Jalil's table, beneath the watchful gaze of another mullah.

Mariam spent ten days in prison. She sat by the window of the cell, watched the prison life in the courtyard. When the summer winds blew, she watched bits of scrap paper ride the currents in a frenzied, corkscrew motion, as they were hurled this way and that, high above the prison walls. She watched the winds stir mutiny in the dust, whipping it into violent spirals that ripped through the courtyard. Everyone the guards, the inmates, the children, Mariam burrowed their faces in the hook of their elbows, but the dust would not be denied. It made homes of ear canals and nostrils, of eyelashes and skin folds, of the space between molars. Only at dusk did the winds die down. And then if a night breeze blew, it did so timidly, as if to atone for the excesses of its daytime sibling.

On Mariam's last day at Walayat, Naghma gave her a tangerine. She put it in Mariam's palm and closed her fingers around it. Then she burst into tears. "You're the best friend I ever had," she said. Mariam spent the rest of the day by the barred window watching the inmates below. Someone was cooking a meal, and a stream of cumin scented smoke and warm air wafted through the window. Mariam could see the children playing a blindfolded game. Two little girls were singing a rhyme, and Mariam remembered it from her childhood, remembered Jalil singing it to her as they'd sat on a rock, fishing in the stream:

Lili lili birdbath,

Sitting on a dirt path,

Minnow sat on the rim and drank,

Slipped, and in the water she sank.

Mariam had disjointed dreams that last night. She dreamed of pebbles, eleven of them, arranged vertically. Jalil, young again, all winning smiles and dimpled chins and sweat patches, coat flung over his shoulder, come at last to take his daughter away for a ride in his shiny black Buick Roadmaster.⁵ Mullah Faizullah twirling his rosary beads, walking with her along the stream, their twin shadows gliding on the water and on the grassy banks sprinkled with a blue lavender wild iris that, in this dream, smelled like cloves. She dreamed of Nana in the doorway of the kolba, her voice dim and distant, calling her to dinner, as Mariam played in cool, tangled grass where ants crawled and beetles scurried and grasshoppers skipped amid all the different shades of green. The squeak of a wheelbarrow laboring up a dusty path. Cowbells clanging. Sheep baaing on a hill.

On the way to Ghazi Stadium, Mariam bounced in the bed of the truck as it skidded around potholes and its wheels spat pebbles. The bouncing hurt her tailbone. A young, armed Talib sat across from her looking at her. Mariam wondered if he would be the one, this amiable looking young man with the deep set bright eyes and slightly pointed face, with the black nailed index finger drumming the side of the truck.

"Are you hungry, mother?" he said.

Mariam shook her head.

"I have a biscuit. It's good. You can have it if you're hungry. I don't mind."

"No. Tashakor, brother."

He nodded, looked at her benignly. "Are you afraid, mother?"

A lump closed off her throat. In a quivering voice, Mariam told him the truth.

"Yes. I'm very afraid."

"I have a picture of my father," he said, "I don't remember him. He was a bicycle repairman once, I know that much. But I don't remember how he moved, you know, how he laughed or the sound of his voice." He looked away, then back at Mariam. "My mother used to say that he was the bravest man she knew. Like a lion, she'd say. But she told me he was crying like a child the morning the communists took him. I'm telling you so you know that it's normal to be scared. It's nothing to be ashamed of, mother."

For the first time that day, Mariam cried a little.

Thousands of eyes bore down on her. In the crowded bleachers, necks were craned for the benefit of a better view. Tongues clucked. A murmuring sound rippled through the stadium when Mariam was helped down from the truck. Mariam imagined heads shaking when the loudspeaker announced her crime. But she did not look up to see whether they were shaking with disapproval or charity, with reproach or pity. Mariam blinded herself to them all.

Earlier that morning, she had been afraid that she would make a fool of herself, that she would turn into a pleading, weeping spectacle. She had feared that she might scream or vomit or even wet herself, that, in her last moments, she would be betrayed by animal instinct or bodily disgrace. But when she was made to descend from the truck, Mariam's legs did not buckle. Her arms did not flail. She did not have to be dragged. And when she did feel herself faltering, she thought of Zalmai, from whom she had taken the love of his life, whose days now would be shaped by the sorrow of his father's disappearance. And then Mariam's stride steadied and she could walk without protest.

An armed man approached her and told her to walk toward the southern goalpost. Mariam could sense the crowd tightening up with anticipation. She did not look up. She kept her eyes to the ground, on her shadow, on her executioner's shadow trailing hers.

Though there had been moments of beauty in it, Mariam knew that life for the most part had been unkind to her. But as she walked the final twenty paces, she could not help but wish for more of it. She wished she could see Laila again, wished to hear the clangor of her laugh, to sit with her once more for a pot of chai and leftover halwa under a starlit sky. She mourned that she would never see Aziza grow up, would not see the beautiful young woman that she would one day become, would not get to paint her hands with henna and toss noqul candy at her wedding. She would never play with Aziza's children. She would have liked that very much, to be old and play with Aziza's children.

Near the goalpost, the man behind her asked her to stop. Mariam did. Through the crisscrossing grid of the burqa[6], she saw his shadow arms lift his shadow Kalashnikov.[7] Mariam wished for so much in those final moments. Yet as she closed her eyes, it was not regret any longer but a sensation of abundant peace that washed over her. She thought of her entry into this world, the harami[8] child of a lowly villager, an unintended thing, a pitiable, regrettable accident. A weed. And yet she was leaving the world as a woman who had loved and been loved back. She was leaving it as a friend, a companion, a guardian. A mother. A person of consequence at last. No. It was not so bad, Mariam thought, that she should die this way. Not so bad. This was a legitimate end to a life of illegitimate beginnings.

Mariam's final thoughts were a few words from the Koran, which she muttered under her breath.

He has created the heavens and the earth with the truth; He makes the night cover the day and makes the day overtake the night, and He has made the sun and the moon subservient; each one runs on to an assigned term; now surely He is the Mighty, the Great Forgiver.

"Kneel," the Talib said.

O, my Lord! Forgive and have mercy, for you are the best of the merciful ones.

"Kneel here, hamshira And look down."

One last time, Mariam did as she was told.

Notes

1. goh:粪便

2. hamshira:太太(madam)

3. ambagh:姐姐(sister)

4. sahib:老爷,先生,阁下

5. Buick Roadmaster:别克汽车

6. burqa:布卡(伊斯兰国家妇女穿的蒙面长袍)

7. Kalashnikov:冲锋枪

8. harami:私生子

Questions:

1. What's does the description of the prison reveal about women's status in Afghanistan?

2. How did Mariam feel before her death? What is the epiphany?

下面选读为小说第50章,描写了莱拉去玛丽雅姆童年生活的窝棚看到的情景。

Laila thanks him[1]. She crosses the streambed, stepping from one stone to another. She spots broken soda bottles amid the rocks, rusted cans, and a mold coated metallic container with a zinc lid half buried in the ground. She heads toward the mountains, toward the weeping willows, which she can see now, the long drooping branches shaking with each gust of wind. In her chest, her heart is drumming. She sees that the willows are arranged as Mariam had said, in a circular grove with a clearing in the middle. Laila walks faster, almost running now. She looks back over her shoulder and sees that Hamza[2] is a tiny figure, his chapan a burst of color against the brown of the trees' bark. She trips over a stone and almost falls, then regains her footing. She hurries the rest of the way with the legs of her trousers pulled up. She is panting by the time she reaches the willows. Mariam's kolba[3] is still here. When she approaches it, Laila sees that the lone windowpane is empty and that the door is gone. Mariam had described a chicken coop and a tandoor, a wooden outhouse too, but Laila sees no sign of them. She pauses at the entrance to the kolba she can hear flies buzzing inside.

To get in, she has to sidestep a large fluttering spider web. It's dim inside. Laila has to give her eyes a few moments to adjust. When they do, she sees that the interior is even smaller than she'd imagined. Only half of a single rotting, splintered board remains of the floorboards. The rest, she imagines, have been ripped up for burning as firewood. The floor is carpeted now with dry edged leaves, broken bottles, discarded chewing gum wrappers, wild mushrooms, old yellowed cigarette butts. But mostly with weeds, some stunted, some springing impudently halfway up the walls. Fifteen years, Laila thinks. Fifteen years in this place. Laila sits down, her back to the wall. She listens to the wind filtering through the willows. There are more spider webs stretched across the ceiling. Someone has spray painted something on one of the walls, but much of it has sloughed off, and Laila cannot decipher what it says. Then she realizes the letters are Russian. There is a deserted bird's nest in one corner and a bat hanging upside down in another corner, where the wall meets the low ceiling. Laila closes her eyes and sits there awhile. In Pakistan, it was difficult sometimes to remember the details of Mariam's face. There were times when, like a word on the tip of her tongue, Mariam's face eluded her. But now, here in this place, it's easy to summon Mariam behind the lids of her eyes: the soft radiance of her gaze, the long chin, the coarsened skin of her neck, the tight lipped smile. Here, Laila can lay her cheek on the softness of Mariam's lap again, can feel Mariam swaying back and forth, reciting verses from the Koran, can feel the words vibrating down Mariam's body, to her knees, and into her own ears. Then, suddenly, the weeds begin to recede, as if something is pulling them by the roots from beneath the ground. They sink lower and lower until the earth in the kolba has swallowed the last of their spiny leaves. The spider webs magically unpin themselves. The bird's nest self disassembles, the twigs snapping loose one by one, flying out of the kolba end over end. An invisible eraser wipes the Russian graffiti off the wall. The floorboards are back. Laila sees a pair of sleeping cots now, a wooden table, two chairs, a cast iron stove in the corner, shelves along the walls, on which sit clay pots and pans, a blackened teakettle, cups and spoons. She hears chickens clucking outside, the distant gurgling of the stream. A young Mariam is sitting at the table making a doll by the glow of an oil lamp. She's humming something. Her face is smooth and youthful, her hair washed, combed back. She has all her teeth. Laila watches Mariam glue strands of yam onto her doll's head. In a few years, this little girl will be a woman who will make small demands on life, who will never burden others, who will never let on that she too has had sorrows, disappointments, dreams that have been ridiculed. A woman who will be like a rock in a riverbed, enduring without complaint, her grace not sullied but shaped by the turbulence that washes over her. Already Laila sees something behind this young girl's eyes, something deep in her core, that neither Rasheed nor the Taliban will be able to break. Something as hard and unyielding as a block of limestone. Something that, in the end, will be her undoing and Laila's salvation.

Notes:

1. him:指玛丽雅姆童年生活的村落的村民,玛丽雅姆请他带路

2. Hamza:毛拉法苏拉赫的儿子,哈姆扎此时在带莱拉去看玛丽雅姆童年时的棚屋(kolba)。毛拉法苏拉赫是玛丽雅姆童年时的村里的长者,玛丽雅姆童年时法苏拉赫教玛丽雅姆念《古兰经》,教她识字,关心安慰她。

3. kolba:简陋的棚屋

Questions:

1. What does the detailed description of the kolba reveal about Mariam's life?

2. How did Laila feel when she saw the kolba?

3. What was Laila's epiphany at that time?

参 考 文 献

[1] 芮渝萍.美国成长小说研究[M].北京:中国社会科学出版社,2004.
[2] 陈嘉.英国文学作品选读[M].北京:商务印书馆,1982.
[3] 李宜燮,常耀信.美国文学选读(上下册)[M].天津:南开大学出版社,1991.
[4] 张立新.二十世纪美国文学导读[M].沈阳:辽宁人民出版社,2002.
[5] 张伯香.英国文学教程[M].武汉:武汉大学出版社,1997.